One More Chapter

A Strangers-to-Lovers, Spicy Lessons Romance

RS Barry

RILEY PAWS PUBLISHING

To my Fellow Spoonie Warriors.

Just because you carry it well, doesn't mean it isn't heavy...
Your worst days don't define you.
I see you, and you dazzle.

Author's Note

While all my books reflect pieces of me, this one is especially close to my heart. I live with the same chronic conditions as the FMC, though in my case it took over thirty years and countless close calls to reach a diagnosis. Like many chronic illnesses, Mast Cell Activation Syndrome (MCAS) and Postural Orthostatic Tachycardia Syndrome (POTS) exist on a spectrum. My doctor once said, "The only thing consistent about this disease is its inconsistency." This novel is influenced by my experience and a healthy dose of fiction, but everyone's journey looks different. I'm fortunate to mostly manage my disease through diet changes and medication, but there are others in my community who are reduced to only a couple "safe foods" and a carefully regulated environment.

If you or someone you know is looking for information or support, I encourage you to explore these wonderful organizations:

Mast Cell Disease Society / The Mastocytosis Society (TMS)(MCAS)

Standing Up to POTS (POTS)

Dysautonomia International (POTS)

CHAPTER 1

Four Rules

I t starts like something from a romcom. The crowd parts to reveal a conventionally beautiful woman. The bodycon dress, heels, purse, nose, and lips all match the current standards. Green eyes meet mine for a moment before lush sooty lashes fall artfully. She approaches, perfectly positioned under the light so her skin and hair glimmer.

"What can I get you?" It's ladies' night at Pop. My best night of the week. Okay, who am I kidding? Every night is ladies' night for me. The damp cloth slides across the dark wood bar. I'm fully aware of how my arms flex in my work shirt—and of how her eyes drop to them. My mouth curves in a way that guarantees double the tips.

"Oh, how about sex on the beach?" Her lips split into a seductive smile.

I grit my back teeth to maintain my expression and force a chuckle, like that's the first time I've heard the come-on. Believe me, as the head bartender in a popular bar in Florida, that isn't as original as she thinks. "Coming right up."

My mind wanders as I grab bottles and pour various liquids into a cup. Keeping tabs on who has drinks and who is trying to catch my eye for a refill. Technically speaking, I'm not the head bartender anymore. I've been at Pop since Anna, Bree, and Nic opened six years ago, but recently I bought in to officially become a partner. Minor partner, anyway.

Pop is a nice place, upscale but not so stuffy you can't bring the family. We see all kinds. Big suits from the city working deals, families celebrating milestones, young singles looking for love. It's the first and last categories that can be a major pain in the ass.

As I give the alcohol a firm shake, the woman's eyes darken and follow my movements. Add a fruit skewer and it's done. "Anything else?" I ask.

Without breaking eye contact, she lifts the skewer, rubbing the cherry around the rim of the drink. Her head cocks, sending her blond curls shimmering about her shoulders in a practiced motion. "Not sure yet." Those fake lashes fan along her cheeks for a moment before her eyes return to mine. The cherry drifts to her matching lips, and white teeth close around the plump fruit. "I'll let you know if I see something I like."

Oh, she clearly sees something she likes.

Bree and Anna have teased me for years about being "the hot bartender" mentioned in our reviews. They claim I'm the only reason the place stays in the black—we all know it's actually Anna's cooking, though. Normally I simply smile, flirt with the pretty girls, practicing some line or other. Call me a player all you want, but it is most certainly a game for two, and I have very clear rules.

Rule 1. Never Kiss First—I never make the first physical move. Consent is key, and I want zero questions about whether she wants it.

Rule 2. Her Place, Never Mine—my home is my haven. No one is allowed over, not even my guy friends.

Rule 3. No Sleeping Overs—it's a one time only thing with no strings. Set clear boundaries and expectations up front, and there will be no surprises.

I appreciate a woman who knows what she wants and goes after it—inside and outside the bedroom. Lately though, the string of one-night stands has grown a bit repetitive. The game has lost its appeal.

My knuckles whiten on the bar, not that she notices. "The special tonight is shrimp scampi. It's good."

Without waiting for a response, I turn to the back wall of the bar and fill a cup with ice before ducking into the mini-fridge for my special stash of Anna's authentic sweet tea. The slight bitterness of the tea and lemon hits my tongue moments before sugar happiness floods my senses. I take a deep breath and release it with a sigh.

Calm down, man; you actually like this job most of the time.

"Hey, Ash?" Jessie, our newest bartender, approaches me. There's a tightness around her eyes that instantly puts me on edge. "Would you mind switching sides of the bar with me?" She's paired her black work shirt and jeans with stiletto-heeled boots, which brings her head level with my nose.

My gaze scans over her head. A group of men in fancy suits laugh in her section as they grope rocks glasses. Problem category number one. Two seem harmless enough, but one of them is staring at Jessie with hunger in his eyes and a hard curl of his lips.

As much as I gripe about the women who eye me like a piece of meat—the ones who don't even try to whisper as they discuss all the ways they'd like to see me naked. At least I've never been even momentarily worried that they would harm me physically. "What did they say?"

She shakes her head, her inky straight hair swishing along her back from a high ponytail. The spikes through her ears glisten in the LEDs. "Nothing I can't handle, but it's getting harder not to deck him. I have shit to do tomorrow and can't afford to end up in lockup. Again." The emotion in her eyes is rage and not fear.

I laugh and clap her muscled arm. "Sure thing, Jess. I could use a different crowd as well."

She raises one perfectly plucked, whip-thin brow at the woman no doubt watching this entire interaction. Pushing up on her toes, she leans into my ear, her hand softly resting on my shoulder. "You're so weird, boss." Then she saunters off with a wink to pour a second drink for the now pouting blond.

It's all for show. Neither of us has a lick of interest in the other. I'm the unofficial big brother at Pop. Need a walk out to the parking lot? Scare off an eager suitor? Plus-one for a reunion or wedding? All the female staff know I'm happy to help, no strings attached. Because...

Rule 4: Sex and Business Don't Mix—I will never sleep with someone I have a professional relationship with.

Yet, none of the girls at work thought to return that favor until Jessie. Her first day, she stepped in when a handsy girl wasn't taking the hint. She rushed in like a jealous girlfriend, and the situation immediately deescalated. Having Jessie helps limit the embarrassing situations where letting a lady down gently doesn't go well.

"Can I make you boys another drink? Or are you ready to close out your tab?" I rest my hands on the bar, effectively blocking dickbag's view.

He sneers at me. "We're good with the hot piece over there."

"Well, now you'll have to settle for me." I flex my biceps as I lean on the surface.

Bro finally gets the hint he can't take me in a fight. "I guess we'll take the check."

I don't even try to hide a shit-eating grin as I ring them out. No one messes with my Pop family.

After they begrudgingly leave, my buddy, Johnson, comes up to the bar. "Hey, man," I say as I clean up the empty glasses and wipe down the surface. "Didn't know you were coming in tonight."

He gives me a fist bump. "Can't stay, but wanted to say hi. I'm here for the talk next door."

"Oh yeah?" I rack my brain about what's going on in the new event space tonight. Since it opened at the beginning of the year, there's been non-stop bookings. Weddings. Retirement parties. Women's business lunches. Sorority formals. Book signings.

"Have you read the *War of the Witches* series?" He pushes a hardcover towards me. I flip it over to read the blurb and see the author smiling on the back. "It's so good! When I heard Gabriella Boyle was going to be here, I begged Bree to snag me a ticket."

I chuckle as I toss the dirty rag under the bar. Johnson works for Bree at her day job at an engineering firm, but he's also friends with her husband. It's a weird dynamic, but they make it work.

"Hey, Ash, the grapefruit IPA kicked. Can you go grab a fresh keg?"

With a nod to Johnson and a wave at Jessie, I head to the back storeroom.

CHAPTER 2

The Limit Doesn't Exist

The metal edge of the shelving digs into my back. It's borderline painful but a welcome distraction, something to focus on other than my pounding ears and the spinning room. My smartwatch vibrates yet again. I don't bother checking whether it's my agent or my heart rate alarm. Most people would be living it up if Netflix optioned their book for a movie. They'd be toasting everyone in that event hall and smiling for all the photos. I've never been "most people." Nope, I'm sitting on the floor of a supply closet, disassociating into a romance novel like a boss, trying to will my BPM under 110.

I wonder how long I can hide here?

The powers that be clearly are laughing at me, because no sooner does the thought cross my mind than the door opens and a figure appears. I peek through the racks of liquor and napkins and nearly fumble my paperback as the most gorgeous man I've ever seen enters. His piercing blue eyes scan the shelves; they glitter iridescent in the fluorescent bulb. Bright blond hair slicks back from his face in a topknot. This man is a Viking god among men. My imagination couldn't dream up a more perfect man, and it's pretty spectacular if I do say so myself.

He steps up to a silver keg on the floor and deftly lifts it with one arm. And oh, what an arm. The sleeve of his black shirt stretches around a bulging bicep. He turns to leave, so I lean out for a better view of his exceptional denim-clad ass.

The shelf is still in my way, so I shift a little more, letting the book slip from my lap, utterly forgotten. My hand darts out to snatch it before it can give me away. I catch it, but lose my balance in the process, landing on my side with a grunt and in full visibility of the doorway.

The Viking whirls, startled, but thankfully doesn't toss the keg at me.

I wonder if passing out would make things better or worse? Totally worse, right?

"You okay, ma'am?" I flinch at the honorific—thirty-two is way too young to be a ma'am. Misreading my reaction, he sets the barrel down and strides towards me in those delicious jeans, completely short-circuiting my brain. "Let me help you there. Do I know you?"

Wide-eyed, I only shake my head at him. For a woman who pays the bills with her words, I'm surprisingly mute.

Blond brows pinch, then suddenly rise. "You're the author from the event tonight. Gabriella Boyle. Shouldn't you be giving a speech or something?"

"It's too people-y out there." Holy shit, did I really just say that?

The Viking laughs. Great big belly laughs that make me shiver. "Fair enough." Still chuckling, he reaches down, grabbing me under my arms like a small child and lifting. "Up you go."

My body tingles where his fingers touch. Standing, my eyes are level with his chest. The rushing in my ears increases, and my vision goes black along the edges. Shit, I stood up too fast. His hands tighten as I blink away the fog. "Sorry, didn't eat much."

"Around here, that's a crime; Anna's cooking is amazing."

"It smelled good. I just have food... issues... and my nerves were already making me queasy." Oh my god, Gabby, shut the fuck up!

"Well, we can't have that. Come on." He walks out the door, holding it open for me with a confidence I'd kill for. Completely under his spell, I follow him down the narrow hall and into an industrial kitchen. A small army of chefs populates the various stations in pristine white coats.

The Viking approaches a striking blond woman manning a table with heat lamps. She immediately smiles when she looks up at him. I bet he gets that reaction from all women. "What's up, sugar?"

"Hey, Anna, do you still have some of that chicken and rice from dinner?"

"Sure do. Want me to have Meeka warm some up?"

"Naw, I got it, thanks."

She returns her attention to the plates in front of her as the Viking leads me away. I really should figure out what his name is. He pushes me into a small office at the rear of the kitchen and points to the only seat. "Sit."

I'm too damn curious to be offended, so I comply. For all I know, I'm actually passed out in that storage room and this is all some dream. Better take mental notes for future novels.

Mystery man returns in minutes with a steaming bowl and a serving set, placing both on the desk in front of me.

"Thanks." I pull out my fork and pick up a juicy-looking piece of grilled chicken. One taste has a moan slipping from my lips. My stomach gurgles, demanding more food, and I happily tuck in.

"So, Gabriella..."

"Gabby," I correct him around a bite of velvety rice.

"Gabby, what is a best-selling author doing in a supply closet reading *Lacrosse My Heart?*"

My head jerks up at my forgotten paperback held up in his hand. Gulping, I slowly lift my head until my eyes meet those electric blue ones that will be living rent-free in my head forever. I need to write a character with eyes like this. A hero on an epic quest to save his kingdom. Or maybe a wizard with snow powers.

Fucking focus, Gabby!

"Market research?" My voice cracks at the end, making it sound more like a question.

The Viking—shit, I still don't know his name—merely smiles at me. "Lacrosse players? I thought you wrote fantasy."

"Pretty sure that cover model is every woman's fantasy." I clamp my lips together, but it's too late. The train of thought has left the station with zero filter in place. My cheeks burn with the telltale sign of a furious flush followed by cold electric zaps along my skin.

I expect him to laugh, but he doesn't. He simply looks down at the novel, and I swear his ears turn a sympathetic rosy hue. The cover in question features a shirtless man from the neck down, holding a lacrosse stick behind his shoulders as muscles flex and sweat drips down his chest. Viking's discomfort leaves me oddly disappointed. I expected him to be more evolved than that.

"My editor wants me to add more romance in book three—write to market and all that—but I've never written spice before. Every scene I draft is completely terrible, so I was looking for inspiration."

It shouldn't be all that surprising. They say write what you know, and as a terminally introverted bookworm, who stereotypically lives alone with her cat, I know dragons a hell of a lot better than I know dick.

He makes a choking noise, and I realize I mixed up my inside and outside voices.

Again.

"Y-you're a virgin?" His eyes rake up and down my body.

Embarrassment and anger spark. "No. I've had sex. Not that there's anything wrong with being a virgin. Or sleeping with dozens of people. I don't judge; you do you. Oh my god, why am I talking about this? I don't even know your name. This is going to end up all over the internet. My agent is going to kill me. How the hell did I even get on this topic?"

"Write what you know, cats, dragons, dick." His lips tremble like he's holding back a smile. "It's Asher, by the way."

"Huh?"

"My name, it's Asher." His lower lip disappears behind impossibly white front teeth. I'm staring, but I can't help it—it's like magic. He taps the paperback against his impressive thigh twice, then holds it out to me. "I could help you. If you wanted."

My jaw drops. Help me how? My active imagination immediately provides suggestions. Very graphic suggestions of different scenes he could help me choreograph.

Before I can kick my brain and mouth into gear, my agent, Roger, appears in the doorway. "Where the hell have you been? I looked everywhere for you. Your fans are waiting."

Viking—no, Asher—turns to the door, keeping his body between me and Roger. "She was having something to eat. Your team failed to inform our staff about her dietary restrictions."

Roger looks at me, clearly exasperated. "You didn't eat beforehand? Are you done now? Everyone is waiting for your reading."

I go to push the bowl away, but Asher stops me with a subtle shake of his head. Those blue eyes must put a spell on me because I lift the fork to my lips and take three more bites, all while maintaining what can only be described as aggressive eye contact.

As the utensil clinks into the now empty dish, Asher smiles. He leans forward to gather the dishes, and I imagine him saying, "Good girl."

Damn, I've been reading way too much romance lately.

The limit doesn't exist, my inner voice helpfully supplies.

"Thank you." So lame, but they're the only words that come to me. I square my shoulders and silently follow my agent back to the event space and the looming stage.

The Collection

The talk is in full swing when I reach the event hall. Rows of chairs sit in even lines facing a single armchair on the small stage. Two giant banners flank Gabriella. One displays the cover of her first book, *Rise of the Covens,* and advertises the upcoming film adaptation. The other advertises book two, *The Road to War.*

With a curt chin jerk, the bartender on duty leaves to take his break, and I replace him behind the bar. All the attendees are in their seats, focused on Gabby with great expectations. So obviously, I'm free to do the same.

Quirky.

That's one word to describe her, with her run-on sentences and putting herself in situations that drive her to hide in supply closets.

Fucking breath of fresh air is another apt description.

Maybe that's why I jumped to her defense in the office. Sure, I can tell myself that I was protecting Pop's reputation by ensuring the client got fed, but who am I kidding? When that asshole spoke down to her like that, something in me snapped. Must have been my big brother complex again, right?

A young woman stands up and approaches the mic for open questions. "Miss Boyle, will Catrina and Lucian finally be together in book three?"

Gabby's smile is well rehearsed, brittle, and it doesn't meet her eyes. "While I'm so touched that you all have enjoyed the interactions between these characters, my goal is to tell Catrina's story of growth and self-exploration. How she can overcome obstacles and a corrupt society to save the day."

An awkward hush falls over the crowd. Then Gabby's dick of a manager grabs the mic. "Rest assured, there will be plenty of fireworks in the next installment."

The room erupts in applause. Poor thing. Gabby grimaces as she squirms in her seat.

What is it like to be forced to compromise your art? So many authors set out with hopes of publishing traditionally, but it's not always the dream people imagine. You have agents, publishers, and marketers all telling you what your book should be. It's no longer yours.

Absolutely, it can be a tremendous opportunity. You can find that agent who believes in your vision. The editor that totally gets you. The marketing team who understands your message. But what happens to those authors whose stars don't align? I'm not sure I could do it. Give up full control like that.

I take a drink order from a woman in a *War of the Witches*-themed t-shirt. Only half my mind is on the task as hands fly from muscle memory, flipping bottles and pouring liquids. The rest of my brainpower is devoted to my favorite activity: people-watching.

My sisters are always after me to "get a real job." In their eyes, I'm fifteen years out of college with a mountain of student debt and no aspirations. It comes from a caring place—I'm the baby and only boy, they can't turn it off.

Becoming a partner in the restaurant last year helped ease their concerns—and it's certainly helped me pay off my loans faster. My one condition was to stay behind the bar. It's not about the tips or the pickups. If I sat at a desk in the back, my hobby would be over.

Some people collect gems or trading cards; I collect people. A speech tic here, an expression there—I file them all away in my brain to analyze later.

And right now? I'm collecting an adorable redhead with curves for days and a terminal case of verbal diarrhea.

"Hey, Ash. What are you doing out here?"

My gaze snaps to Brianna, one of my fellow partners here at Pop. She started the restaurant with Anna, our head chef, and their friend Nic shortly after graduating college together. I was their first hire, but we've been more friends than coworkers for years.

"I could ask you the same thing. You know Anna and I are both here to handle things, right?"

"Oh, I know, but I would not miss this one. I love this series. After doing all the planning, it seemed a shame to skip the actual event."

As a professional project manager, Bree naturally took the role of coordinator at Pop. Since we opened the banquet room a few months ago, she's been stretched thin, though.

"We really should look into hiring a full-time event planner, Bree. You do a great job, but you also have another career and a toddler."

Bree and her husband, Colin, are executives at a nearby engineering firm. They met there while working on a new product and now practically run the company—when they aren't at home with their daughter and two dogs.

She smooths a hand over her already perfect ponytail. "Yeah, you're right. I'm just not ready to let go of this place. You know?"

"Who says you have to? You can still be involved; just let someone else do the heavy lifting. Wedding season is starting, and we're booked straight through August. With Nic busy in New York, you can't do it alone."

"Can't do what alone?" Johnson comes up beside Bree, handing me an empty drink.

"Plan all these events by herself," I say.

"I can help out—can't be that much harder than running a product launch." Johnson is a project manager at Bree's research and development firm.

"Really? You don't mind?" She sounds relieved.

He shrugs. "I'm here all the time, anyway. Everyone else either works here or is married to someone who does, I was starting to feel left out."

Gabby's agent grabs the mic again. "We'll now move on to the signing portion. If you could all form a line."

"That's my cue. Catch ya later." Johnson heads off to the queue, Bree beside him.

Gabby smiles at each fan as they approach her table. She shares a little small talk, signs the book with a flourish and then hands it back. Gone is the shaking girl from the closet who didn't want to face the people.

After the final fan leaves, Gabby shakes Bree's hand and the two chat for a moment. She takes a deep breath and, without a look back, she walks out the door.

My shoulders slump with a sigh. I'm not sure what I expected. A goodbye? Thank you? Something.

It's well past two in the morning when I finally walk through the door of my apartment. Such is the life of a bartender. It will be hours yet until my head hits the pillow, though. I have work to do.

The light flares as my computer comes to life in the otherwise dim space. I open a blank document and stare at the empty screen. It's not bare for long as my fingers fly over the keyboard, a satisfying clack the only music to my ears.

People who collect figurines or art can display their collections on the walls. When you collect characters, the only place to put them is into a book.

Words fill the page, but in my head I only see her. Instead of sitting in a small apartment on the outskirts of Friendship Springs, Florida, my mind is in Boston, where the gorgeous bookstore owner is the only one who can identify a serial killer on the loose.

As the sun rises, my fingers finally slow. Somehow I've drafted eight thousand words in a few hours. Gabby Boyle has completely captivated me and inspired me like no one else. I want more.

War of the Witches – Book 3 – V1

by Gabriella Boyle

~~~

As Lucian looked at Catrina, he felt a stirring in his loins. It was likely the result of the love potion the enemy coven had dosed him with. Grabbing her about the waist, he pushed her back against the tree and lifted her skirts. "I want you," he growled.

Catrina wrapped her legs around him and opened herself to him. "Finally." She wrapped her fingers around his quivering member and...

SHIT.

This is all shit. adcskl;v kjjb
~~~

Big Bossy Sister

I collapse onto my keyboard with a groan. Why is this so hard?

Well, isn't hard the point?

Ugh, so not the time for my inner voice to make dick jokes.

I can write intricate fight scenes, design whole magic systems, so why can't I describe two people having sex without it sounding like some teenager's diary? Maybe if they were dragons this would be easier... Can I dose them with a transformation potion instead?

The doorbell rings, saving me from exploring that harebrained idea further. I blink at the clock on my screen. I've been at it for hours, might as well take a break. Padding to the door in my fuzzy onesie, I don't bother to check the peephole before throwing the door wide. There's only two people who know where I live, anyway.

My sister, Deidre, sails through the opening without a word, heading to the kitchen with two totes, her long red curls bouncing behind her. Her wife, Corinne, enters more sedately, stopping to smile at me in the entryway, hands also full.

I grin back, taking one of Corinne's bags as I lean in to kiss her cheeks. "Well, hi to you too, Dee."

She waves at me dismissively as she pulls out a bottle of wine and then moves about my apartment like she owns the place. Fair though, since she lived here with me until she got married. "We're here to pull you out of your funk and feed you, because I'm sure you haven't eaten."

Corinne smiles at her wife, shaking her head slightly, as she unpacks the bags on the counter. There's a growing stack of Tupperware. Each has a Post-it note with reheat instructions.

My heart warms at the sight. I went no contact with my parents years ago, and writing can be isolating—which I'll admit was half the appeal. I can always count on Dee and Corinne. They're my family.

We stand around the island as Corinne preps a casserole for the oven. It's my favorite—cream of mushroom soup, rice, and chicken breast. So easy, but I never manage to make it for myself. Probably because once I realize I'm hungry, I can't wait forty-five minutes for it to cook.

Dee snags a grape from the fruit platter, popping it past her scarlet lips. "So, what's the problem with the book? I don't think I've ever seen you this stuck."

"It's this damn sex scene the publisher wants. I literally have the rest of the plot figured out, but every time I try to write the big deed..." My fingers thread through my unruly curls, tugging until I'm sure it's a ratty puffball.

"It sounds like some D-grade adolescent fanfic?"

"Deidre!" Corinne admonishes, wearing her best disappointed teacher's face. Dee only shrugs her shoulders with wide, innocent eyes.

"No, she's right. That's exactly what it sounds like. I don't know what I'm going to do." I collapse onto the barstool, taking a healthy swig of my drink.

"Do you have to include the sex scene? Can you just tell them no?" Corinne asks as she puts the dish in the oven.

"Roger says it's part of my contract. I could lose my entire deal, and the Netflix one, too." I take another sip, the telltale tingles and heat rushing up the left side of my face. "My face is doing that flush thing, isn't it?"

Dee winces at me, then switches out my wine for some water. Every time I drink, this blotchy red rash breaks out around my mouth and cheeks. Sometimes it gets so hot to the touch, I feel like my face is on fire. "I can't even Hemingway my way out of this writing slump."

"There's got to be something you can do," Corinne starts. "Have you tried a course? A coach? Porn?"

"Yes! All of that. Every time I try to write anything remotely sexual, it just comes out awkward. Like me." I drop my forehead to my crossed arms on the counter, doing my absolute best dramatic princess impression.

"What about getting laid?" My sister puts her hand on her hip as she waits for my answer.

I lift my head, looking to Corinne for help, but she stays silent. "You can't possibly agree with her?"

"Well, you said you tried everything else. Maybe some real-life experience would unblock you."

Oh, you know exactly who you want to unclog those pipes.

The heat spreads to the right side of my face and ears. A certain Viking has been running through my head constantly... and his offer.

"Woah! The rash just spread. I'm grabbing the Benadryl." Corinne rifles through the medical cabinet in the kitchen, but Dee narrows her eyes at me.

"No, that's an emotion flush." Did I mention I break out at any strong emotion too? Makes interviews super fun. "Spill it."

My black cat, Draco, jumps onto the counter, nuzzling my arm as he walks by. I pull him onto my lap for a cuddle to buy time. Okay, and so I don't have to make eye contact as I say this. "Remember the guy at the book reading in Florida I told you about?"

They nod. "Tall, ripped, and hunky. Yeah."

I bite my lip at the thought of him. "He kinda sorta offered to help me with the book. It was after I let slip that I'm having trouble writing the sex scenes because I'm inexperienced."

Corinne gasps. "Like sex lessons? I thought that only happened in romance novels."

Dee's auburn brows raise to her hairline. "What exactly did he say?" Trust the lawyer to want specifics.

"He said, 'I could help you. If you want.' What else could that mean other than sex lessons?"

Dee taps her nail on my counter, lips pursed in thought, before pulling out her cell, fingers flying across the screen. She turns the device to me with a picture of Asher. "Is this him?" I nod, and she goes back to her typing.

After a few more minutes of this, she presses the button and raises the phone to her ear. "Pack your bags, Gabby. You're going to Florida." She pulls her attention away from me as someone picks up the call. "Hi, my client Gabriella Boyle was at your restaurant for an event last month. No, there isn't a problem."

What the hell did I just agree to? And why am I vaguely excited about it?

Beauty and the Butcher

by Asher Ramstead

~~~

Cathy's stomach dropped as James's words registered. "You don't believe me."

He sighed. "I never said that. Your points make a lot of sense, but the proof against Greyson is overwhelming. The lab matched his fingerprints at the last scene and found a bloodstained steak knife in his kitchen."

"I guess." She had to trust the police to do their job. He didn't think she was crazy, at least.

"They caught the guy, Cathy. You can relax now," James said.

Something still bothered her, though, about the evidence. The receipt tucked in the book at the
~~~

crime scene, the bloody footprint. It had been too easy. Maybe that was the years of Agatha Christie novels talking, and real-life mysteries aren't as complicated.

Cathy glanced around her store and saw abandoned piles of books, dusty shelves, outdated events boards. Her recent moonlighting as a detective had left little time for her beloved bookshop, and these copies were not going to reshelve themselves. She guessed it was time to force her head back into her work.

"So listen," James said, "I was thinking, now that the investigation is over, we should go out to dinner."

A stack of mysteries in her arms, Cathy paused, trying to make sense of his words. "Dinner?"

"To celebrate. I couldn't have closed the case without you."

"I'd think you'd be sick of me by now." She felt her cheeks blush. Her time with James had been invigorating, and not only because they were catching a killer. It had occurred to her at least once that arresting the perp meant considerably less time with the handsome detective. After months of late nights studying reports over pizza, he'd become a bit of a constant in her life, and she dreaded going back to meals alone.

"No one could be sick of you, Cathy."

Her heart skipped a beat, and she admitted her newfound hatred of solo dining was more about missing him specifically rather than company generally.

James misunderstood her silence and rushed on. "It doesn't have to be dinner—lunch or even coffee would be nice. You do have to eat eventually, right?"

She listened to James rattle on as she skimmed the shelves to find the correct place. Her hand froze over one particular title: Nancy Drew 7 The Clue in the Diary.

"Of course, it's so obvious. James, I gotta go."

"Cathy, wait—" but she hung up before he could finish, her mind already whirling over the facts.

The police swore the killer merely hunted for victims at bookstores, but they didn't care about the why, simply the who. So desperate to close the case, they glossed over the most important detail. The books left at the scene weren't arbitrary; each was a clue. Gabby had analyzed them all: And Then There Were None, Rebecca, The Girl with the Dragon Tattoo, My Dark Vanessa. A wide range of publication dates, genres, and authors, but all shared a theme of justice—the murderer identifies themselves as the hero.

At first glance, the targets seemed just as random—a teacher here, loving father there, philanthropist CEO, and dentist. Different towns, economic brackets, but there must have been a common link. Then Cathy got a hit on the CEO, a passing mention of a lawsuit for wrongful termination, but it was something. The plaintiff? His twenty-something secretary, who claimed he fired her when she wouldn't sleep with him.

So Cathy dug deeper, tried a new angle, and struck gold. All the supposed victims had sexual assault complaints against them posted anonymously in a subreddit. Now that she knew what to look for, Cathy found arrests and trials. Every single one had charges dropped or cases dismissed.

She merely had to find the right common thread to pull. A quick search of public records, and one officer appeared on all of them. Cathy had a name and an address. She should go to the police, but they'd rejected her once already; she knew they would never believe her over one of their own.

James's face came to her mind—maybe one of them would.

He didn't pick up. After the third try, she sent him a text with all the information she'd found. Check marks appeared, telling her he'd read the message, but no response came. After half an hour, Cathy couldn't ignore the twisting in her gut any longer. She flipped the sign to "Closed" and jumped in her car.

~~~
~~~

CHAPTER 7

Hands-On Learner

My fingers fly across the keys. The continuous clacking sound of the mechanical keyboard gives instant dopamine hits with every strike, urging me to type faster and faster as I hurl the words onto the screen.

Mid-thought, a knock sounds on my door. Probably a delivery. It can wait until I finish this scene. My brows pinch as I try to focus.

The words haven't been consistently flowing this well. Sure, I had an explosion of productivity when I first started this project, but then it petered out into fits and spurts. Today is the first real burst I've gotten, and I'll be damned if I waste it.

The knock echoes again, louder this time, distracting me just long enough that I completely lose my train of thought. Grumbling, I stomp across my apartment to the door, ready to chew out whatever solicitor ruined my flow. I throw open the door, the snarl in my throat freezing as I take in the unexpected sight before me.

Underneath a mop of curly copper hair, wide brown eyes stare up at me through black-framed glasses. A loose hoodie covers her frame, but I remember those curves; they're stamped in my memory. Gabby fucking Boyle is standing at my front door.

"Maybe I should have called first. Is now a bad time?"

Yeah, it is, but I don't want to tell her that. I'm too curious about why she's here. After the signing, I'd half expected to find an email from her, but as the weeks passed, I'd pushed our meeting to the back of my mind.

At least I'd tried to.

She's not my usual type. Okay, up to now my type has been simply "women," but they've all been variations on a theme. Confident and polished, only looking for a good time and to say they've snagged Pop's hot bartender. I'm not complaining or judging—it's not like I got nothing from the arrangement—but they all blend together into a forgettable lineup.

This little firecracker is hard to forget.

Silently, I step back and watch her walk in. Is that a suitcase? Is she in town for another signing?

"I've been thinking about your offer." She nibbles on that plump lower lip, and I want to pull it free with my thumb.

Instead, I fist my hands and bury them in the pockets of my gray sweatpants. Her eyes follow the motion, and I swear they darken. The not-so-little-guy twitches in appreciation.

Her cheeks redden, confirming she was watching. Her tongue darts out to wet her lips as she raises her eyes back to mine. "I'd like to take you up on it. If you still want to... help, I mean."

Oh, I do. I want more time with this walking ball of chaos. "Of course. We could have done this over email or video, though."

Her brows pinch in confusion. "I'm more of a hands-on learner. I wasn't sure how long it would take, but I packed light. Figured I wouldn't need much, anyway. Unless you want that. Oh, god." The red flush spreads all the way to the tips of her ears.

What is she talking about? My eyes drop to the bright purple roller bag. Yup, it's a suitcase. "Gabby, what are you doing here?"

"For your offer... to help with my... Are you really going to make me say it?" At my silent stare, she gulps and then raises her eyes to the ceiling. "I'm here for the sex lessons."

I choke on my fucking spit. Those are the last words I expected her to say. How the hell did she come to that conclusion?

Mentally, I replay our conversation in the office. She complained about being sexually inexperienced, and I offered to help with her book. Right? Did I say "writing" explicitly or did I offer to help and her mind filled in the dots?

Mortification spreads across her face, the color draining so fast I'm worried she'll hit the floor. "I totally misread this situation, didn't I? Of course. Why would someone like you be willing to sleep with someone like me? Great job, Gabby." She grabs her bag and heads towards the door.

Within three steps I catch up, my six-foot-two frame coming in handy. I slam my hand on the door above her head as she tries to open it, looming over her body.

She whirls, leaning back against the surface. Her head slowly raises until her eyes meet mine. I can read her emotions like a book. Want. Need. Shame.

"Don't you run away, little Imp. For the record, I haven't stopped thinking about you since we met."

She gulps, and the muscles in her throat constrict. Her pulse races, the skin by her delicate jaw fluttering like a hummingbird. With a stuttering breath, her breasts brush my chest, burning my skin. Those plump lips fall open, and I lean in, catching the faintest whiff of rose.

"Hands-on demonstration wasn't exactly what I meant." I'm so close, every sense filled with only her.

"Wh-what did you have in mind?" Her eyes drop to my mouth, and she leans the slightest bit towards me; it's all the invitation I need.

"Doesn't matter. I like your idea better." I slam my mouth down on hers.

~~Rule 1. Never Kiss First.~~

CHAPTER 8

Down the Rabbit Hole

She pauses for only a second before leaning into the kiss, clutching my shirt as she arches her entire body into mine.

I groan. My hands trace every curve until they reach her ass. Cupping each cheek, I lift her higher against the door. The wood scrapes my knuckles, but I don't care.

Her lips part on a gasp, and I take full advantage, plundering her mouth. She matches my movements, her tongue teasing in a seductive dance, her hips rocking in a matching rhythm.

I carry her to the nearby counter, allowing my hands freedom to fully explore the body that's starred in my dreams for weeks. My fingers brush along the cotton leggings, which expose every curve to my eyes.

Continuing upwards, I slip underneath the hem of the hoodie, finding her bare skin. I trace each vertebra on her back.

Gabby trembles as she clings to me, clawing at my shirt. Blindly, I pull it off, only breaking the kiss when I absolutely have to. Her fingers immediately move to explore my abs.

Every nerve lights up like I've been struck by lightning. Each moan urges me on more. I've never felt like this before, and if I'm being honest, I've kissed a lot of women. My lips travel along her jaw and to her neck, drinking in the new sounds she makes. My body is buzzing. Hers must be too based on her gasp. I grind against her hot core. Some part of my brain is yelling that this is all too fast, and I should stop.

I've never been one to listen to my own advice.

I lay her back on the counter as I grip her hips to haul her even closer to my hard cock. My hands glide her sweatshirt up her pale stomach as I stare into her brown eyes. Her pupils are blown wide, making them appear almost black. I trail soft kisses along her skin until her white cotton bra blocks my path. Deftly flipping the cup inside out, my lips latch onto an already pebbled nipple as she arches her back into me.

Fifth Harmony's "Work from Home" starts blaring from my bedroom. I freeze. My cock is still buzzing—no, like literally vibrating. I curse as I drag myself back, digging into my pocket for my cellphone. The words "Get Ready for Work" flash across the screen as the alarm goes off again.

"What is it?" Gabby pushes herself up on her elbows, looking like a fucking wet dream. Her curls form a wild halo, and a flush colors her cheeks.

I can't believe I have to say this. My fingers grip the back of my neck as I try to push away the lust still riding my body. "I have to go to work. That's my backup alarm."

"Backup? Where was the first?"

I hold up my phone. "It was vibrating in my pocket, but I was, uh, distracted."

"Oh. Oohhh. That explains a lot. I thought you just had a magical dick." Her eyes widen, and she surges up, pulling her clothes back in place. "Not to say it wasn't enjoyable. I'm sure it's a perfectly adequate dick. That's not better, is it? What I mean is, it was quite nice before the vibrating. I'm just going to stop talking now."

My cock twitches, fully willing to show her how much more than adequate he is. I bite my lip to fight a smile. There's something invigorating about how this girl talks. She has abso-fucking-lutely zero filter, and I love it. Before I think twice about it, I drop another lingering kiss to her lips and lift her back off the counter. She stumbles slightly, blinking rapidly.

"I have to jump in the shower and change. Why don't I drop you off at your hotel? We can pick up where we left off after my shift." Not waiting for a response, I rush into the bathroom, jumping into an ice-cold blast in an attempt to calm my still-raging erection.

Showers are usually one of my most productive times. Some authors plot while driving; others wake up from a dead sleep with a fully formed novel. I'm a shower thinker. The brief contact with Gabby has reignited my creativity, and the solution to my latest plot hole immediately forms as my fingers rub shampoo into my scalp. I dive back out of the stall, careful not to slip on the tiles as I type the idea into the notes app of my phone, cursing as the suds sting my eyes.

After the fastest shower of my life, I reemerge in a pair of jeans and my Pop polo shirt. With the time crunch, I pulled my hair up into a messy bun. A droplet runs down the back of my neck, but give the Florida heat five minutes and it'll be dry enough.

"Okay, Imp, where am I dropping you off?" I swing my keys around my finger by the ring.

"Oh, about that..." Her fingers grip the hem of her sweatshirt, twisting the material. "I didn't book a hotel."

"Where are you staying? "An Airbnb?"

"I assumed I'd stay with you, which sounds dumb now that I say it out loud."

I pause, catching the keys in my palm. "Here?"

Her cheeks are scarlet, and the flush is creeping below her collar too. I wonder how far the blush goes? "It's efficient..."

I still, it somehow only now dawning on me that she's in my apartment. The same place I don't invite anyone to because it's my sanctuary. Okay, also because I don't share well and I like my shit a particular way.

Do I honestly want to tell her to leave? Will she just fly back to Boston?

My stomach clenches at the thought, and I realize I really don't want her to go. I've been struggling with writer's block for a week, fifteen minutes with her, and the juices are flowing again—not to mention other juices I'd like to see flowing again.

"Can't argue with that," I say slowly. "Come on, you can hang out at Pop while I work. My shift is only a couple of hours."

Gabby lets out a relieved huff, her shoulders relaxing as I guide her out the apartment door, trying to ignore how quickly I'm throwing out all the rules for this girl.

~~Rule 2. Her Place, Never Mine.~~

Welcome to Pop

Sitting in a small car next to a near stranger 2.3 seconds after he's had his tongue down your throat and hands all over your body is super cool. Not awkward at all. And going to work with him is completely normal. Nothing to see here.

Okay, it's been more like fifteen minutes, but that doesn't make this any less weird.

My eyes stay firmly glued to the window as we drive and I study the town. Last time I was here, it was a rushed visit, and I barely saw anything as my agent jetted me from the hotel to the event hall. Roger even booked radio interviews over commutes. Plus, it's way easier to simply ignore the hottest man I've ever seen, who appears completely unaffected by our make-out session, while I'm sitting here praying my pants don't catch on fire.

Friendship Springs is charming. Most of the buildings are older brick facades along tree-lined streets. Farther from the center, there are slightly more modern stucco and concrete constructions that are still a few decades out of style. Once-bright colors faded to pastels but still cheery, giving a nostalgic vibe rather than tragic. It's cozy.

Asher pulls into a parking lot behind the buildings. He turns off the car and smiles at me. "Ready?"

I try for a smile of my own but, considering how awkward it feels on my face, I've probably missed the mark. "I could have just stayed at your apartment, I really don't want to be in the way."

"You won't be. Plus, I couldn't leave you alone there all day—there's no food in the place. Pretty sure that's a war crime."

"Oh. Is that like a normal bachelor thing? No groceries in the house?"

"Naw, that's an I-work-at-a-restaurant thing. Just makes sense for me to grab most of my meals here. We'll stop at the market after my shift. I want to make sure there's stuff that you can eat."

I blush, reminded of our first meeting. Having food sensitivities is so frustrating. People make such a big deal out of it when I honestly would rather ignore it. Not that I want to feel sick, I don't, but I wish meal planning was as easy for me as everyone else.

"Okay. I brought a book, so I can just sit somewhere and be out of your way." I wave my paperback like the awkward fool I feel.

Asher peeks at the cover, then shakes his head. "More market research? I see you've moved on from lacrosse."

My cheeks burn. What does this guy have against romance novels? "Not exactly. I kind of got hooked and have been reading through the whole backlist." This one is baseball. There's a certain magic to the way AR Storm writes. The spice is absolutely... well, spicy, but the characters are so well rounded and the speeches so heartfelt. I can't help myself.

Asher leads me through the back door into the kitchen. I pause by the back office, assuming I'll be hiding out in here again, but he keeps walking. A handful of men and women stand at the counters, chopping vegetables, preparing sauces, or cubing meat. He greets each by name and gets an enthusiastic reply. It's clear Asher is well-liked here.

"Hey, Ash." A striking woman calls to him from her spot by the pass. She wears her chef's coat with confidence as she checks plates.

"Hey, Meeka. This is Gabby, she's going to be hanging out front with me today."

She turns her smile on me. As I shake her hand, her eyes widen. "You're Gabriella Boyle. I love your books. You'd better run before Tony catches you, though. He's a huge fan." She jerks a thumb over her shoulder at a man stirring a vat of soup while jerking his hips to a Taylor Swift song.

"Come on, Gabby." Asher grabs my hand and pulls me towards the double doors. My heart stops at the casual action. I wave weakly at Meeka as I let him drag me through to the dining room.

We enter by a massive wooden bar. Bottles of alcohol line glass shelves stretching to the ceiling with LED lights. A pink neon sign sits prominently with a champagne bottle, the cork shooting out, sparks surrounding the spout, and the word "Pop."

Asher places a hand flat on the bar top and leaps over the surface in a fluid motion. The sleeves of his work polo stretches around his biceps as the muscles bunch. My mouth goes dry as all the liquid pools lower.

This man is a walking thirst trap.

Rolling my tongue back into my mouth, I survey the rest of the room. Large paintings and photographs hang on the walls in various groupings.

The architecture and furnishings themselves are simple, clean lines in modern chrome, black, and white.

A couple waitresses sit in a booth together, laughing as they roll napkins and fill salt shakers. They don't even spare us a glance.

I love it here. There's something so welcoming and comfortable. I'm sure I'll feel differently when it's filled with people, but when it's like this, it's perfect.

"Here, grab a seat."

"I don't want to take a spot away from paying customers."

"Gabby, it's barely eleven and the bar rush won't be until five. Pop a squat, Imp."

Despite myself, I smile at the nickname and do as he says. "So, how long have you worked here?"

"Since we opened almost six years ago. Bree, Anna, and Nic opened the place and hired me on as head bartender." He pushes a cup of pale amber liquid over ice in front of me. "That's Anna's special sweet tea."

"Thanks. Have you always been a mixologist?" I may have gone on a wine-driven Google spiral after we met.

"Pretty much. I started in college for some extra cash and then realized I really liked it, so... here we are." His hands fly behind the bar, checking bottles and unloading the dishwasher. The veins in his hand bulge as he grips the glass.

My fingers slowly stroke the straw in my tea, the cold glass biting my palm as I hold it aloft. I realize he's stopped talking and rip my eyes back up to his.

His eyes are intense, but I can't name the expression. Quickly licking my parched lips, I take a sip. Those icy blue eyes darken and his grip tightens. I gulp my drink, of course, sending it down the wrong pipe and start choking.

My lungs burn as I cough and sputter. A vein throbs to a drum line at my temple, and my eyes tear.

"Shit." Asher is over the bar again in a heartbeat with a bottle of water and a napkin. His giant hand covers half my back as he rubs it. "Breathe, Gabs."

One stuttered breath in, then a second. My whole body hurts, and my face is on fire—either from the embarrassment, lack of oxygen, or both. The bottle shakes in my hand as I bring it to my mouth.

"Easy."

"Yeah, wouldn't want to choke."

He laughs, his hand pausing on my back, practically burning my skin. "You good?"

I give him a thumbs-up. Real fucking smooth, Gabby.

CHAPTER 10

Affirmations

My eyes dart around the room, desperate for a distraction or escape. The pink neon sign for the restroom is like a beacon from Gondor.

"I'm just going to..." I jerk my thumb over my shoulder towards the bathroom. For the love of god, Gabby, put the thumbs away. Shooting to my feet, the edges of my vision darken and I stumble off the stool, wrap my arms around myself to hide the offending digits, and blindly trudge to the bathroom door.

Instead of the harsh lighting I expect, dim sconces line a wallpaper-covered accent wall with tall mirrors ringed with LEDs. It acts as an impromptu ring light that I'm sure the girls go nuts for. Bright red patches mottle my face and neck. I pull my soft t-shirt away from my chest and find the blotches continue down, like I'm the world's most uncool leopard.

Well, that couldn't have gone much worse. I definitely proved why I need sex lessons at thirty-three. Maybe I should have chosen a less hot teacher. That must be the problem: when I'm near Asher my brain short circuits.

Those kisses at his apartment made me forget to breathe, then I tried to drown myself just looking at his face. If we ever actually have sex, I'll probably find a way to die.

The cold porcelain of the sink is a welcoming shock to my senses as I grip the edges. I turn the tap on and let the sound of the rushing water chase away the voices in my head for a moment.

I grab a handful of paper towels, soak them, and press them to my face, desperate to bring down the color.

You've got this, Gabby. This is not life or death. It's a fling: two consenting adults mutually benefitting from the arrangement for an agreed-upon amount of time. Well, I'm not actually sure what Asher is getting out of this, but he definitely wasn't opposed. I gulp, vividly remembering the press of his erection against my center. The Viking is packing. My thighs squeeze together, trying to ease the ache left from our unfinished make-out session.

Taking a deep breath, I look at my reflection. The red is better, but my skin is still mottled. My eyes slide off and focus on words printed on the mirror above my head.

Fix your crown, Queen. You were made to shine!

Glancing at the other mirrors, I see more affirmations scrawled across the glass. Somehow I found the one that said exactly what I needed, though. My shoulders relax and my lips tip into a smile. Thank you, universe!

I head back to the bar with a new sense of confidence.

The sound of Asher's throaty laughter guides me back. I'm so distracted by the view of his throat muscles flexing as he throws his head back in amusement, the rest of the room fades away. A feminine snort draws me short, and that's when I see her.

She's fucking gorgeous. Like one of the dark witches in my books. Inky hair falls in a smooth waterfall down her back, almost to her waist. Toned, tanned arms with an intricate floral sleeve from shoulder to hand. I'd kill for her figure, prominent bust on tasteful display in a Pop-branded tank top and a firm round ass perfectly displayed in black Lycra.

I'm wearing the same pants, but my rump is more square than globe-shaped—she definitely doesn't spend hours sitting at a keyboard. Should I buy one of those standing desks? And a walking pad. Isn't that supposed to help with computer butt? Or maybe that's a yoga ball... I tried one of those but ended up flipping backwards and almost cracking my head open.

"Gabby!" Asher's lips tilt in an amused smile, but it's clear he's called my name more than once. "You good?"

The flushing I'd calmed down reignites with a vengeance. "Yeah, sorry, zoned out there for a minute—professional hazard."

"Mmhmm. Gabby, this is Jessie. She's my right hand behind the bar. If you need anything, she will get it for you."

Dark brown eyes sweep me from head to toe as an inky brow arches higher. "Is that so?"

"Hi." My hand jerks in some pathetic impression of a wave.

The mauve lips quirk, but I wouldn't call it a smile. "How long are you in town for?"

"Not really sure yet. It's awesome to escape the cold, though."

My phone rings in my pocket, saving me from the inquisition. "Shit, it's my agent. I should take this."

Asher's brows pinch in concern. "You can take it in the office through the kitchen." He steps towards the opening in the bar.

"I remember the way. Nice to meet you. I'd better..." Backing through the double doors, I waggle my thumb in some strange wave and thumbs-up combo.

If they weren't critical for typing, I'd cut my hands off. There's always dictation, I guess.

Putting the cell to my ear, I duck my head and speed through the now bustling kitchen to the quiet room I remember. "Hello."

"Gabriella, where are those pages? Your editor mentioned you're late with the new pages."

My head jerks as if slapped. "You've been talking to my editor?"

"I'm worried about you. You've never missed a deadline before."

I sigh as guilt and my endless need to please swells within me. "It's these changes they requested. I'm struggling with the sex scenes. It just doesn't fit with the story I want to tell."

"It's what's going to sell this book and land you another contract. Just buckle down and write it."

Gee, real supportive, Roger. "I'm trying."

A pan clatters in the kitchen, startling me.

"Where are you?"

"It's a sort of writing retreat to help with the romance. Uh, like an intensive course." I mouth *what the fuck* to the room.

"What's the name of it? I should be vetting these things."

I bristle. "Roger, that is outside your job description. Let me worry about the novel; you worry about getting a little more time from the publisher."

"Okay, okay. Just send me those pages."

I collapse into the nearby rolly chair, letting my head fall back. A dull throbbing in my temple builds. Great, add "find aspirin" to the ever-growing to-do list. It can go right before "make a deal with a crossroads demon to write a romance I never wanted to in the first place." Sometimes I wish I could tell the story I want, not worry about the market or my editor or my agent.

A throat clears. In the doorway stands a young man with dark brown hair, olive skin, and a nervous expression. "I'm sorry to disturb you, but I saw you walk by and... well, I'm a huge fan."

This must be Tony. Great.

CHAPTER 11

Bring Your FB to Work Day

The double doors swing shut behind Gabby. I'm still chuckling over her goofy thumb guns as I turn back to the bar.

Jessie leans with a hand on her cocked hip, giving me that patented ice glare.

"What?"

"What's up with the cling-on?" She jerks her chin towards the kitchen.

"Gabby? It's not like that." I go back to emptying the dishwasher, finding comfort in the routine.

"The girl has heart emojis in her eyes when she looks at you."

My heart gives a traitorous leap. "Don't be ridiculous. If anything, it would be eggplants—we're friends with benefits."

"So what? Is it bring your fuck buddy to work day and nobody told me?"

With an overly shocked expression, I turn to her. "You have one? I thought you were a no back-to-backs girl?" She rolls her eyes at me and tosses her cloth at my face. "Figured here was better than being alone and bored. Plus, we're hitting up Tucker's on the way back to the apartment."

Jessie freezes, her entire body going stiff. "She's staying with you?"

I borrow Gabby's words. "It's efficient."

"Uh-huh. This is going to end poorly." She retrieves her towel and flips it over her shoulder.

"Stop it, Jessie. She's here for work and needs a place to stay. I like hanging out with her. Win-win."

"Whatever you say, boss." With a sarcastic salute, she heads off as the lunch crowd trickles in, ending our conversation.

There's not a large population of day drinkers in Friendship Springs, but a lot of people who work in the nearby businesses will sit at the bar to eat, or pick up a to-go order. There's a constant slow flow to keep the day interesting.

Not busy enough to stop me from checking the kitchen doors a dozen times.

I'm not waiting for her to return; that would be silly for someone I barely know. It's that manager of hers; there's something about him I don't like. When an hour goes by and she still hasn't returned, I grow worried.

Gabby's a grown woman; she doesn't need me rushing in to save her. She's probably writing on her phone in the office. Going in would only distract her, plus Meeka sent out a sandwich for me, so I don't even have an excuse to go back there. Meanwhile, there are drinks to make and front of house management duties to see to.

When my shift is over, I finally give in to the urge to go look for her. It doesn't take much effort; the door barely swings shut behind me when I see her. She's perched on the table we use for meals. Her head tilts back as she laughs, exposing her long neck. Copper strands escape her ponytail and curl around her face in the kitchen heat. A bowl rests in her lap, cradled with one hand. She leans forward, her eyes alight.

She's gorgeous.

Her other hand reaches out and pats the arm of the man next to her, and my stomach clenches. She says something to him, and they both laugh together.

What the fuck was that?

"Like I know why Lucian is all about Catrina in your books—the woman kicks ass—but what's in it for her? She's trying to save the world and keep the dark coven's curse from spreading, and the kingdoms are at war. She doesn't have time for a roll in the leaves!"

"Thank you! And can you imagine how uncomfortable sex would be in the forest? What if you rolled over onto a stick?" She wrinkles her nose. "I just can't wrap my modern brain around it."

"Well, there is a psychological and biological explanation. Between the adrenaline rush and the fear of death, many people turn to sex for comfort." They both look at me with wide eyes. My ears tingle with embarrassment as the silence turns awkward. "But yeah, a stick up the ass sounds terrible."

Gabby and Tony share a look and burst out laughing.

I shove my hands into the pockets of my jeans. "Hey, Gabs, ready to head out? We still need to pick up food."

"Yeah, sure." She inhales the last couple of bites in her bowl, then hops off the surface. "Thanks, Tony. I'll text you about that coffee."

"It's a date. See ya, Asher."

Date? How did these two get so chummy? Gabby was hiding from people the first time we met, for fuck's sake. A few hours ago, she was in my apartment with my hands all over her, and now she's making coffee dates with other guys? I'm totally not jealous... only mildly offended.

Gabby brings her dish over to the sink station, placing it in the pile and smiling at the kid washing dishes.

"Hey Miss Boyle, I'm a big fan. I was wondering if you could take a look at the manuscript I've been working on? It's a paranormal romance set in a restaurant where all the waiters are vampires and the customers don't realize they're dinner."

Gabby freezes, her lips curving in a smile that looks more like a grimace. "Gee, that sounds wicked interesting. I'm not allowed to take manuscripts for liability reasons, but I can totally give you my agent's email address, and you can pitch it to him."

"Thanks."

After another one of her wacky waves, we head out to the car. Her earlier high spirits dimmed, Gabby sighs heavily in the passenger seat.

"What's wrong?"

"I just hate having to disappoint people like that. It's probably my least favorite part of this whole business."

"Even more than launch parties where you hide in supply closets?"

Her lips smirk, and she gives me a huffy side-eye that has my cock twitching. "Supply closets are growing on me, thank you very much."

I smile, darting glances at her as I pull out of the parking lot. "So why do you have to turn people away?"

She sighs again, turning her body in the seat to face me a bit more. "I wasn't lying about liability. If someone hands me their manuscript, even if I don't read it, I'm opening myself up to a copyright infringement issue. The last thing I need is a lawsuit from some aspiring writer claiming the big bad trad author stole their idea."

I take in her crossed arms and pinched brow. "I get that, but that doesn't explain why it made you mad."

Her eyes widen. "I don't know. I guess I hate that most people only want something from me. You know? They don't see Gabby the person, just Gabriella Boyle, the author who can give them a big break. Everybody wants something from you in this business."

"So what did Tony want?"

She laughs. "He had a head-cannon question he was dying to ask and traded food for intel."

"Is that why you're getting coffee?" My eyes stay on the road like I'm not anxious to hear the answer.

"I always love to talk books—we're both fans of this other series that we have different theories about the next book on—but I offered to sign his copy of *Rise of the Covens*."

"You know, I like books."

"Oh, yeah? What do you read? And where do you keep them? I didn't see any bookshelves. Though I was a bit distracted." That charming flush rises again.

"Mostly crime and suspense. I prefer audiobooks and podcasts, that way I can listen while I work out or clean."

"Huh." She looks thoughtful.

I chance a look away from the road, my eyebrows pinching. "Huh, what?"

"Nothing, I just could never get into audiobooks."

I bristle. "Audiobooks are just as valid as other mediums."

"No, totally—but they don't smell as good."

I never know what Gabby is going to say next, but that couldn't have been right. "What?"

She flushes. "I'm a physical reader through and through—I barely touch my e-reader. There's just something about that paper and ink smell I can't live without. Maybe they could create a book-scented candle. Then I could save some trees... Nope, I'd probably still want my shelf trophies."

I shake my head as I pull into the small market on the edge of downtown. It's not much, but it has all the staples and is convenient. Oh shit, what if Gabby is some health food nut? I know she has dietary restrictions. "This should be good enough for a few days, at least. I can take you to the chain store in the next town tomorrow if you want."

She waves a hand at me as she unlatches her seat belt. "I'm sure this is fine. I'm easy."

My cock twitches. Down, boy, that's not what she meant.

Gabby's already bounding out of the car before I get my shit together enough to join her. She doesn't seem bothered. Hands shoved in her hoodie, eyes darting around taking in the area.

Resting my hand on her back, I guide her to the door.

CHAPTER 12

Groceries

The grocery store is small but well stocked—somewhere between a bodega and a local market. The aisle markers call out everything from lightbulbs to carrots.

Asher drops his hand from my back and grabs a cart. "So where to first?"

"Hmm, how about produce and work our way back?"

He leads the way and I keep pace.

We fall into my general circle of hell—awkward silence. This is about the point where I break out into anxious chatter.

"So bartending…" Yup, right on cue. "How does one get into that? Is it a calling? Or more a vocation? Ooh or are you Liam Neeson and you 'have a particular set of skills'?" And there we go—complete with a terrible Scottish impression.

Asher chuckles. "Not a bad Irish accent—you should try that on my buddy, Colin."

Apparently my terrible Scottish accent is actually a decent Irish accent. Who knew?

He tosses a bunch of bananas into the cart and continues, "Nothing like that. I was just looking to earn some cash in college. It was easy, in demand, and under the table. Already had the skills, so I worked in a bar after graduation while I looked for a real job."

"Pretty sure bartending is a real job." A bag of baby carrots joins the bananas.

He shrugs noncommittally. "Then I saw the ad for a head bartender at a new restaurant, and the rest is history."

"So you've been at Pop since the beginning? What's that like?" I grab a jar of sauce and a couple boxes of pasta from an end display.

He studies my face for a beat, probably judging my intention behind the question. "Honestly? It's great. I work with some of my best friends. The atmosphere is very chill—well, you saw it. With the event space now, there's something different every day."

His eyes grow distant as he grabs a six-pack of energy drinks, then a sleeve of Gatorade I point to. "At first I wasn't sure I'd like more responsibility, you know, when they let me buy in, but it's been good. I like the freedom, and as a night owl, you can't beat the hours." He's grinning as he finishes; it's clear he loves what he does.

I hold up a bag of ground coffee and individual pods. Asher points to the pods, and I toss them in the cart. We continue in silence for a few aisles.

"What about you?" Asher asks as he grabs some white bread. "How did you decide on writing?"

"You know my aversion to people?" Asher chuckles and nods, no doubt thinking of how we met. "Well, I've always been like that. As a kid, I'd escape into books. Late at night, when I couldn't sleep, I'd tell myself stories. Eventually, I started writing the stories down to get them out of my head."

"And now you've made a career out of it. Your parents must be so proud."

A lump rises in my throat. I tuck a stray curl behind my ear. "Not exactly." I toss a bag of bagels with a little too much force. "Dad's a lawyer and Mom's a surgeon. They wanted my sister and me to follow in their footsteps. We stopped talking to them after high school."

Asher stops the cart as emotions play across his face. "I'm sorry, Gabriella."

I lay a hand on his arm, and the muscles dance under my fingers. "It's really okay. Dee and I still made our dreams come true."

He smiles and then pushes the cart again. "So why high fantasy?"

That's an easy one. "What little kid doesn't dream of magical powers?" I give him a goofy grin as I grab a package of ground chicken.

"Especially ones who feel powerless in their own lives." He adds hamburgers to the filling cart. "Why not urban or paranormal?"

I pause, surprised at the turn in conversation and impressed he knows the differences between subgenres. "It's all about escapism for me. I want my readers to be transported to a completely different world, far away from their current issues."

We approach the only cashier line. Asher blocks my path and starts loading the selections onto the belt. It should be macho and insulting, but it's somehow hot. Maybe it's the way his muscles bunch as he hauls the heavier items.

"Hey, Nate. How's it going?"

I tear my eyes away from the free gun show and towards a teenage boy with a red apron manning the cash register. He's tall, definitely over six feet, though his face still holds the roundness of youth. With his blond hair and brown eyes, he looks the very definition of "all-American."

"Hey Mr. Ramstead, doing pretty good. Wow, don't think I've ever seen you buy this much food before. Having a party or something?"

Asher's knowing grin and those electric eyes draw me in. "Or something." He winks at me and then turns back to the boy. "This is my friend Gabby. She's staying with me for a bit. Be sure to take care of her if she comes in."

"Yes, sir, Mr. Ramstead." The kid looks up at Asher with obvious hero worship. His hands fly as he rings up the items with ease.

Asher steps over to the bagging area to give a hand, and I swipe my card through the reader before Asher can protest.

He calls out a farewell to Nate and grabs three bags to my one. I feel his eyes on me as we move to the car, but I break the silence first. "So how do you know Nate?"

"Oh, I'm the assistant coach for the football team. Nate was on JV last year. Kid's got potential, though."

"How many jobs do you have?"

He freezes. A careful look enters his eyes. "What do you mean?"

I put my bag in his trunk and start counting on my fingers as I answer, "Bartender, part owner, assistant coach? When do you sleep?"

He chuckles awkwardly as he runs a hand over his head, messing his topknot. Once again, my eyes snap to the biceps on display. "I like to stay busy." He snaps the lid shut with a clunk.

Clouds darken his typically sunny expression as he climbs in. "Why did you do that?"

"Huh?"

"I could have paid for my groceries."

Uh-oh, looks like I stepped in something, but I have no idea what. "Never said you couldn't, but I'm staying with you, and it seemed easier to pay for it all at once rather than split the order. Take it as a host gift." His knuckles are white against the steering wheel. "Are you going to charge me for water?"

"What?" Blond brows pinch in confusion.

"Well, I assume I'm going to shower at some point. And when I write I'll use your electricity and internet—are you going to invoice me for part of your utilities?"

His lip curves slightly, and his shoulders finally relax. "No."

"I benefit way more from this arrangement than you do. Let me pay for the damn groceries."

Sunny expression restored, Asher turns the ignition. "Okay, Imp. Let's go home."

My heart flutters. Those words sound entirely too good. Easy, Gabs, this is only a temporary thing. Keep your emotions and your hoo-ha separate.

CHAPTER 13

New Rules

Arms full of groceries, I stare at my front door with no way to open it. Didn't exactly think this one through when I was insisting on carrying all the bags in one trip.

"What's wrong?" Gabby stands beside me, huffing a little from climbing the stairs.

"Can you grab the keys? They're in my right pocket." I tilt a hip towards her, lifting the sacks higher to make room for her.

She swallows so loudly, I can hear it. Her hand tries to push in, but the thick fabric resists. "They're a little tight," she mutters. The tip of her pink tongue peeks out of her lips as she pushes harder until her fingers glide across my hip, completely missing the keys and grasping my cock instead—which immediately twitches to say hello. Gabby gasps, freezing with her fingers still loosely gripping my rapidly hardening dick.

"That's not the keys, Gabs."

"Oh, shit, sorry." She quickly grabs the keys and steps up to the door, avoiding eye contact.

I grin as I trail behind her to the kitchen. Gabby empties the bags, grouping the items into categories and still averting her gaze.

"We should probably set some ground rules."

"Ground rules?" Her brown eyes finally meet mine, a gorgeous blush still staining her cheeks.

I scratch at my stubble, realizing I missed my shave this morning. "Yeah, can't say I've ever given sex lessons before. What exactly are you looking for tutelage on?"

She hugs a box of pasta to her chest. "I have had sex."

"You said." I can't help but smirk as I turn to the cabinet, spaghetti sauce in hand.

"Look, I understand the mechanics—tab A goes in slot B, repeat until desired result."

I nearly drop the jar, but save it with a bark of laughter.

Her way with words continuously surprises me. Maybe that is why I want to keep spending time with her. I've spent my life accurately predicting the events of the world around me—there has never been a plot twist I didn't see coming—but with Gabby, I never know what's going to tumble out of her mouth next.

It's fucking exhilarating.

"Well, that might be your problem. There's a lot more to good sex than insert P into V, and I'm starting to doubt you've had good sex before." I approach her, my taller frame forcing her to look up at me.

Her eyes darken moments before they drop to my mouth. Lips part, and that pink tongue swipes the bottom one. This girl has no idea how sexy she is, because it's clear she's not even trying—which gets me going even more.

I lean into her space, breathing in the subtle scent of rose. Her breath catches, her head falling the slightest bit backwards to expose her throat. My fingers grasp the box of pasta from her grip, and then spinning on one heel, I set it away in the cupboard.

Down, boy. If my alarm hadn't gone off for work, I have no doubt we would have ended up naked in my bed without having this conversation—which is so not my style. Even when I have no intention of ever seeing the girl again, I make sure boundaries, expectations, and preferences are fully communicated before any tabs enter any slots.

Groceries put away, I keep the kitchen island between us, not trusting myself to keep my hands to myself. "Okay, so you've got the mechanics down. What is holding you back in your writing? That's why you're doing this, right?"

"Everything I write is very... cold?"

"Like an instruction manual? With your slots and tabs?" I smile, and she rolls her eyes at me. "So you're missing the emotions, the sensations. It's not all about the... how did you put it? Results? The journey is just as important as the destination."

"Well, duh. Most women don't even orgasm during sex. If it were just about the result, I doubt couples would keep doing it."

My fingers grip the counter as I lean towards her. "Oh, honey, I guess that depends on the sample size. I've never left a woman unsatisfied." Gabby exhales with a slight moan, and damn, I want to hear that noise again. "So, I think my earlier theory still stands. You haven't had good sex, so you have nothing to draw from in your writing. I can help with that."

"Cocky much?"

"You were the one with her hand in my pocket, you tell me?" That flush spreads across her face like lightning. "So, what are your limits?" She looks at me as if I'm speaking another language. "What do you like and not like in bed? Do you have a favorite position? How do you like it? Rougher? Light touches? Spanking?"

Her cheeks shine brighter than her hair now. "Jesus, I don't know. Is this just something people openly discuss?"

"Okay, I guess I know what the first lesson is then. If you can't tell me what you like, you'll just have to show me."

"What?" Gabby grips the counter, paling under that furious blush.

"Tonight I'm going to watch you touch yourself. Show me how you get yourself off."

"And you're just going to... what? Sit in the corner like a perv?"

"No, Imp, I'll be touching myself as I catalog all the ways you want me to touch you." She gulps. "Now make yourself comfortable on my bed. I'll be there in a minute." She still looks scared. I walk around the island and rest my hands on her arms, rubbing soothingly. "How about this? Go take a shower, change, do whatever you need to relax, and I'll wait thirty minutes before coming in. Okay?"

Gabby is gnawing on her lip so hard I'm afraid she'll draw blood, so I gently tug it free with my thumb as she stares up at me with wide eyes. "Okay. Thirty minutes."

She walks through my door, looking back at me with the biggest doe eyes that almost bring me to my knees. This girl winds me up in ways I didn't know existed.

What am I going to do for thirty minutes? My eyes fall to the desktop in the corner of my living room. A scene comes to mind instantly, and I need to write it down. With one last look at the closed bedroom door, I set a timer. No way do I want to get lost in my manuscript and wait even an extra minute.

CHAPTER 14

Getting Wet

I lean back against the shut door as my heart races so fast I'm sure my watch alarm will go off any second. Relax, he said, like it's so simple. Like crawling into a stranger's bed naked is an everyday thing—well, maybe for some people it is.

Oh my god, he does this all the time—he's probably slept with hundreds of women. *All the more reason he should be our teacher.*

How the hell do I compete with that? *Calm the fuck down, Gabby. You don't need to compete; this is a temporary arrangement. Wham, bam, thank you, ma'am. Have the experience, then haul your ass back to Boston to finish the book.*

Right. I guess my inner voice is good for more than just dick jokes sometimes.

Asher suggested a shower, but the idea of my wet curls dripping down my back or all over his pillow almost sends me into a tailspin. Plus showers usually send me into full-body blotches, which are distinctly un-sexy, but then again after three hours sitting on a plane, I probably have swamp ass. I could take a ho-bath in the sink, or do a quick pits-and-privates wash with cold water.

Shit, how long have I been arguing with myself? I have only thirty minutes!

Per usual, the threat of a deadline and absolute panic are the magic touches to spur me into action. I pull my hair up into a hasty bun as high as I can and angle the showerhead down. That's when I realize I didn't grab my toiletries and I'm already in the shower. I snatch his body wash, trying not to overthink it, and lather it up. A hint of smoke and cedar hits my nose; it smells like him, and the slightest whiff sends vivid flashbacks to the minutes I've spent in close contact with him.

Rubbing his scent into me creates a naughty thrill. As I slick the gel across my skin with my hands, I shut my eyes and imagine it's his instead. My nipples harden—whether it's from the cold water or my dirty thoughts, who knows? My mind wanders, and I picture Asher coming into the bathroom and finding me touching myself in his shower. Would he join me? Strip off his clothes, step under the spray, grip my thighs, and pin me against the wall? Or would he take over washing me? Lather every inch of my body until I beg him to take me?

Oh shit, how much time do I have left?

The water flows across my skin as I rush to rinse off. A fluffy towel hangs by the door. It's soft as a cloud as I wrap it around my body.

Now what? He told me to make myself comfortable. I could lay there naked, but that's not me. I dive for my suitcase and pull out the silky night shift I packed. It's thin and clingy, with lace at the breast and hem, but the material caresses in the best of ways.

I lay down on his covers with my head on the pillows, staring up at the ceiling. There's a weird texture to it, and I imagine pictures from the shapes, like passing clouds. This is fucking awkward though. I'm not a Victorian bride waiting for her deflowering while thinking of the queen.

Loosen the fuck up, Gabby!

Okay, how do I usually relax? My eyes land on the paperback sticking out of my suitcase. Reading has always been my escape. A way to distract the voices in my head and shut out the stresses of the real world. I'd barely started a sex scene when the plane landed. Relaxation and stimulation in one. Perfect.

Quick as lightning, I dart across the room to grab the book and back like my parents are about to walk in and catch me out of bed. Flipping to my bookmark, I'm immediately sucked in. My breath catches along with the female lead as our hero worships her body. Her words are so vivid, I can almost imagine I'm the heroine. Right before she orgasms, the door opens and Asher walks in.

His eyes rake over me, widening when they reach the book. "Seriously, Gabby? You're waiting in my bed, reading?"

"You said to relax; this is how I relax. Plus, I'd just gotten to a spicy part, and I thought that'd help get me in the mood."

His lips quirk slightly before he wipes the expression away. "Whatever works for you." My heart speeds up as he approaches me. This is actually happening. Instead of coming closer, he sits at the foot of the bed, well beyond touching distance.

"What are you doing?"

"I recall you having an objection to me standing in the corner like a perv. Is this not better?" A single blond brow arches at me.

Yeah, I did say that. Chalk this up to one more thing Gabby got wrong. *I don't know, the corner would definitely be worse... unless he was in a trench coat. That might be hot.* My eyes clench shut as I wrestle my inner voice for control.

"Look, if you've changed your mind, that's completely fine. We can go watch a movie or something and go back to lecture-based learning instead."

"N-no, I still want to do this; it's just..." He arches a brow. "You're still fully dressed and I'm very much not. Hardly seems fair."

His eyes darken as they scan my nightgown again. "I'm all about fairness." With one bicep bulging, he reaches behind his neck and pulls his shirt off in one fluid motion, exposing sun-kissed skin stretched across muscles. I want to trace every curve with my tongue.

"Now, Imp, show me how you make yourself feel good."

CHAPTER 15

Lesson 1

His electric blue eyes bore into mine, and I'm compelled to obey him. I want this gorgeous man to keep looking at me like that. I squirm as an ache rises in my core. "I'm not sure where to start."

"You said you were a hands-on learner; I want a hands-on demonstration. How do you like your pussy touched?"

My cheeks burn—half embarrassment and half desire. No one has talked to me like this before, and I find I like it. No, I fucking love it. Having Asher here, the filthy things he says in that growly voice is like my own romance novel come to life. This man could take home any woman he wants, but tonight he's all mine. The thought emboldens me, and I don't want to miss a moment of this experience.

I hold his gaze as I let my knees fall open, exposing my lace-covered center to his view. My fingers seek the seam of my folds through the cloth and press with the slightest pressure. Slowly, I trace the slight indent up and down, barely teasing my clit before slipping away again.

"What kind of pressure do you like?"

"Light at first, then harder once I'm wet." My core clenches at the boldness of my words, the fabric growing damper still.

Asher groans and palms the bulge at the front of his jeans. "Are you wet for me, Imp? Can I see?"

My fingers grip the lace of my nightgown, slowly easing it up my thighs to give him a better view. His eyes follow every movement as if there will be a pop quiz. *Oh, there will be, when it's his turn to touch. I bet he gets an A.*

"I believe I was promised a show, but your pants are still in the way." Where did that come from?

"As you wish." His fingers deftly undo his fly as his hips lift from the mattress in an impressive display of strength. I'm so distracted by the clench of his ass finally free of restricting denim that I don't immediately notice his hard cock. Not that it isn't eye-catching. I could tell he was going to be massive from the outline of his sweatpants, but not even my imagination did him justice. As his hand glides from base to tip, I start to have concerns about logistics. *It will be so worth it, though.*

"I showed you mine; can I see yours?"

Hooking one finger under the triangle of fabric, I pull it to the side, fully exposing myself.

Asher licks his lips. "I want to taste you, but that will have to wait for lesson two. I promised I wouldn't touch you tonight."

My body shudders at the thought. No one's ever gone down on me before. Something about the idea was always off-putting, but suddenly this man between my thighs is all I want. With a moan, I return my fingers to their earlier exploration, this time dipping slightly into my opening and gathering the wetness there to spread on my clit for a better glide.

I circle the sensitive bud, increasing in speed and pressure. A whine escapes my lips. Asher answers with a groan, one hand still working his shaft as the other grips the covers until his knuckles turn white.

When the friction becomes too much, I slip a finger into my channel again, seeking more lubrication. My pussy greedily clenches around the digit.

"Does that feel good, Imp? Work that finger in your pussy while your other hand works your clit." This isn't how I usually masturbate, but I came to him for lessons, so I comply. "That's it. Find that soft spot, then curl your finger up and stroke it."

It takes a couple of tries, then I discover the magic location. My head falls back against his pillows with a moan, and my back arches.

"Fuck, yes. Now work a second finger in that hungry pussy."

There's a slight stretch as I comply; pumping both in and out. Pressure builds in my lower belly. My breath comes in short pants.

Asher's hand moves faster over his cock as he leans closer to me, eyes fixed on my hands.

Sparks tingle across my toes, and I clench them to ease the sensation. Moans of pleasure and torment vibrate through my throat. My fingers glide so easily now, but it's still not quite enough to get me there. I'm desperate to cum, but I need something else to push me over the edge.

I meet his eyes, begging him silently to offer me the answer.

"Give me another finger, Imp."

My head thrashes on the pillow. "No, that's too much. I can't."

"You have to, baby, if you ever want to take me."

My eyes drop to his cock with a hungry moan, imagining that man meat inside me. Hand shaking, I add a third digit. There's a slight sting as I stretch, but it's immediately swept into pleasure. A rush of liquid coats my hand, my pussy so wet I can hear every pump of my fingers.

"Look at that pretty pussy drip. I can't wait to feel you on my cock."

His words send me over the edge. Half strangled, I call his name as my muscles clench down and wave after wave of satisfaction courses through my body. The shocks have not quite settled when Asher curses and spills himself in great ropes of fluid against his stomach and hand.

CHAPTER 16

Strange Magic

Gabby lies limp on the pillows, a gorgeous blush across her skin. One hand rests on her chest as it moves up and down in slow movements. She looks utterly satisfied, and a rush of masculine pride fills me. A couple more lessons like that and she won't remember any of her disappointing exes' names.

"I'm going to clean up." I grab my polo and wipe myself off, then head to the bathroom to finish the job. The granite counter is cold under my hands as I lean on it to catch my breath. Who knew parallel play could be so damn hot? The experience definitely sparks a few new ideas for future encounters.

Our make-out session earlier told me she was responsive—not that I expected anything else with her unfiltered honesty—but who knew she'd also be a bossy little firecracker? She must have dated only idiots.

Gabby pads in, toiletry bag in hand. With one shy smile at me, she places it next to the other basin—the one that's never been used. Bottles and potions of every shape and color appear on the counter. Methodically, she applies them to her face and hands, leaving a clean, dewy glow. It's no wonder she writes about witches—I'm half convinced she is one.

Or maybe this is what all women do, and I've never seen one in the wild?

She opens a small case, about the size of her hand. What magic device could this hold? Will it be for her hair? Her skin?

Gabby pulls out a bright purple retainer and pops it in her mouth. She checks the fit in the reflection, smiling to reveal a wire line crossing her teeth. Absolutely adorable. Her eyes widen as she catches me staring in the mirror. "What?"

"Don't think I know anyone who still wears their retainer."

"I already wore braces for four fucking years; I'm not doing that again." I laugh at the mix of swearing and slurring, causing her cheeks to blush again. She steps towards me, and I turn to meet her, assuming she's approaching me. Instead, she jerks to the right and freezes in some robot dance move. "I've gotta..." She waves at the water closet with those crazy finger guns.

I'm still chuckling as I settle under the covers, waiting for my new temporary roommate to return. When she does, Gabby stands by the bed, her eyes darting around the room.

"What is it?" I ask.

"Do you have any extra pillows?"

"Are you trying to build a pillow wall? Gabby, you've read too many romance novels. I promise to stay on my side."

With one more unsure look, she crawls into bed, and I draw the sheets over her shoulder as she turns towards me. This close, I can see flecks of amber in her irises. She gnaws that lip again, giving me those big doe eyes that make me hard and soft at the same time. "You don't snore, do you?"

I laugh. "Naw." Then I freeze and tip my head to the side as I consider. "Actually, I don't know. I've never slept next to someone before. You'll have to tell me in the morning."

She smiles slightly, a blush tinging her cheeks. "Good night, Asher."

"Good night, Gabby."

Her blinks grow longer until her eyes remain shut. She wrinkles her nose and squirms a bit before settling.

It's strange lying this close to someone. I half expect it to be unnerving, but it's surprisingly comfortable. Sleep is the last thing on my mind though, so I study her. Watching her is quickly turning into my newest obsession. Gabby bounds through life with this honesty and bubbling energy. Spending time with her is like drinking champagne—it sends tingles that can be intoxicating. I have no idea how long I have to catalog every one of her mannerisms, but I don't want to miss a moment.

Her openness is even starker when she orgasms. Following each new sensation dancing across her features was the most erotic experience of my life, and I didn't even touch her.

Gabby's red curls float on the sheets next to me. I want nothing more than to reach out and tug a ringlet to see if it springs back, but I don't want to wake her.

"I can feel you staring. Go to sleep," she mumbles from the depths of her pillow.

"Yes, ma'am."

Normally, it takes me ages to fall asleep. Story ideas fight for dominance along with every stray thought and to-do of the day. Tonight, all my thoughts are aligned on her, and I drift off easily, hoping to see her in my dreams.

~~Rule 3. No Sleeping Over.~~

Beach, Books, & Bods

S unlight peeks through the blinds as I open my eyes. I've always been one to wake up with the sun—fucking annoying, honestly. What is it that princess said? The sky's awake, so I'm awake? That shit only works when you have servants and the ability to take an afternoon nap.

I wiggle on the mattress a bit, trying to find a comfortable spot, but my back aches at the movement.

Asher grunts in his sleep, my movements no doubt disturbing him. He sleeps on his stomach, golden hair splayed against the pillow and equally golden skin on display. My eyes trail the planes of his back muscles, snagging on the dimples of Venus exposed above his boxers. His arm lifts, and I freeze as a large, hot hand lands on my thigh. Holding my breath,

I wait for him to say something without a single idea of what I'll say in response.

What does someone say the morning after the best sex of her life? Especially when there was no actual sex that occurred. I'm an awkward ball of words on a good day, and waking up next to a near stranger who's seen all my bits and bobs is certainly not a common occurrence.

When Asher doesn't move again, I'm confident he's still out. There's no fucking way I'm falling back asleep, so I might as well get up and start typing away at my manuscript. Lifting his hand like a bomb that might go off any second, I slip from the bed and pad out to the kitchen as quietly as I can.

I'd kill for a cup of coffee, but I have no idea where he keeps the mugs. Well, at least I now have a topic for the inevitable morning-after interaction. Should I leave? We never discussed whether this was a one-time thing or how long I'd stay. If I go in there to pack, he's definitely waking up, and I need a game plan before that happens.

Without any better ideas, I turn to my usual coping mechanism—ignoring the real world for the literary one. In no time, I'm lost in the words of my manuscript. Restructuring the scene, refining word choice. It's still not there, but it's shaping up a bit more by the time Asher emerges, looking deliciously rumpled.

"Hey there, I was wondering where you'd run off to. How'd you sleep?"

"Sorry, I'm a morning person. This is usually my writing time."

"No need to apologize. You have coffee yet?" I shake my head, following him with my eyes as he opens a cabinet and grabs a mug and places it in the machine. "How do you take it?"

I cough to clear my throat. "Light and sweet, there should be a creamer in the fridge. I can..." He's already in the refrigerator before I can finish the sentence. The spigot sputters its final bit of caffeinated glory, and

Asher wastes no time grabbing the mug and topping it off with delicious decadence before sliding the concoction across the counter.

"Thanks." I grip the warm ceramic in my hands, happy for the distraction as I continue to figure out what the fuck to say. When Asher doesn't turn back for a second cup, I tilt my head at him. "None for you?"

He waves a silver can at me and then raises it to his lips. The muscles in his throat dance as he gulps. Damn, girl, dial it back a notch. "I prefer the high-octane stuff. You didn't really answer how you slept."

"Okay."

"Just okay?" His eyes narrow, and I blush. "Shit, do I actually snore?"

"No, it's not that. I'm a little sore—I usually sleep with a bunch more pillows for support."

"Oh." He drains his can, then tilts his head at me. "What are your plans for the day?"

"Uh... I didn't really make it that far..."

"Get ready. I'm taking you to the beach. You're looking a bit pasty there, Imp."

"Well, I'm a ginger, fucker, we can't all be sun-kissed by the gods." He smiles, and I lose my nerve as I realize what I said. "Plus, I didn't bring a suit."

"It's Florida; there are shops on every corner. Or you can just wear shorts and a tee. Either way, some vitamin D and fresh air will be good for you."

Oh, I could use some vitamin D alright, but not from the sun. I squeeze my thighs at the sudden ache. Is there a gas leak in this apartment? That's the only sane explanation. Fresh air is definitely in order.

The warmth of the sand under my back soothes my sore muscles. I'm a big enough gal to admit when I'm wrong: the beach was a fantastic idea. The crashing of the waves tickles my brain in the best of ways as my stress simply melts away.

I take a sip of my icy drink and turn back to my paperback—I could absolutely grow used to this.

"Having fun?" Asher plops down on his towel beside me, splattering droplets of cold water on my bare legs. "I see you're still reading those damn novels."

"I'll have you know, beach reading is the ultimate ginger sport. Keeps us from scaring the children with our radioactive glow."

"Umbrella keeping you from spontaneous combustion?" His smirk is downright devilish but filled with humor.

"Yes, thanks for buying it." Asher had thrown the shade into the cart when we stopped for a suit and towel for me. "You'll be grateful too when your skin doesn't look like leather by forty."

He chuckles. "Speaking of which, can you reapply to my back?"

Pushing up to my knees, I approach him as he hands me a can of sunscreen. "Sure." Concentrating on my task, I spray sweeping paths of lotion across his broad back.

Asher looks over his shoulder, tendrils of his long hair curling around his ears as they drip salt water. "You have to rub it in, otherwise it won't absorb."

Gulping, I place the can on his towel and lay a tentative hand on his back. The firm muscles dance under my fingers, his skin smooth and cool from the ocean. Asher moans slightly. Growing bold, I skate my hands down his back, tracing his spine until I reach its base, then run up his flanks. "There."

"Thanks," his voice is gravely. "I'm going to take a quick sun nap, then gotta head back before my shift." I nod, and he flops down, tossing his t-shirt over his face.

I try to focus on my paperback, but fail spectacularly. No offense to Ms. Storm, but she can't hold a candle to the man beside me. My eyes keep darting to his abs as they glisten, shifting with each breath to catch the light. It truly is criminal for any man to be this gorgeous. I've read the same paragraph a dozen times by the time Asher stirs and starts packing up.

CHAPTER 18

Shower

We climb the stairs to my apartment. I have the umbrella and a beach cooler while Gabby carries the towels. As we near the landing, Gabby's watch blares, bringing her to a stop.

"All good?"

Her breath comes out in hard puffs. "Yeah, my heart rate's a little high. I don't take the stairs that much... little out of shape." After a couple more puffs, she gives me a thumbs-up and finishes the climb.

Once in the apartment, I take care of the damp suit and umbrella and then realize Gabby isn't behind me. I find her still in the entryway, staring at the mirror by the front door.

"This Florida humidity is doing a number on my hair." She picks at one fuzzy ringlet that is standing on end and groans.

"What do you mean?"

She raises a brow at me. "Look at it."

"What? You have beautiful curly hair." It's the first thing I noticed about her. Like a living flame around her face, as untamable and chaotic as her trains of thought.

"No, my sister has beautiful hair. It's auburn instead of orange with these gentle waves. Mine is such a pain to take care of—special shampoos, blowouts for events. Not to mention the comments."

"Comments?"

She turns to me with an arched brow. "Come on, you know?" I merely shrug. "Fire crotch. Hot head. You must be a freak in bed. Soulless Ginger. I bet every freckle is just a soul you stole. And everyone's favorite: does the carpet match the drapes?"

Can't say I expected each example to be worse than the last. "Are you serious? That's disgusting."

"Yup, people really feel entitled to say anything. Growing up in Boston wasn't so bad—there's a lot of Irish DNA—in college I started noticing the jokes, and of course the floodgates opened when I became an author."

Her words hit home. It's not that I'm surprised at the audacity of some people—I'm no stranger to comments about my appearance. I guess I never noticed the stereotypes about redheads; I was too busy focusing on myself. Sure, people assume I'm dumb, but otherwise they fall over themselves to compliment me. What would it be like if the assumptions were all negative?

"I'm sorry, Imp, that's horrible. For what it's worth, I think you—and your hair—are beautiful."

She blushes. It's barely noticeable against her already flushed cheeks, but I've been studying the color changes of her face more closely than I care to admit.

"Thanks, and thank you for not being weird about it. Some guys make the redhead thing into a fetish."

I shake my head, disgusted and angry for her. As I open my mouth to respond, my work alarm goes off. For the best, honestly, I'm not quite sure what I was going to say. "I've got to clean off before heading in. Why don't you shower with me?"

Her eyes widen. "Oh, no, it's okay. I'll just wait until you're done."

My lips curl as I use her argument against her. "It'll be efficient. We'll call it an anatomy lesson—a look-but-don't-touch anatomy lesson." She's still looking at me like a cornered animal. It hurts more than I expected. "Don't you trust me?"

"It's not that... I've never showered with anyone before. Not because I'm shy, well, not really. I take cold showers because of my skin; otherwise, I get all red and blotchy."

I shrug. "Okay, just don't judge me for shrinkage." Without another word, I head for the bedroom to turn on the water.

Gabby jogs to keep up. "Seriously? Just like that?"

"It's Florida, honey. Cold showers aren't a big deal." I adjust the dial. "Is that good?"

She checks it as I grab a couple of towels, then adjusts it slightly warmer. Muttering under her breath, she strips and climbs in. I wish I could hear what she was saying—her inner-outer dialogue never fails to make me laugh.

I undress, tossing my clothes on top of hers, and step into the stall behind her. Gabby keeps her back to me as she lathers silky lotion over her body, filling the space with the scent of roses. As she leans back to wash her hair, she bumps into my chest, then lurches forward as if burned; her elbow smacks into the tile wall.

"Shit. Fuck. Hell. Damn!" she yelps, jumping up and down under the spray while clutching her arm.

"Here, let me help." I hold my hand out over her shoulder for the shampoo. She hesitates for a moment and then hands it over. I squeeze a dollop into my palm, then lather it gently and work my hands through her wet hair. I've been dying to dig my fingers in her curls, and this is a perfect opportunity. They're thick, the ringlets perfectly gripping my fingers as I massage the shampoo into her scalp.

I've never done this for anyone before. It's oddly soothing. There's this cozy feeling I can't quite describe. Maybe that's just her, though.

Gabby moans, and the sound sends a hot curl of desire through my belly and blood straight to my dick. As much as I want to move closer to her, touch her, I step back until my ass hits the cold tile, hoping that will offset the heat in my groin, knowing it won't help at all.

She rinses the suds out, then hands me the conditioner. I repeat the process, this time combing my fingers through the lengths, gently detangling. The water streams across her head and shoulders, creating sparkling droplets down her back. As the last white sud slides off her hips and onto the floor, she turns, eyes still closed.

I take my first unobstructed view of her breasts, the cool water leaving her nipples hard. Gabby pushes her sodden hair out of her face, arching her back slightly, pushing those tantalizing tits closer to me. Any hope I had of the cold deflating my erection is gone.

"Thanks," she begins. "Never considered the benefits of being with a guy with long..." Her words cut off as she opens her eyes and stares directly at my cock. Her mouth drops open like a cartoon character—I'm not sure if I should feel offended or flattered. "Fucking hell, if that's shrinkage, I may need to reconsider this hands-on learning arrangement." Her brows pinch together, and she leans slightly closer. "Is-is that a piercing?"

Unsure what to do with my hands, I push my hair out of my face. "Uh, yeah. You didn't notice last night?"

"No... well, I might have thought I saw something sparkly, but from the angle..."

"Oh. Is that a problem?" I'm suddenly self-conscious. I've never gotten any complaints—quite the opposite. Normally, it's an added excitement for the women who take home the hot bartender of Pop, but those women aren't Gabby Boyle.

"I don't think so; I've just never seen one before." She's looking so intently, my cock can't help but wave at the attention. At least her expression has morphed from horror to something closer to fascination.

That I can work with.

With gentle pressure on her arms, I swap positions with her so I can wash myself. As my hand works the soap over my cock, I might give it an extra stroke for her benefit. Her eyes follow the movement. "Does it hurt?"

"It did when I got it, but not anymore. Sure, if something gets caught on it, it hurts like a bitch, but I imagine that's like any piercing." She nods and continues to study me. My backup alarm blares in the bedroom, so I rush through the rest of my shower and turn off the water. When I hand Gabby the towel, she looks up at me with blown pupils.

I've never wanted to call out of work more than I do now. It takes every ounce of control not to carry her to the bed and worship her body. Add it to the list of firsts with this one. "Leave in ten?"

"Yeah." Her voice is husky. I can almost imagine she's thinking the same as me.

This shift will be the longest of my life. The sooner it's over, the sooner I can claim her. If the anticipation doesn't kill me first.

CHAPTER 19

We Want the Redhead

Gabby laughs beside me between sips of her frozen coffee. I've been telling her stories about Pop during our drive to town. Each one more ridiculous than the last because, selfishly, I want to keep hearing that laugh.

Happy hour is in full swing when we arrive. Spotting a familiar face, I guide her to the far side of the bar. "Hey man, what brings you in?" I clap Johnson on the shoulder in a friendly greeting.

His smile is wide as he returns the clasp. "Was talking to Anna and Bree about the event planner position and decided to grab some dinner." One inky brow arches as he takes in Gabby beside me. "Hello there."

With his dark, clean-cut looks and designer duds, Johnson is the perfect foil to my golden coloring and laid-back vibes. He's the boardroom bosshole to my surfer summer fling, and we've always used it to reel in the ladies. Funny how I find that less beneficial tonight. If my hand remains on the back of her neck longer than necessary once she sits, it's only to make her comfortable. Not because I don't want my best friend eyeing her.

"Gabby, this is my best friend, Johnson."

"I've met you before." She tilts her head slightly as she studies him. Her eyes widen with sudden recognition. "You were at the signing here, but you had me write a different na…"

His smile turns brittle as he interrupts her. "Big fan. What brings you back to Friendship Springs? And with this guy, no less?"

I flip a halfhearted finger over my shoulder as I duck under the service pass. Johnson has always been tight-lipped about his name—I don't even know what it legally is. Maybe I can get it out of Gabby later.

"Asher's helping me with my next book." Her eyes dart to me, and that flush stains her cheeks. Without breaking eye contact, I fill a glass of ice water and place it on the surface in front of her. With a grateful smile, she raises the straw to her lips.

"Is he now?" The arched brow now turns to me, and reluctantly, I turn my attention to my best friend.

"What can I say? I have hidden talents." Gabby's watch lights up, the alarm barely audible in the crowded room. "Is that your heart rate again?"

She glares down at the notification, hitting a button on the side. "No, it's my agent."

"So how is a man who doesn't know the difference between a wizard and a sorcerer helping you with a novel about witches?" Johnson asks with a smirk on his face.

Her wrist flashes again, making Gabby groan.

"Do you need to take that? You can always use the office," I offer.

A V forms between her eyebrows, giving me the strangest urge to smooth the spot with my thumb. Her eyes suddenly fill with determination. "No, it's late. He can wait until tomorrow." She pulls out her phone and turns it off. "Now where were we?"

"You were about to tell me exactly how my magically ignorant friend is helping you with your best-selling fantasy novel." He leans towards her on his barstool. It's not quite flirty, but it still has my back stiffening.

Gabby's lips curve in a confident smile as she matches his posture. "Well, I could tell you, but then I'd have to kill you."

At a loss, I mumble something about getting to work and move to the other side of the bar. They barely notice. First Tony, now Johnson? How can she be so comfortable with these men she's only just met when I've seen her naked and still get stutters and blushes?

Despite my shit mood, the shift flies by fairly quickly. I serve my section like a man possessed, but my eyes keep darting back to the two in the corner. A few patrons attempt to flirt, but it does nothing to console me. What is wrong with me tonight? It's never bothered me before when a woman goes for Johnson instead of me. So why this time?

"What will it be, gentlemen?" I wipe down the bar in front of two guys in suits, but Gabby's laugh immediately draws my attention. I try to shake it off and force myself to stay present as I draw beers.

"I bet that one's a firecracker between the sheets," the man on the left says to his friend. "You ever had one of them before?"

"What a redhead?" My hand clenches around the glass. What are the chances they're talking about someone else? "Naw, I like my girls a bit more manageable."

"With her hair around your fist and your cock in her mouth, she'll be plenty manageable."

The pint glass slams onto the surface, jolting both assholes on their stools. The first guy opens his mouth, but one glare from me has him quickly shutting the fuck up. It's too bad; I would have liked to knock those white teeth down his throat.

I think that's about enough for the night. "Jessie, you got the bar, I'm out of here."

She salutes me. "Aye, aye, boss. Have a good night."

Oh, I fucking plan on it. My eyes focus on Gabby. She's still having an animated conversation with Johnson. Her eyes sparkle with emotion as she talks. With a palm on the bar top, I'm over it and beside her in a moment. She stops mid-word and stares up at me, biting that lush bottom lip.

Could I have walked around or ducked under the pass? Yes. But then I wouldn't be enjoying the way Gabby is currently eye-fucking me. "Come on, Imp. I promised you a big burrito." With a nod at Johnson, I anchor my hand on the small of Gabby's back and guide her to the door.

A cry rings out as we walk by. The jackass stands blotting his suit with cocktail napkins as beer soaks his crotch. An empty pint glass lies on the bar, its bottom cracked off.

Insane Burritos

I nstead of the car, Asher guides me further down Main Street to a parking lot with food trucks lining the curb. We join the line at a blue truck with green palm fronds and bright hibiscus painted on the side claiming to have "Insane Burritos."

The man's eyes light up when we approach the window, and he reaches down to clap Asher's hand in a high-five squeeze combo. "Hey man, good to see ya. The usual?"

"Hold the beans tonight." Asher turns to me, earning a wink from the cook. "Kai makes the best burritos in the state—just don't tell Anna I said that. Trust me, pick the insane burrito, any meat, and you won't regret it."

"I'll have chicken, please."

Asher has his wallet out before I can blink, and we move to the side to wait for our food. He shifts his weight from foot to foot, hands shoved deep in his pockets. The muscle in his jaw ticks every so often, like he's chewing something over.

"What?" He jerks towards me, like he forgot I was here. "Awkward silence is sort of my ninth circle. What's on your mind?" He opens his mouth, and I can tell from his expression exactly what he's going to say. "And don't say 'nothing'. I may not know you that well, but I can read tension a mile away. What's up?"

"I'm trying to figure you out, but you threw me tonight. Our whole arrangement is based on your feeling so socially awkward you can't write romance, but I've seen you confident and flirty. So I guess I'm not sure what you think you need me for."

My jaw drops open as all the words promptly escape my brain. It's a truly impressive feat for someone to leave me speechless, and I'd probably be more impressed if I weren't trying to figure out what the fuck he was talking about. "You were there yesterday when I literally choked on my own spit, right?"

He runs a hand through his hair, pulling out the elastic and snapping it on his wrist. "Yeah, that's part of my confusion. When we're together, I see this quirky girl who's authentic and, yeah, maybe a bit awkward sometimes, but then I see you with Tony or Johnson and you're like a totally different person. What is it about them that I don't have?"

Is that a hint of jealousy? *Fuck yeah, slay girl, slay!* My inner voice preens her feathers like a damn peacock—though I'm pretty sure it's only the male peacocks that have the pretty feathers. Oh my god, focus, Gabby!

Shaking my head, I concentrate on Asher. "Well, the answer is kind of obvious." He glares at me, clearly conveying it's not obvious to him. "My social mask stays in place with them; it's easy because one, I have the books as common ground, and I can always talk books. And two, I'm not attracted to them. It's a lot easier not to sound like an asshole when half your head isn't busy picturing someone naked." My eyes widen as my brain catches up with my mouth. My cheeks burn as my hand slaps over that traitorous body part that is constantly outing me in front of this man.

The silence hangs heavy for a moment as I pray the ground will open up and take me. Then Asher's laugh breaks the tension like a whip. His hands grip my hips, pulling me against him moments before his mouth captures mine. I've never kissed someone while they're smiling before, but his lips are definitely curled in a grin as they stamp mine. It's not a lengthy kiss like at his apartment, but it is the first time he's touched me since our make-out session.

My body melts into his, softness to his hard muscles. I clutch his arms, not quite sure if it's for support or simply to touch him. My lips open for him eagerly. I have no idea why he's kissing me in the middle of downtown, but I'm not about to start complaining.

I'm debating how okay I am with public sex when he breaks the kiss. His hands keep my hips still, and the evidence of his arousal presses against my stomach. "Don't ever change, Imp. I like this side of you exactly as you are."

I'm still reeling from the one-two punch of hormones and emotions when Kai calls Asher's name, and we carry our dinner back to the car. Our pinkies brush slightly as we walk, my stomach flutters with every graze of skin, and I have to lecture my inner self to calm the fuck down because this is not a date.

Back at Asher's apartment, a giant box blocks the door. "Oh good, it came. Can you grab that for me? It should be light." He juggles the to-go bags in one arm as he holds out his keys.

The package is surprisingly lightweight for its size. "Where do you want it?"

"In the bedroom," his voice calls from the kitchen. I leave the delivery by the bed and return to find Asher already sorting burritos onto plates. "I hope these will be okay. I probably should have asked you first."

"What do you mean? I ordered my own dinner." I unwrap the end and take a hefty bite, the fluffy rice and juicy chicken melding perfectly with the cheese and sour cream. An unholy moan escapes my lips before I can hold back. "Fuck, that's good."

Asher blinks as he runs a hand over his mouth. "Not the food, I, uh, bought some more pillows for you."

"You did?" I lower my food onto the plate.

He shifts, avoiding my eyes. "Yeah, it's nothing. I just thought... If they're not right, we can return them, no big deal."

But it's a very big deal. Not only did he listen to me, but he actively tried to do something about it. Gorgeous and extremely thoughtful? *You are so falling for him.* Why did I think I could keep emotions separate? I think I'm well and truly fucked... and we haven't even had sex yet.

CHAPTER 21

Fire and Gasoline

Gabby pushes a stray piece of rice around her plate, not quite meeting my eyes. "So, do you have to open tomorrow?"

The atmosphere in the room shifted, and I don't know why. Was it the pillows? "Nope, I'm all yours until dinner. You have my undivided attention."

"Good." She looks up at me through her lashes. It's a move I've seen a dozen times a night for years—I'm practically immune by now—but with Gabby there's nothing artificial about the motion, nothing practiced or forced, and my gut clenches.

"Good." I grin at her.

Her shoulders drop as she huffs. "In hindsight, burritos might not have been a good choice prior to a sex lesson."

My cheeks sting as my smile grows. Damn, she's funny. "Don't worry, there are no beans."

"I guess you've thought of everything, then." Her lips twist in that little impish smirk that inspired my nickname for her.

My stomach gives a strange lurch. God, I hope there wasn't something off with Kai's pork today. "Wouldn't want to disappoint my student." My words are flippant, but I'm nervous as hell. Why does this feel so much bigger? Is it because I know she's going to be judging me? The stakes of inspiring a potentially best-selling novel's sex scene are weighing on me more than I expected. "We should probably set some ground rules."

"Oh, right! Damn, I can't believe I almost forgot." She lowers her burrito to the plate with a longing look, then lifts again for a giant bite and dashes into my room. In a moment, she returns with a stapled packet of papers. "I hope this is alright; it's not like I've ever done this before. If you want to change anything on it, let me know, but I think it's pretty standard stuff. Crazy what you can find on the internet these days."

I hold a whole page of legalese. Holy shit, did she write up her limits and preferences in a contract? She's been reading too many romance novels.

My eyes scan the document again and finally dial in on the title at the top: Non-Disclosure Agreement. This isn't a sexual contract at all. My brow pinches as I skim the verbiage. It states that neither of us will reveal any personal details or participate in malicious publications. I can't share any information about her upcoming novel or the nature of our "research sessions." Oddly, discussing our relationship itself or the fact that we've had sex doesn't seem to be a no-go, only where it connects to her book.

Gabby fidgets a bit. "I'm sorry; this is probably a mood killer. It's not that I don't trust you, but my sister's a lawyer and she's drilled these kinds of things into me. I tried to make sure it protects you, too. We didn't really discuss compensation before."

My muscles freeze. It never occurred to me she'd question what I get out of this agreement, or how weird it'd be to randomly offer sex to a stranger. I can't tell her about my writing or how having her here alone is powering my creativity—not after she made it clear how sensitive she is about other authors.

Misreading my reaction, she rushes on. "Oh my god, I didn't mean to imply you were a sex worker. Not that there's anything wrong with sex work! Fuck, this is going terribly. It's just that I know this arrangement is incredibly one-sided, so if you help me hit my deadline, I'll pay you the $1500 bonus in my contract. If you're not so completely insulted you just want me to leave, that is."

Swallowing acid back down, I lay my hand over hers on the counter. "Gabby, I have no problem signing an NDA—you're right, it protects both of us—but I don't want your money." I grab a pen from the drawer and scrawl my name across the line before she can object. "This wasn't what I meant by ground rules."

"It isn't?" Her eyes are huge behind her glasses.

"No, we need to discuss what is and isn't allowed in bed. I want to make sure you're absolutely comfortable when we're together, and things can progress naturally. So it's better to have this conversation now than stopping every five minutes to ask if you're alright. Let's start with an easy one. What's your safe word?"

"Safe word? Do people outside of sex dungeons have those?"

I chuckle. "Don't worry, I'll keep it vanilla... until you ask me not to." Her nostrils flare. "Safe words just make it clear to communicate your needs in the moment. So what is it?"

"Muffin."

"Muffin?"

"Yeah, I'm pretty sure I've never said 'muffin' during sex before. Unless we're getting busy on the counter and I accidentally stick my hand in a pastry, I think it's a solid choice." She takes the last bite of her burrito.

Well, can't argue with her there. "Muffin it is. Are there any areas on your body you're particularly sensitive or ticklish? Places that if I touched them, it would completely take you out of the mood."

She shakes her head slightly. "Not that I can think of…"

"Okay, well if anything makes you uncomfortable or you don't like it, just say… muffin… and I'll stop." I finish my dinner and clean up the containers as Gabby fidgets by the counter. "What is it? Better to lay everything out in the open now."

"I'm a little nervous about your…" she gestures at my crotch, "…piercing. Is it going to hurt?"

"It shouldn't. The barbell should add a little extra stimulation to your G-spot, like when you curled your finger last night."

She nods slightly as she bites her lip. "Is that why you got it?"

I laugh as I rub the back of my neck, my ears burning. This isn't something I've ever admitted. "Actually, it was a stupid bet in college. Can't remember what I got for doing it, but I've never been able to stand down from a challenge. One minute a guy on the team throws a dare in my face, the next I'm at a tattoo shop with my pants around my ankles."

"Oh." Her eyes widen.

"It was pretty dumb. I thought about taking it out a bunch of times, but after it healed, I kind of forgot it was there." My lips lift in a sorry excuse for a smile. "You've got to admit, it's a good conversation starter."

She laughs, then lays her hand on mine on the table. "I think it's really brave. You just did it and kept going without looking back. Owned it as you stared down the world. I could never do that."

An unfamiliar warmth spreads in my chest. I flip my hand so my fingers can intertwine with hers. "I think you already did, Imp. Or was it someone else who tracked me down to show up on my doorstep requesting sex lessons?" I look around the apartment as if another person will appear, earning a giggle from her. "You ready?"

With a small smile, she leads the way to the bedroom, eyeing the bed like she's never seen one before. I'd be lying if I said I wasn't nervous too. At this point in the evening, it's usually all hands and mouths and stripping clothes as quickly as possible. Everything about this thing with Gabby is a first for me. I rest my hand on her side, startling her.

"I'm just going to go freshen up, change into something..." she looks down at her jeans, tank, and loose cardigan, "...not this." She grabs something from her suitcase and heads into my bathroom, shutting the door.

My skin itches with the need to move; if I keep standing here, I very well might explode. The box catches my eye, giving me a perfect outlet. Tearing the cardboard brings a welcome burn to my muscles. First, a half-moon cushion emerges from the package, then a round bolster, a kidney-shaped thing, two long rectangles, and finally one that looks like a regular head pillow and a mermaid had a baby. The stack is a solid two feet high at the head of the bed. Maybe I went a little overboard. I searched for supportive pillows and bought every kind I saw.

Most have a microfiber shell, but the last one I remember is for her head and should probably get a cover. I grab one from my dresser, and pop it over the pillow but pause as my mind pictures that purple suitcase. Back into the drawer I go, scooping up the rest of the contents and dumping them into a nearby laundry basket.

Guess I might as well change, too. I've only pulled off my polo when the bathroom door slides open, revealing Gabby in the doorway, and I drink in every inch of her, committing this moment to memory.

The light behind her halos her curls and the clingy material of her nightgown as it hugs her curves. She's left her glasses off, and I vaguely miss them. "You look beautiful."

Her posture is straight, but her teeth digging into her lip give her away. Can't have that.

I'll just tell her about the drawer tomorrow.

My legs eat up the distance between us. Her head tilts back as she tries to compensate for my height, highlighting the gentle curve of her throat and the delicate edge to her jaw. My fingers skim the soft skin there, as if I want to confirm she's real, because Gabby Boyle is like no woman I've ever met.

I capture her mouth. Is this only the third time I've kissed her? How does it feel like both the first time and the hundredth? I already know the shape of her lips, the sweet fullness, how they'll open at the first gentle request for entry. How her fists will cling to me, like she's also afraid any moment this will disappear.

My hands clasp her bare thighs and lift, gliding up the smooth skin to her ass as she wraps her legs around my waist. I groan as I realize my fingers never touched fabric; the Imp has a thong on.

Gabby's knees grip my side as she grinds herself against me. For all her talk about being inexperienced, she's a fucking natural... uh, literally. Her eagerness is like gasoline on a fire—it's the reason I almost lost control that first time. The asshole at the bar's words echo in my brain, and I wish I'd decked him. It's not her hair color that makes Gabriella Boyle incendiary; it's all of her. The raging chaos in her soul, I'd happily burn alive for one taste.

I carry her to the bed, placing one knee on the mattress so I can lower her onto her back. She clings to me with a desperate whimper as I try to lift my head. A chuckle escapes as I tear my lips off hers to speak. "I'm just getting started, Imp. We have all night for me to explore every inch of your body. To show you how you were meant to feel."

Her pupils are completely blown as she stares at me. She wants this as much as I do, and it drives me onward. My mouth and hands map her skin, taking note of which spots make her tense and which make her melt, piling all the data points away until I'm confident I can make her scream.

As I kneel between her spread knees, I look down at her prone form splayed across my pillows. This is it. I'm finally going to have this imp to myself with no interruptions or distractions. This is the moment when I finally have sex with Gabriella Boyle.

~~Rule 4: Sex and Business Don't Mix.~~

Chapter 22

Lesson 2

"You still with me, Imp?" Asher's electric blue eyes bore into me as he kneels between my legs.

Gulping, I nod my head, afraid to speak.

Asher's lips skim along my thighs. It tickles, but also sends tingles shooting across my skin. This is it. I'm finally going to know what it's like to have this Viking between my legs. My heart pounds, but not entirely from excitement. A thousand thoughts ricochet around in my head, none of them helpful.

He works the lace trim of my nightgown up, the rough texture at odds with his gentle lips. My breath comes in quick pants. The edge of one knuckle traces the seam of my thighs along my underwear—tonight a cotton thong. The string threatens to split me in half from its location somewhere past my colon, but supposedly, this is attractive. Asher strokes his finger again, a teasing light touch that leaves me wanting more.

This isn't so bad.

That same finger slides beneath the teeny-tiny triangle of fabric. I jerk against the covers as Asher touches me intimately for the first time. He settles more fully between my thighs, alternating gentle strokes to my clit and tracing of my folds—exactly how I did it.

The man's a quick study.

Warmth pools in my belly as his talents take effect, but I can't quite settle. What do I do with my hands? Should I lie here and think of the queen? Am I supposed to make noises? Is there such a thing as too much noise? Does that crack on the ceiling look like a pentagram?

Humid heat caresses my clit moments before his mouth closes over my pussy. With a squeal, my knees lock together—around Asher's head. He gives a muffled shout of surprise—or maybe it's suffocation. Oh my god, can you suffocate someone with your pussy?

I release him and scramble up against the headboard, the telltale fire already crawling up my chest and face. "Fuck. I'm so sorry."

"It's okay." But he's rubbing his temples with a slight wince. Can I just die now? "What's going on, though? Did I do something you didn't like? Do you prefer non-clitoral stimulation during oral?"

"No, I mean, I-I'm not sure. It wasn't bad, just surprising?" It sounds like a question.

A look of understanding crosses Asher's face as his eyes widen. "Gabby, has no one ever eaten your pussy before?" My face flames more, and I cover it with my hands. "Hey now, there's nothing to be embarrassed about. It's their loss."

"Guys have tried, but I've never really liked it. I feel so awkward lying here doing nothing, and then I think about where their mouth has been and... Usually, the guy is more than happy to skip ahead."

"Baby, if you're thinking about all that, they're not doing it right." The bed shifts as Asher moves.

That's it. He's giving up. Not that I blame him—I knew I was hopeless.

The mattress dips again, and Asher's warm palms cuff my wrists, pulling until I meet his electric blue eyes. I expect to see pity or exasperation, but there's only understanding in his eyes. "Here." He hands me my latest paperback, *Blindsided*, a football forbidden romance where the MMC falls for the coach's daughter.

"What's this for?"

"You said reading helps you relax. I want you to pick a sex scene, read it to me and I'll reenact it with you. If there's anything you don't like or that makes you uncomfortable, just tell me to stop."

That could work. I wouldn't be awkward Gabby, I'd be irresistible Sarah—plus I wouldn't have to worry about what to do with my hands; there's literally a manual. "Okay." I flip through the book until I find the spot I want.

"Woah, did you have the scene marked?" His tone is teasing as he draws back, encouraging me to lie back down.

"Maybe." I clear my throat and start reading, immediately pulled into the story, and relax into the pillows. *"Sarah's back hit the lockers as Bradley invaded her space. Her breath caught as his lips brushed against her sensitive neck."*

Asher follows my directions, and I squeal at the sudden contact. Undeterred, he lowers his mouth again for another nibble. Tiny shockwaves feather out from the touch. I close my eyes and moan at the sensation. It's all the encouragement Asher needs as he works a slow line down my collarbone, his hands once again gliding up my thighs. "Keep reading."

"Sarah's head fell back as his lips trailed across her exposed skin. Bradley's hands slid up her pleated skirt until he found her center, already wet and betraying her lust for him."

Asher's fingers reclaim my opening, slowly tracing my slit until I squirm against his touch.

I keep reading, remembering where this scene is heading and anxious to experience it. *"Bradley ripped off her panties, shoving them in his back pocket as he knelt at her feet. 'You'll be screaming my name, sweetheart, then you'll never again deny this pussy belongs to me.' With those words, he lifted Sarah's thigh over his shoulder and plunged his tongue into her weeping passage."*

My foot slides along Asher's smooth back as he moves me into position. Even knowing it is coming, I gasp as Asher's tongue penetrates me. This time, my knees spread wider, granting him full access. With a satisfied groan, Asher digs his fingers into my hips and hauls me closer. There is no need; I'm already arching my back, desperate for as much contact as I can manage.

He changes his pace, pausing every so often to circle my clit with the tip of his tongue. With a slurping sound that I should find embarrassing but can't spare the brain cells to care about, Asher lifts his head. His lips glisten with my wetness, but his eyes gleam with challenge. "Don't stop there; you know what Bradley does next."

"Soon he switched his attention to her aching clit, replacing his tongue with two fingers." I moan as Asher's thick digits stretch me and move. *"Bradley was determined to make her cum on his mouth before he would claim her with his cock. Angry that she would deny this growing bond between them, he set a punishing pace with his fingers, his tongue equally unrelenting on her swollen bud."*

Asher works a third broad finger into my already stretched pussy. I whimper at the onslaught of sensation threatening to pull me under, and he immediately freezes. "Are you okay? Do you want me to stop?"

"Don't you dare. It's just thicker than I'm used to."

His lips curl with male ego. "Oh, baby, you haven't seen thick yet."

With a frustrated growl, I grip his topknot and direct his fresh mouth back to my aching core. His chuckle vibrates against my clit, sending me that much closer to the edge. My fists stay locked in his hair, holding him exactly where I need that devilish tongue. His expert digits find some secret spot within my channel, and I scream his name as my body explodes. He continues to move as the waves of pleasure slow, extending the orgasm as far as he can for me.

I collapse onto the pillows, panting as I finally release him.

Asher kneels between my spread thighs, wiping my juices from his face. "Delicious. Can't wait for you to read the next part when you've caught your breath."

I toss the forgotten novel onto the nightstand, barely caring when it overshoots and thuds on the floor. "Would you shut the hell up and fuck me already?"

His eyes darken as his lips smile. "Yes, ma'am."

Free Fall

Eating Gabby while she read to me was hands down one of the top ten sexual experiences of my life. I can't believe she chose that scene, and I find myself wanting her to keep reading the rest of it.

My cock aches in my jeans as I stare down at Gabby. Watching her relax and shift into a vixen is the hottest thing I've ever experienced. When she grabbed my hair and forced me closer to her pussy, I almost came in my pants.

With efficient motions, I push my pants and briefs to the floor. As I stand, my cock proudly does as well—level with Gabby's face. Her eyes widen as she takes it in. The cocky bastard knows it too and waves at her. "Do you want to keep your nightgown on?"

She blinks. I'm about to assure her she's beautiful no matter what she wears, or doesn't, but a new confidence enters her eyes. Holding my stare, she grips the hem of her shift, lifting it and leaving herself bare to me.

"Magnificent." It kills me to look away as I reach into the side drawer for a condom, quickly working it onto my length, careful of the barbell through the crown, then return to the space between her knees, drinking in the sight of her. She squirms slightly, blushing. I was right; she does flush all over, and it's fucking intoxicating.

Pink may be my new favorite color.

Not giving her a chance to freeze up on me, I capture one rosy nipple with my lips, swirling the hard peak with my tongue. She arches, all seeking hands clasping me close.

My fingers find her opening. She's wet from her orgasm, but I need her soaked if she's going to take me. I start again with three, tilting them to massage her G-spot with each stroke. Her grip tightens in my hair, the slight stabs of pain surprisingly welcome as she guides my mouth to her other nipple.

Her hips buck against my hand, and I have to concentrate to keep contact with that spot that drives her wild. Fresh wetness coats my fingers, and I know she's ready. My lips wander back up to her throat. She gives a disappointed whine, which quickly transforms into a moan as I rub my cock along her slit, coating the condom in her juices.

"Are you still sure, Gabby? It's not too late." I'm not positive who my warning is for, but something tells me I'm standing on the edge of a precipice.

"Absolutely. Show me what I've been missing, Viking."

I notch myself at her entrance, gently pushing against the resistance. I watch her chocolate eyes, I want to see her face as I take her for the first time. Her mouth widens on a gasp as I press further—her pussy so tight it grips my cock like a vise. I grit my teeth as I struggle to slow down. My fingers squeeze her ass as I try to angle her up. Another inch in and she whimpers, immediately having me pull out completely.

"No, don't stop."

"I don't want to hurt you, Imp." Glancing around for a solution, I spy Gabby's mountain of pillows and inspiration strikes. I snake one arm under her thighs, hauling her towards me and her knees over my shoulders. Then I grab three of the firmest cushions and shove them beneath her back and hips for support.

Gabby watches me with glassy eyes. My girl likes to be man-handled. Noted.

Lining myself up, I push into her, the new position allowing for easier progress. This time Gabby moans as I slowly enter her.

"Oh my god, Asher, the barbell... I've never felt anything like it."

For the first time, I'm insanely happy I took that bet and never removed the damned thing. I flex my hips to withdraw slightly, pausing at the same spot she liked. Her head sinks into the pillows as she arches up, trying to pull me deeper into that greedy cunt.

My fingers glide across her smooth skin, anchoring her waist so she doesn't slide off. I press further still. Sweat drips down my back with the effort to go slow until I'm fully seated.

"Fu-uck." The word falls from my lips, half curse, half prayer, all praise.

"Asher... please." Her brows furrow as she begs for something only I can give her. At this moment I feel like the Viking she constantly accuses me of being, and her body is the treasure I most want to plunder.

I set the pace, slow at first to let her grow accustomed to my size. It's a delicious kind of torture for us both. Every sensation plays across her face in an open display of carnal satisfaction. Gabby fucks the way she lives—loudly and unapologetically. I catalog each change in expression, noting which angles bring her the most pleasure.

Her pants quicken, her head tosses on the pillow in a gorgeously mussed halo of red curls. I pick up my speed, spurred on by the sounds Gabby makes.

She grips my arms, her nails biting into the skin, as she tries to gain leverage to meet my thrusts. This is my lesson, though. I'm in charge here, and I want her to realize exactly what her body can experience. Reaching between us, I rest my thumb on her swollen clit. Just that briefest of caresses has her legs falling open. My lips twist into a grin, and I circle her clit in earnest, switching the tempo as her pussy clenches, effectively edging her without stopping completely. Each time, she groans and grips me harder.

Abandoning her nub, I lean down to capture her lips, my pubic bone taking up the job of my fingers. She tries to kiss me back, but she can barely catch her breath.

Her walls tighten in a chokehold, and I know she's close. Arching back to better see her face, I snap my hips fast and hard, and it's enough. Her eyes widen with surprise as she climaxes, two endless pools of darkness and mystery, and her mouth opens on a silent scream. The emotions playing over her face send me over the cliff, letting the spasms of her orgasm milk every ounce of cum from my aching balls. I'm in free fall.

I bury my face in her neck, breathing in the subtle scent of roses. She shifts under me, but I hold her still. "Still coming," I grit through my teeth.

Slender fingers tentatively stroke down my back, and I spasm inside her again. As my breath calms, my heart doesn't slow. I drop a kiss onto her lips before pulling out. It's not until I'm dealing with the condom in the bathroom and wetting a facecloth that I realize how odd my behavior is.

It's not that I'm an unfeeling lover—though I'm not sure you could factually call a one-night stand a lover—but I'm not the aftercare-and-cuddle kind of guy. I'm usually a put-your-pants-back-on-and-get-the-hell-out guy. With Gabby, there is no urgency to leave.

Is it because this is my apartment?

I push the thought aside as I return to Gabby's side. She's still lying where I left her. She flinches slightly as I rub the wet cloth over the inside of her thighs. My eyes snap to hers as she blushes. "Are you sore?" Fuck, was I too rough with her? I'm supposed to be showing Gabby how fantastic sex can be and inspiring her novel, not maiming the girl.

"It's cold, and it tickles."

Oh, oops. I finish wiping her off and hand her the discarded nightgown from the floor. She knocks the pillows down and stands up. I pull her against me for another kiss, refusing to overthink the impulse.

I trace her lips with my tongue. A momentary pause, then she melts and grants me full access to explore. Too soon, she pulls back slightly, and I let her go. Watching her walk naked into the bathroom is almost worth it. There's a swing to her hips that wasn't there before, and as she smiles over her shoulder at me when she catches me staring, it's dripping with feminine satisfaction.

I gave her that, and, fuck, it feels good.

Pulling on a pair of briefs, I slip between the sheets and type some story ideas into my phone while I wait for Gabby's return.

She eyes the mountain of pillows. I might have gone a bit overboard, but there were so many options. A pink tongue peeks out of her lips as she concentrates on her task as if it were rocket science.

Watching this woman do anything is absolutely fascinating. I've spent my life predicting everything—I honestly thought I had magic powers as a kid before I realized I simply had superior pattern recognition—but I never know what Gabby's going to do next.

A firm half-moon bolster goes halfway down the mattress under the sheets. A small kidney-shaped one sits a bit higher, then she adds two longer pillows to form a square.

I'm about to ask her where she's supposed to sleep when she crawls on top of the arrangement. She wiggles around until she's on her back, knees bent over the bottom pillow and the other three supporting her back. With a contented sigh, she smiles at me. "That's better. Thanks again."

Giving into the urge, I tuck a loose ringlet behind her ear. It's springy but surprisingly soft. "You have everything you need?" She bites her lip and nods. "Are you sure? You've got to be fully rested for your lessons."

She blushes even as she rolls her eyes at me and smacks my arm. "Good night, Asher."

"Good night, Gabby."

Even after her breathing evens out, I continue to watch her. Something settles in me, like a constant itch I couldn't quite satisfy. It's a hell of a lot like peace, and that scares the shit out of me. I've always had an addictive personality. If I like something, then I'm obsessed, and it quickly becomes my entire identity. It was like that with sports, and the frat, and writing, and then bartending. I've never felt like this about another person before, and I'm worried Gabby is a drink I might happily drown in.

My last thoughts as I drift off are simply: I'm fucked.

CHAPTER 24

Gator Golf

The palm trees sway in the breeze, and the sun shimmers on the water's surface. It's truly picturesque down here, but even that isn't enough to get this scene moving from my head. I glare at the words on the screen as if they have personally insulted me. Maybe they have, though that's extra insulting since I wrote them.

Today I brought my laptop down to the apartment pool area to write. Okay, to the covered patio next to the pool—I'm no fool, and gingers and sunshine don't mix.

My stomach grumbles, as if it's feeling left out of the bitching session. Might as well head up for a snack and to refill my water.

Tossing my supplies back into my bag, I trudge up the stairs to Asher's unit, using the key he gave me this morning to let myself in. It takes my eyes a moment to adjust to the dimness of the room compared to the brightness of the day, so I pause in the doorway, happily soaking in the blessed relief of the air conditioning.

"You're back sooner than I expected." Asher sits at a desktop computer. It took me a couple of days to notice it there, kind of tucked behind the couch in the corner. I've never seen him at it before, but we've not exactly had a lot of downtime when we're in his apartment. *Unless you mean down and dirty.*

My cheeks would be flaming, I'm sure, if they weren't already red from the Florida summer heat.

"Every word was shit, and I got hungry, so I called it a day."

"Still blocked?"

"Yup," I answer with my head in the refrigerator. There was a piece of peach cheesecake shoved in the back here somewhere I'd been saving. "I was hoping the change of scenery would knock something loose. Well, there are words; they're just not the right ones."

"Hmm." His voice comes from the other side of the door. "Maybe you need to get your blood pumping and stop thinking so hard."

My pulse picks up a bit at that suggestion. Abandoning the thoughts of cake, I close the door and step into his space, making a big show of running my eyes up his impressive body. "Oh yeah? What do you propose?"

He leans down, and my breath catches when his lips are a whisper away. "Mini-golf."

I blink. Then again. "Excuse me?"

He smirks as he stands up to his full height. "Mind out of the gutter, Imp. Come on, let's have some fun."

"Pretty sure my idea would have been fun, too," I mutter.

Asher laughs as he drags me from the apartment and to his car. Before I know it, we're getting on the freeway and speeding off to the next town. This is obviously a more touristy area, with souvenir shops and chain restaurants along either side of a divided highway. He pulls into the lot of our destination. Overhead, giant statues of gators leer down with their toothy smiles and out-of-place golf clubs. I'm still staring at the garish decorations as Asher ushers me to the stand and then to the first hole.

"Ladies first." He drops my purple ball onto the starting mat. My eyes dart between him and the ball, but I make no move. "What's wrong?"

"I've never played before."

"Seriously?"

"I understand the general principles—my dad took us to the driving range a few times—but we weren't exactly a mini-golf family."

"What about high school? It is a go-to first date option."

My heart gives a traitorous lurch at the word date. *Calm that shit down, Gabby. You know the deal here.* To cover my emotions, I prop a fist on my hip and raise an eyebrow at him. "Well, obviously you went on more dates than I did."

Asher scratches the back of his head. "Not really, but my sisters went a lot."

With a sigh, I look down at the ball and then at the windmill five feet away. How hard could this be? I line up my feet, interlace my pinkies on the grip of the putter, pull back the club, and let her rip.

The ball goes flying down the course, leaving the ground with the velocity of a rocket before bouncing off a windmill blade with an ungodly bang and ricocheting right back at our faces. I stand there in shock as a purple projectile flies at me with my name written on it. Asher jumps in front of me, blocking the projectile with a grunt.

"Shit, are you okay?" I drop the club I'm still clutching and jump around him to see his face. Asher's brows pinch in pain, and he rubs his arm tenderly. I push his hand out of the way and find a blue circle already forming. "I'm so sorry." Not knowing what else to do, I kiss the spot as if that will magically take the sting away.

"It's fine. I've had way worse. Let's try that again, and this time I'll help you."

I return to my position on the rubber mat. Asher places the ball on the ground and stands behind me, wrapping his arms around me as he also grips the club. Every spot his body touches comes alive, and I'm almost afraid I'll explode. If the Florida heat doesn't kill me, Asher Ramstead will.

"Easy does it, slugger. Just a gentle back-and-forth motion." His lips tickle my ear as he speaks, making my core ache. I try to concentrate on the game, truly I do, but my mind fills with him. With Asher's help, I send the ball on a perfect path through the windmill and at the hole on the other side.

I turn my head towards him, our mouths so close. "Th-thanks." It takes all my willpower not to kiss him. It would be so easy to bridge the distance and give in to this magnetism. That would be against the rules, though—wouldn't it? Kissing is reserved for lessons. Well, except for that time at the food truck... and the door-lean incident.

A fresh wave of desire courses through me at the memory of that first heated kiss when I showed up on his doorstep. Pretty sure I'll be replaying that moment until I die.

"Good job! Do you want to go knock it in before I take my stroke?"

"Huh?"

Amusement sparks as those icy eyes drop to my lips and back to my eyes. "Do you want to take your next shot, or wait for me to hit the ball?"

"Oh, I'll finish, thanks." I stomp off to the other end. No wonder mini-golf is popular on dates. I had no idea how fucking raunchy it was. Asher's laugh pulls my focus back. "That was my outside voice again, wasn't it?"

He laughs harder. "Yup."

Still muttering under my breath, I try to concentrate on the offensive purple rubber. This time I'm too gentle with my hit, and it barely moves five inches towards the goal. Third time is the charm, and I tap the ball into the cup with a satisfying clunk.

Asher waits for me to clear the green, then expertly sends his blue ball through the windmill, stopping just short of the hole for an easy two points.

"Seriously, is there any sport you're not good at?"

He scratches his head for a moment. "Well, pickleball was rough. I kept missing the damn shot."

"Pickleball?"

"Yeah, my buddy Colin dragged me a couple of times. There's this tiny little paddle, and it's easy to hit the ball too hard."

I chuckle, my frustration fading, and as he wraps his hand around my waist to lead me to the next hole, it melts completely.

Asher kicks my ass—not that we actually keep score. I'm not even mad about it. He has an effortless way of making everything fun. Comfortable. I forget all the should do's and just be me with him. He's right—this was exactly the break I needed, and I'm almost sad when we head back to the car.

CHAPTER 25

Too Much Smut

It's fairly busy for a Thursday afternoon at Pop. I haven't gotten to chat with Asher in a while as he works his way up and down the bar, checking on his customers. That's fine, though. With an overactive imagination like mine, full of errant thoughts and voices, I'm never truly bored.

My gaze darts around from group to group, never quite settling on a single one for long, until I see something I like.

A couple across the way catches my eye. He lounges in the booth, one leg stretched out so it rests against hers. Their styles clash. He's in jeans and a black tee, biker boots, and silver chains with tattoos climbing up his arm. She's in a sheath dress and pumps, her brown hair perfectly curled and pinned away from her face, diamonds glittering at her ears and wrists.

A dozen stories pop into my head. He's her bodyguard. She's the girl who got away in high school, their lives taking them down very different paths before dumping them together again.

"What are you staring at?" Asher grins at me as he places a fresh iced tea in front of me.

I blush—though not sure if it's at getting caught or the fact he only shares his special stash with me. "Promise not to laugh?" He draws an X over his heart with his finger. "I have this habit of watching people and making up stories about them in my head. Call it an occupational hazard."

Asher's eyes light up with excitement. "I want to play. Who are we talking about?" He leans across the bar so we're nearly nose to nose.

I dart my eyes at the couple. "They're obviously in love and trying to hide it, but I can't quite decide if it's a forbidden romance, or just the beginning of something new."

He follows my gaze, then chuckles. "You've been reading too much smut, Imp. That's the guy's stepmother, and they're having a family dinner."

My nose wrinkles. "No way."

"Occupational hazard, sweetie." He steals a fry off my plate, popping it into his mouth. "Plus, he's dating one of our waitresses and stops in here every week."

A handsome older man approaches the table. He's wearing a gray suit, and a gold timepiece flashes at his wrist as he runs a hand through his silvered hair. He sits in the booth beside the woman as a waitress appears. The young woman is a bubbly blond who speaks animatedly, dropping off a check. Biker-dude pulls her down onto his lap for a quick kiss then sends her off with a tap on the ass and a couple crisp bills.

"Huh. I could have sworn… doesn't matter! That one doesn't count. Who here don't you know?"

"Hmm. Her." He nods towards a woman seated at the bar as he steals another fry.

She's pretty in an understated way—minimal makeup, and her honey-colored hair is clean and pulled back from her face. Her black dress is pressed, but nondescript. She's surrounded by others in similar business formal attire, but talks to no one as she stares into her glass, her hand shaking slightly. A bubble of sadness hangs around her.

"She's a lawyer at some nearby firm," I begin. "Case finished early, and she came home to her husband banging her best friend. She's licking her wounds with a drink while he packs his shit."

Asher squints as he studies her. "No ring."

"She threw it in his face when she told him to get out, obviously."

He chuckles. "No tan line either. It's unavoidable here in Florida, no matter how pale you are." I raise an eyebrow at him. "I always check, don't want some jealous spouse coming at me."

A wave of jealousy rises at the reminder of the dozens—no, probably hundreds—of women who throw themselves at him and have made it to his bed. I'm the one in there now, ladies, so suck an elf.

Asher sputters on his drink. "What?"

Dammit, I used my outside voice again. "Nothing. So what's your read then, expert?"

He studies her for another minute, then leans back to me to whisper conspiratorially. My grumpiness evaporates as the mischief in his eyes is contagious. "That woman is lost. She's standing at a crossroads in life, and isn't sure which way to go—her heart and her head are at war. The weight of the world is on her shoulders—some great responsibility. She's terrified of making the wrong decision, because she feels like she has once before."

"Wow. I've heard the jokes about bartenders being a poor man's therapist, but that was like an episode of *Profiler*. Maybe I should pick up a few shifts here."

Some of the excitement dulls on his face, but he's still smiling. "Actually, that would be the psychology degree I got."

"Really?"

His brows pinch. "I told you I went to college. What did you think? That I majored in basket weaving?"

I sit back, surprised by the anger creeping into his voice. "Of course not. I just assumed it was business since you own part of a restaurant, but I never asked. I'm sorry."

His eyes soften. "It's alright." Asher leans in and kisses my forehead. "I better get back to it. Want to explore Main Street after my shift?" I nod as he stands. "Cool, we can grab some ice cream and see if we can squeeze in a lesson." He winks at me as he walks over to the lonely blond to see if she needs a refill.

Heat travels along my nerve endings as thoughts of potential lessons race through my head. Did he mean a lesson on Main Street, or after? Maybe I should ask for clarification before jumping to conclusions again. *I don't know; that worked out pretty well for us last time.*

The family dinner is breaking up. Silver-fox-dad heads to the front, his phone to his ear as his wife and son follow behind. Biker-dude drops his hand as he walks beside his stepmother, his finger deliberately stroking the inside of her wrist.

That was weird. I blink as I finish my fries. Maybe Asher is right; I should lay off the romance novels for a bit. Ha! Never going to happen.

CHAPTER 26

Ice Cream Cones

The sun is a perfect golden glow between the buildings as we walk down Main Street, casting a radiant halo around Gabby's hair. It may not quite be summer yet, but this close to the equator the days are already longer, and it is doing wonders for my mood. I take a deep breath, happy to be done with work and enjoying this time with Gabby.

The thought pulls me up short. I love my job at Pop. Going in used to be the highlight of my day. I could recharge my extrovert batteries, collect new idioms for my characters, and hang out with my friends all while getting paid. Lately though, it's merely been a distraction from Gabby, time away from her when all I want to do is make every moment count. *It's because you know this will all end soon, then what will you do for inspiration?*

The manuscript is going well. I'd gotten another few thousand words in while Gabby was writing by the pool. I've managed some scribbling on my phone at the gym or between customers, but not much. Normally, time away from my work in progress would leave me irritable, but not with her here. How could you be grumpy with a drop of sunshine so nearby?

Gabby's eyes dart left and right as we walk, studying each building we pass. "They're all closed already." She pouts a little.

"Yeah, Friendship Springs doesn't exactly have a booming nightlife. Most of the shops close around six; the restaurants a bit later, but only Pop and the dive bar on the other end of Main Street stay open past ten." Her watch lights up on her wrist. "Agent again?"

"Yes, like the twenty emails weren't enough of a reminder about the deadline." She groans as she silences it. "I'll call him back tomorrow. Where are we going?"

"Right here." I stop in front of a small storefront that's barely wider than a door and pass-through window.

"Hey, Mr. Ramstead, what flavor would you like?" Nate stands behind the counter in a vintage soda shop hat and white apron.

"You working here, too?" I ask.

"Trying to save up as much as possible over the summer. Won't have many options once the season starts."

"Come see me at Pop—we're always looking for bussers or event servers, and I can schedule you around football."

"Gee, thanks, Mr. Ramstead! Now, what flavor can I get you?"

"I'll have a double scoop of black walnut. Gabs, what do you want?" I draw Gabby closer and slightly in front of me, keeping my hand anchored on her hip. The scent of rose tickles my nose as I keep her close.

"Single scoop of sweet cream, please." She doesn't pull away from my hand, and something in my chest goes a bit gooey.

I've never technically dated before—not that we're dating; this is purely a friends with benefits situation. In school, I spent every moment I could playing sports, and then in college, working my ass off to afford it. Oh, I fucked. There was never a shortage of girls who wanted me, and it's not like I had a reason to turn them down, but nothing resembling a relationship.

As Gabby and I walk down Main Street licking our ice cream cones, I'm seeing the appeal for the first time. Sure, I've hung out with the ladies at Pop in completely platonic ways, but this doesn't feel like that. Time with them is like a beer—low stakes, fun, but fleeting—but time with Gabby is like a finely aged bourbon, complex, full-bodied, and can knock you on your ass if you're not careful. Must be the combination of sex and friendship.

"Tell me about your book."

"My book?" Gabby's tongue darts out to catch a creamy droplet, momentarily distracting me. "What about it?"

I gulp, then lick my own dripping cone as I will my cock to stand down. "What's it about? Tell me about the characters and their relationship. It'll help me plan our lessons."

She shrugs, gives one more lap around the base of the scoop. "The story is about Catrina. She's a light witch whose coven was destroyed—or so she thinks, anyway. She's on a journey to save the world from the dark witches, who are slowly poisoning it because of the imbalance of power."

"But there's got to be a guy if there's spice."

She glares at me over her ice cream. "Hey, it could be a sapphic fantasy!"

I hold a hand out in defense. "That would be cool, but you wouldn't need me."

"Oh yeah, good point." I chuckle and eat my treat as I wait for her to continue. "There's this warrior, Lucian. He was once the most revered in the land…"

"But?"

"He figured out how corrupt the government was and pushed back. Now he's disgraced and fighting to bring down the very organization he previously swore to protect. So he's conflicted a bit."

"Why?" She looks at me like I'm crazy. "If he's loyal to his kingdom or country or whatever and it's threatened, in his mind, bringing down the system is being patriotic."

She tilts her head to the side. "I hadn't thought of it that way. That makes a lot of sense." Another long lick of her cone.

"What's Catrina's motivation? Is she equally driven to fight because it's the right thing to do? Or does she fear there's no one else?"

Gabby looks thoughtful. "More the latter, I guess. There is a bit of a revenge aspect—she lost her family at a young age and has spent her life focused on defeating the dark witches that destroyed her life."

"You said she was the most powerful of her kind?" She nods. I continue, "So she has some survivor's guilt mixed with a chosen one mentality, probably resulting in a reforged hero archetype." She stares at me, slack-jawed and wide-eyed. "What?"

"Maybe I should have gotten a psych degree instead of liberal arts. You're wicked good at this."

My stomach warms at the compliment. I want to bask in her praise, but a flicker of guilt nags me. Should I tell her about my writing?

The moment passes as she rushes on. "No, you're totally right. Lucian is sort of a lone wolf meets fallen knight character. The two of them are journeying in parallel rather than together, if that makes sense."

I nod. "Do they meet as enemies, or are they allies from the beginning?"

"They fight at first—both conditioned to distrust the other on sight—but as they banter between strikes, they realize they could help each other."

"That sounds like a fun scene. I assume there's still some doubt at first, but do they ultimately trust each other and form a truce?"

"Yes. They make it through a bunch of scrapes, so the rocky partnership turns to admiration, and then with time they do genuinely like each other. Not that they sit around the campfire talking about it—they're too busy trying to overthrow a corrupt government."

"Good old forced proximity with a dash of trauma bond. Do they dream of a life together, or are they always planning to separate as soon as the fight is over?"

She licks her cone as she thinks. "I wouldn't say they're thinking about the future—they're too focused on the job at hand. Which is exactly why I never planned to focus on their relationship in the books."

"So why are you?"

"Huh?"

"Why even include the sex? I know you said it was what your publisher wanted, but is there an alternative? Maybe a scene with other characters? A dream or vision?"

"Roger says it has to be Catrina and Lucian. So I'm having the enemy coven slip them a potion." I chuckle at the irony. "What?" She side-eyes me as her tongue makes another swirl around the scoop.

"It's sort of art mimicking life—they're forcing you to write the scene so you're using a potion to force the characters to participate—fitting. It also forces them to stop and face the emotions they've been suppressing this whole time. You'll have to work those constant doubts into the rest of the plot. How would Lucian react if he had to choose between saving Catrina and defeating the big bad?"

Gabby lazily licks the cone, swirling her tongue around the very tip before working her way back up to the creamy scoop. I've been sporting a semi this entire time, but that motion has my cock swelling painfully behind the zipper, wincing slightly as I try to adjust as we walk.

"Hmm, you have a point," she says, sounding distracted.

My eyes meet hers, and I realize I've been caught by the gleam in her eyes. She holds my stare as she continues to lick the dessert, her motions increasingly erotic. My cone sits forgotten in my hand until the cold liquid drips across my hand, melting rapidly in the Florida heat.

Cursing, I quickly switch hands. Why didn't I take napkins? Gabby grabs my hand, bringing it to her mouth where she closes her lips over my fingers, gently sucking the smoky ice cream. "Hmm. That's good."

Glancing around at the emptying street, I grip Gabby's hand and pull her into an alley between two buildings, tossing the rest of my cone into a nearby trashcan.

"Where are we going?" Her voice is breathless as she tries to keep up.

"I promised you a lesson." This was not what I had in mind when I said that, but I've always been good on my feet.

Lesson 3

My heart races as the darkness of the alley engulfs me. I'm not sure if it's from jogging or the thrill of whatever Asher is up to. At the end of the lane, Asher spins me against the brick wall, caging me with his body as he shields me from the main street. His eyes smolder with molten heat. I knew I was playing with fire when I sucked his fingers. I'm more than ready for the burn.

He removes my cone from my hand and finishes it in two bites.

"Hey, I was enjoying that!"

"I'll buy you a new one," he growls. His lips slam into mine in a demanding kiss. If he thinks he's punishing me, he's sorely mistaken. The icy sweetness of the treat lingers on his tongue, sending my senses into a tailspin. Lifting onto my toes, I mold my body to his, matching his desperation to feel this connection again. His arms cradle me, the gentleness at odds with the harshness of his lips.

I rock, seeking some friction to relieve my aching core. He's too damn tall, though. Growling my frustration only makes him chuckle darkly. The world tilts as he hauls me higher and pins me to the wall. A brick digs into my back, but I don't care; it's the leverage I need. My hips rock as I grind my core against his hard cock, that damn barbell rubbing exactly where I want it.

He groans. "Yes, baby, use it. Take what you need."

Taking him at his word, I roll my hips in wider arcs, fully confident in his ability to hold me up as I ride him. My head falls back as I imagine fucking him in this position. I finally understand the saying "Climb him like a tree".

His lips nibble my neck, and I tilt my head to give him free access. "You are so fucking hot when you're like this."

"Like what?"

"Relishing the power of your body."

I mean to argue, but then his kisses find a particularly sensitive spot behind my ear, and the point no longer seems important. My hips rock harder, seeking a better angle on his erection until it's butting my clit perfectly. Asher pinches my nipple through my bra, and the shock is enough to send me over the edge. He recaptures my lips, drinking in my cries as I shudder in his arms.

My legs shake as he lowers me back to the ground, and he keeps an arm around my waist as if he's worried to let go.

"So what was the lesson, Professor?"

His lips twist into a devilish grin as he leans over me. "Fuck me if I know, but that was hot." He rubs his still-hard cock against my stomach, as if I need further proof.

I frown. "You didn't cum."

"I'm not a teenager, Imp, I can wait."

My eyes dart to the entrance of the alley. The sun has set below the buildings, casting us in full shadow. When I count to twenty and no one walks by, an idea hits me. A wild and crazy, no doubt very bad idea. My lips curl. *Those are the best kind.*

Pushing on Asher's shoulder until his back slaps the opposite wall, I then drop to my knees before him.

"Gabby, what are you..." His words break off as I free him from his jeans and wrap my lips around his cock. "Jesus fucking Christ, Gabby."

I release the head with a pop. "Shut up. It's time for my oral exam."

Asher eyes the entrance. Sensing he's about to turn me away, I lick my lips and take as much as I can fit in my mouth. With a defeated groan, he collapses back against the wall. His fingers comb through my hair, almost reverently, before settling at the back of my head. He doesn't guide my movement; more like he can't help but touch me.

I look through my lashes at him as I bob my head up and down his length. Intense blue eyes gaze back at me from a taught face. His jaw flexes as he grits his teeth.

I take it as a challenge; it drives me to try every trick I've ever read about to make him lose control. I grip the base of his shaft with one hand and cup his balls with the other. My tongue swirls across his tip, the barbell creating an interesting texture change from the smooth skin. I slowly increase the pace, rewarded by his sharp intake of breath and his fingers spasming in my hair.

Blowjobs have never done it for me. They were always something I felt required to do on birthdays and anniversaries. None of those experiences were anything like this.

Asher's entire being is fixated on me. I feel powerful.

Relaxing my throat, I try to take him deeper. His piercing hits the back of my tongue, and I cough reflexively as my eyes water. He tries to pull away, but I tighten my hands around him, keeping him in place. This time I'm prepared for the sensation and take him even further.

His hips jerk slightly, and I can tell he's still holding back. That won't do.

I keep my eyes on his as I take his cock down my throat as far as I can, then I hum before sliding off and repeating the motion.

"Oh, fuck." His fingers tighten in my hair, and he guides my head. Gently at first and then faster. His hips move in small jerks, so different from the controlled thrusts in bed.

A salty taste coats my tongue, and I know he's close. I want to push him over the edge. My fingers stroke his sac, as I hollow my cheeks. With a muffled shout, he cries my name as liquid explodes on my tongue. I swallow it down and keep light suction as he spasms in my mouth. He pulls free and hauls me up against him by my armpits.

He kisses me with hungry desperation, completely uncaring that he can taste himself on my lips. Why is that making me achy again?

"So did I pass?"

With a bark of laughter that ends in a groan, Asher embraces me again, softer this time. "A-plus, zero notes." He tucks himself back into his jeans, then wraps his arm around my shoulders to lead me back to the street. I pull my hair into a quick ponytail with the tie on my wrist—otherwise, anyone would know in a second what we were doing.

"You know, I'm still kind of sad you threw out my ice cream."

His lips caress my temple. "I'll buy you a whole pint on the way back to the car."

"That's a good start, but I want the flavor you got this time."

His chuckle tickles my ear as he lowers his mouth. "One of each it is, but they're going straight in the freezer, because I have some extra credit work for you."

My thighs clench at his tone. *We'll be lucky if we can walk tomorrow.* Pretty sure walking isn't required for what I have in mind. The Viking can keep us horizontal or upside down for all I care. *Damn, now who's the slutty one?*

The smile doesn't leave my face for the rest of the night—not even after four orgasms and some creative use of ice cream. Asher gave me another A-plus.

CHAPTER 28

New Friends

I walk down the sidewalk on Main Street, enjoying the breeze through my curls and the warmth of the sun on my face. It's beautiful down here, so different from Boston. Don't get me wrong, the history, the culture of New England is irreplaceable—the architecture, the theater, the museums. It can be a bit intense though; everything is at breakneck speed and high pressure.

A young couple passes me. They're holding hands and smiling at a toddler waddling ahead of them with wide eyes, peering at the world around her with wonder. I can't help but smile at her too—I'm sure my eyes are equally wide.

Trees and hibiscus bushes line the street, giving a tropical flair. Brick and stucco buildings with big picture windows and pretty awnings stretch as far as the eye can see. It's like its own magical realm.

A few more doors down, I find my destination: Books and Brews. An old-fashioned bell jingles as I open the door. Inside, I take a deep breath of that amazing book smell as instrumental covers of pop songs play.

The walls are a soothing hunter green. Dark-wood bookshelves line the sides and create even aisles along one side of the room. A marble counter with gold accents sits at the far end, with a vintage register above, and three brown leather bar stools on pedestals before it. Nearby, a large gold chandelier retrofitted with LED bulbs hangs over a seating area of brown leather armchairs and a small sofa circling a coffee table on an ornate green and cream rug.

Closing my eyes, I take one more deep breath of that distinctive paper and ink scent. I never want to leave.

A chuckle draws my gaze back to the bar area. A blond woman in a blazer gives me a wide smile.

My cheeks burn. She caught me red-handed. Er, -nosed? "Sorry, there's just something about the smell of books."

"Don't worry, I love that smell, too. How can I help you?"

I approach the counter and lay the latest romance I finished on the surface. "Do you happen to have the next in the series? I've been ordering them online but thought I'd see if you had any. If not, cool beans."

Her smile tilts to one side. "New England?"

"Boston. Is it wicked obvious?"

She laughs. "Well, now it is. I'm originally from Connecticut, so I recognized the slang." She holds out a hand, each finger tipped with gorgeous manicured nails in a bold peach with delicate gold rings at the third knuckle. "I'm Cassie."

Zero reservations plague me as I take her hand in mine with a smile. "Gabby."

Cassie walks around the counter with her head tilted slightly, sending golden curls with peek-a-boo pink highlights over her shoulder. "I'm sorry, you probably hear this all the time, but you're not Gabriella Boyle, are you?"

The bottom of my stomach drops out. "Uh, yeah?" It comes out more as a question than a confirmation.

"Your books are some of my bestsellers—especially after that talk a bit back! Thanks to you, that day put me in the black for the whole quarter. I was sorry to miss the event, but I couldn't close the shop for the day." She walks towards the front of the store without looking back.

My heart rate slows. Cassie doesn't seem to want any more from me.

There's a sign over the section that reads "Indie Romance." A graceful hand hovers over the titles as she scans for the one she's searching for. With a triumphant sound, she pulls a paperback and hands it to me. The cover features another bare-chested man from the neck down, this time with a catcher's mitt over his groin.

"I have the entire series. AR Storm is probably my best-selling indie author."

"Why don't I buy them all now? Otherwise, I'll be in here every day."

"I wouldn't mind the company." She exhales sharply, setting her curtain bangs fluttering. "Friendship Springs isn't exactly full of bookworms. Care for a coffee?"

She strides back to the register, her nude heels clicking across the wooden floor. I envy her easy confidence. Once again behind the counter, Cassie grabs a couple of mugs. "How do you take it?"

"Light and sweet, please." I sit on a barstool, twirling slowly from side to side. "So why Friendship Springs?"

"Came down here for spring break in college and fell in love. Haven't left since." She pauses, the creamer frozen above a mug. "Well, I went back and graduated, but you know what I mean."

I nod my thanks as she pushes the drink towards me. "Do you like it?"

"Adore it. The pace is so much slower down here than back home—no one's in a rush. I definitely don't miss the snow in the winter either."

The ceramic is warm in my hands as I lift it to my lips. Damn, that's good coffee. "There is something to be said for reading by a fire, though, with a nice blanket."

"I still do that, but now it's on my patio with a firepit." Cassie grins at me as she raises a matching mug to her lips. "How about you? What brought you back?"

My cheeks burn. Cassie's eyes widen over her cup. "Oo. Was it a guy? I don't know what they put in the water down here, but Friendship Springs attracts some fine-looking men."

"I'm working on my next book and needed a change of scene."

"Well, this is the closest we have to a coffee shop. So you're welcome to work from here anytime. Hardly anyone will disturb you." Her eyes glaze over for a moment as her shoulders round, almost disintegrating in front of me.

My heart goes out to her. She's obviously hustling and struggling to make her dreams come true. I'm all too familiar with that. I spent years writing my first manuscript, then another five getting rejected by agents, until I finally found Roger, who took a chance on me. For every author that makes it, hundreds don't.

"That sounds like the change of scene I've been looking for. Say, do you mind if I sign some books while I'm here? Whatever stock you have."

Her eyes light up. The mug lowers to the counter with a clink. "Really? That would be amazing."

We sit and talk some more as I sip my coffee. Cassie fills me in on the local hot spots, the real hidden gems only the locals know about. She asks for nothing in return, doesn't pry any further into her assumption that I came here for a guy, or ask for details on my next book. We simply enjoy each other's company, talking about books, booze, and the beach.

Did I just make a friend?

Girl Talk

My eyes trace a bead of moisture as it runs over Asher's hand cupping the long, smooth surface. He gives it a strong jerk that sends veins popping across his impressive forearm. I lick my dry lips as I imagine tracing those lines with my tongue. With a firm whack against the counter, he's done and the frothy liquid pours into the waiting martini glass.

My knees clamp together to combat the thrumming ache in my core as I try to slow my panting breaths. Did I seriously almost cum from him making a drink? Holy fuck, that man could make anything erotic.

Feeling my eyes on him—because how could he not with how hard I'm staring at him—Asher shoots a wink my way, and I swear I nearly die. My watch beeps with a heart rate warning, and I chug my sweet tea, willing some of the blood to return to my brain.

Anna pops out of the kitchen with a paper bag in one hand and a plate in the other. She smiles as she approaches me. "Hey, suga'. Here you go." She yells louder, "Asher, here's Cassie's lunch order for pickup—she should be in soon."

I perk up on my stool. "I can bring it to her."

They both look at me. "You sure?"

"Yeah," I wave around the busy restaurant, "everyone's got work to do except me—might as well be helpful. I want to pick up another book, anyway."

Asher's brows wrinkle. "You need to eat, Gabby. We can stop in after my shift."

"Just throw mine in a to-go box and I'll eat with her." He looks like he's going to argue with me. "You know I can't leave a bookstore in less than an hour—it's like an escape room. If we wait, it'll be that much longer before we get back. Didn't you say you had something planned tonight?" I raise my eyebrows at him so he knows I'm talking about the next lesson he promised.

Without another word, he dumps my plate into a paper box, tosses it in the bag, and hands it to me. "My shift is up in two hours. If you are not back by then, I will drag you from that store."

"Is that a threat, Viking?" I lean across the bar to grab the bag from him, but he holds it higher, out of reach.

His eyes darken as he leans towards me, dropping his voice to a raspy growl. "It's a fucking promise. I'll throw you over my shoulder and carry you down Main Street if I have to." He kisses me. It's brief—more of a physical stamp of the agreement than an affectionate goodbye, but it's still surprisingly public.

I can't help but smirk as I back away from the bar, waving the bag in one hand as I give a sarcastic salute with the other. He growls, and the last dry spot in my panties is a goner.

He's so going to make me pay for that later. *Yes, please!* I never would have thought I'd enjoy pushing his buttons so much, never thought I could! When we started this, I was expecting hands-on demonstrations geared towards blocking and finding the words for the spicy scenes that still evade me, but truthfully, what I've gotten is something so much more. Asher has unlocked this secret power within me, to tease and drive him crazy, and I fucking love it. So, I've been exploring it at every opportunity.

What can I say? Absolute power corrupts absolutely.

My lips still curl in a grin as I walk down the quiet sidewalk to Books and Brews, the delicious smell of fries wafting on the breeze. The bell chimes delightfully as I open the front door. "Delivery," I call.

Cassie sticks her head out from the back room, with a comically confused look on her face. "Gabby? What brings you here?"

I place the paper bag of food on the counter with a flourish. "I volunteered to carry your lunch down when the order was ready. Thought I'd save you the trip and come to eat with you. Plus, I promised to sign your stock of books."

"That's so sweet. I think I've earned a break." Cassie flips the lid open on her chicken sandwich and fries, breathing in the delicious scents with a contented sigh. "There's nothing like grease when you're in a bad mood."

"What's got you down?" I tilt my head at her as I pick up my veggie wrap for a sizable bite.

She shoves a fry into her mouth. "Business. I'm running out of ideas to bring in customers." Another fry waves through the air as if it's a magic wand, warding off her negativity. "But enough about me. I want to hear about you. A little birdy told me that you and Asher Ramstead are a thing."

My cheeks burn.

"Ah-ha! So it's true." She points the fry at me as triumph shines in her eyes, then pops the whole thing in her mouth. "Spill it, sister. I want all the details." She holds up a soda and water.

I point to the water. "Not sure I would say 'thing' per se... Like what are the requirements to be a thing? We are friends... and sort of roommates."

"I'm pretty friendly with my roommate, but we don't see each other naked." A shadow crosses her face and promptly disappears as she focuses on me again.

The bottle lid cracks open as I try to think of wording. "We are friends... with a temporary, beneficial arrangement and no strings."

She hums at me. "Is it true he's pierced?"

I choke on my water. "Cassie!"

"What? I overheard a couple of tourists talking about it after one of them picked him up."

I dim. Of course, I know Asher has experience, but I haven't thought about it much before. *You know why you haven't.* Okay, maybe I've been in a bit of denial.

Cassie's eyes soften. "Oh, shit. I'm sorry, Gabby, that was rude."

"No, it's fine. It's not like I expected a man that gorgeous not to have a past. Plus, like I said, we're not really a thing, so I can't be mad." Pity clouds her face, turning my veggie wrap to lead in my stomach.

Or that might be the dressing—where are my pocketbook antacids? As I dig through my purse, I try to change the subject. "Where are those books for me to sign? Oh, and the next AR Storm novel. Asher only gave me two hours, so I better hop to it."

The conversation steers back to safer topics—mostly books and ideas for social media posts. I autograph stock until my hand aches, but it's a welcome distraction from the ache in my heart.

CHAPTER 30

Words Fail

At five on the dot, I'm out the door and heading for the bookstore. I've been hard as stone in my jeans since I watched her sashay out that door, not exactly an optimal work situation. The little imp has gotten entirely too good at getting under my skin. I'd pretend to hate it if I weren't so fucking proud and turned on watching her blossom.

The bells jingle as I shove the door open. Both women stop laughing and turn to me from their spots at the bar, a pile of books between them, but my eyes are only on Gabby.

"Oh, shit. Cassie, can you grab the next AR Storm book for me?" Gabby checks the time, but doesn't move. I take three long strides forward.

"Okay, okay, I'm coming. No need to throw me over your shoulder like a caveman." She quickly grabs her bag and heads towards me.

Cassie stares open-mouthed at the exchange, then rushes to the front of the store, grabbing a paperback from the shelf. "Here, catch." She tosses it to Gabby as she passes. "You can pay me tomorrow when you bring me lunch... and tea."

Before she can do more than nod, I've got Gabby out the door and halfway to the car.

She's panting from my rushed pace as she sits in the seat. "Damn, I didn't think you were serious about the manhandling."

Leaning over the console, I hover an inch in front of her lips. "Deadly. Do you have any idea how hard I've been since your little challenge?" Her eyes try to drop to my crotch, but I'm too close for her to possibly see. I grab her hand and place it over my throbbing cock. "That's what you do to me, Imp. You're this unrelenting fire until all I can think about is the next time I can bury myself deep inside you and let the world burn."

I slam my lips to hers. It's not gentle, but neither are my feelings right now. My teeth nip her bottom lip, the way I've watched her do a thousand times. She whimpers, and that's enough to bring me to my senses. I sit back in my seat, giving her space to breathe, but she looks spooked. "Gabby, I'm sorry. Are you okay? Was I too rough?"

Her eyes are wide behind her glasses, but her cheeks are lacking their usual color. "N-no. I... I liked it. I've just never... no one's ever." She swallows thickly, squeezing her eyes closed. "I never knew I'd like... th-that."

My hand shakes as I start the car and put it in drive. Great fucking job, man. I thought we were past this. She's been so flirty and confident, I forgot about the whole reason she asked for these lessons in the first place.

With a deep breath, I push down my frustration and hurt and turn to my psychology degree.

With a gentler voice, I try again. "Gabby, why can you still not talk about sex with me? The person you are currently sleeping with."

"I don't know." She's staring at her lap as she fidgets with the sleeves of her hoodie.

"You read smut like you breathe air, and you blew me in an alley for Christ's sake—so I know you're not a prude." Okay, maybe I'm out of practice with therapist mode—I never actually practiced as a counselor. "Is it me? Do I make you uncomfortable?"

"It's not you." She sighs. "I've never talked about this stuff with anybody before. When I reach for the words, it feels... unnatural."

"Was your family very religious? Is it a purity culture thing?"

She shakes her head. "No, we were Easter and Christmas Catholics, but sex wasn't exactly appropriate dinner party conversation, and that's about the only time we saw our parents."

I try to imagine growing up like that. Both of mine worked, but they always made a point of spending time with us. Even if it was something as routine as family movie night every week. "So, who gave you the talk?"

"My mother. She's a surgeon, so it was all very clinical. There was definitely no discussion of positions or G-spots or even what a clitoris does." Her cheeks burn with color again. "Everything else I figured out on my own."

"Or with an inept boyfriend," I snark as I park the car in front of my apartment building. "What about your sister? Don't you ever girl talk?"

"Yeah, but as she's a lesbian, not sure how many pointers she could give me on sucking dick." Gabby flushes deeper, but there's a fire in her eyes too. I'll take it.

"Okay, fair point, though for the record, I'm more interested in your pleasure, and a lesbian would sure as hell know all about that." She only glares at me.

She has the actions, the passion, the enthusiasm. The thing holding her back from writing her scenes is the language. An idea forms. "Here's the lesson: you are going to take the lead. You will control the pace, position, and every touch. I'll narrate your moves so you can hear the words. Like with the romance novel, but in reverse. Do you understand?"

Gabby gives a noncommittal "Mm," but her eyes darken as she stares at me. I raise my eyebrow as I hold myself away from her, waiting for clear consent. "Yes, sir."

The words and the bratty tone have my cock swelling all over again. Oh, what I'd give to have her in a pleated skirt with that fresh mouth and easy access for my palm. "Good girl," I growl, "now move your smart ass upstairs before I smack it."

Her lids hood over dark eyes, and she squirms beside me. Seems like Gabs would enjoy that, too. She's not ready yet, but as I watch her hips sway as she rushes up the stairs, I tuck that thought away for later.

CHAPTER 31

Lesson 4

My heart pounds, setting off the alarm. This time the stairs aren't the only thing to blame. It's the anticipation of full control over Asher's body. To touch him in all the ways I've fantasized but been too nervous to voice.

Beating Asher to the apartment, I let myself in and head straight to his bedroom. Nestled in the drawer he gave me is the sexiest piece of lingerie I own: a corseted top that barely kisses my waist and pushes the girls up, with tiny panties held up by crisscrossing ribbons at the hips, all in black lace. It reminded me of a medieval princess with the boning, and I must have been ovulating because I bought it without a second thought. Could never bring myself to wear it, I'm so glad I saved it for tonight.

Hesitating for only a moment, I grab the matching garter belt and thigh highs and dash into the ensuite to change. It's a struggle to squeeze it all on, and I have to break to catch my breath a couple of times, but one glance in the mirror tells me it was all worth it. I feel sexy, and a little naughty.

When I open the door, Asher is lying on the bed stripped down to his briefs. His abs ripple as he sits up, hooded eyes scan me from head to toe, but I don't flush. "Damn, Imp. You're really trying to test my restraint tonight."

"Oh, yeah?" My voice is smoky, and there's a sway to my hips as I stalk towards him.

His fists clench the blanket as he settles himself back down. "It's taking everything in me not to toss you on this mattress and change my lesson plan."

I crawl up his body until I'm straddling him, rubbing my aching core against his hardness, relishing this power over him. "And what would the new syllabus be, Professor?"

His hand spears my curls, cupping my skull as he pulls me down to him, our mouths a whisper apart. "Fuck if I know."

Our lips meet, and he tries to take the lead, but I'm supposed to call the shots tonight. My nails dig into his shoulders, pinning him down. My tongue dances with him, demanding dominance. When he fights back, I retreat, nipping his lip like he did earlier.

Asher groans as I sit up, rocking against him, teasing us both. "You're a quick learner." His hands knead my sides, tracing the edges of the straps.

"I had a gifted teacher. Didn't you say something about narrating my actions, though?" I roll my hips again, rubbing my slit up his shaft until his piercing bumps my clit.

"She worked her hips against him, teasing them both while denying them the friction they both craved."

The deep timbre of his voice and his words, so like my thoughts, turn me on more. I move again, changing things up, curious about how he'll respond.

Asher groans. "Her heat burned him through the thin layers separating them. Her arousal soaked her panties, and he longed to feel it on his cock, or taste it on his tongue."

A fresh gush of wetness collects at his words. I lower my mouth to his shoulder, pressing open-mouthed kisses against the smooth skin with a groan. My fingers seek the grooves of his abs, tracing each from center to side. A rough edge catches my finger—a condom! "Were you a Boy Scout? Impressive preparation skills."

His laugh is mostly grunt, his hips flexing under me as his hands continue to explore my thighs. "More like I'm impatient as hell and didn't want to wait one moment longer than necessary to have you around my cock."

With a throaty laugh, I lift up on my knees. "Works for me. Off." I tap his briefs and get to work on the wrapper.

"Yes, ma'am." He tugs me closer, so I'm straddling his chest instead of thighs. As he wriggles, he jerks slightly beneath me, knocking me off balance. I pitch forward, catching myself on the wall with one hand. Reflexively, I grind my core against his firm trunk, sending waves of pleasure through my body.

"Fuck, Imp, you're soaked," he growls as he guides me back towards his now uncovered hips.

"Yeah, hurry the fuck up already." I make quick work of rolling the condom on, careful of the piercing. What would it be like to ride him bare? Would it change the way the barbell rubbed? Would there be more friction? Or less?

"Where'd you go, Imp? I'm dying here from blue balls." His face looks pained.

"Sorry, got distracted wondering what it would be like without the condom."

His eyes darken to full navy. "I don't know; I've never gone raw before." But he wants to; it's clear from the desire in his eyes.

Unable to wait another moment, I tug my thong to the side, take his cock firmly in hand, and lower onto him. We both groan as I fully seat myself on him.

In an impressive show of core strength, he sits up so his face is level with my chest. "Finally. I've been waiting for this all day." His palms caress my sides reverently. His eyes trace the curves of my breasts, then his lips follow the same path.

I've never felt more attractive. "Where did my words go?"

His fingers map my arched spine. "Of course, we can't neglect the lesson."

Slowly, I press up until only the tip remains, enjoying the scrape of his piercing on my G-spot.

"Fuck, yeah. Use that cock for your pleasure, baby. Do you know how fucking perfect your pussy feels? Like it was made for me. Keep sliding up and rocking so my piercing caresses that spot. Slow, deep strokes that bring you closer to the brink."

His words, the velvety catch of his voice, are the ultimate aphrodisiac. My head tilts back, eyes closed so I can focus on the ripples of electricity radiating up my spine.

"These tits look fucking amazing in this top. I want to worship them." Asher does exactly that with his hand and mouth. His stubble grazes the sensitive skin, the slight pain shooting straight to my clit.

I cup his hand on my breast, keeping it in place. My nails dig into his opposite bicep as he palms the globe of my ass.

"Fuck, Imp, I can feel you dripping down my balls." He shifts subtly, tilting my hips slightly. The new angle intensifies the building pressure in my core, and I spasm around him. He's stopped narrating, but I'm too far to reprimand him. "Look at me as you come."

I follow orders like the A-plus student I am. The intensity swirling in his eyes sends me over the edge. I cry out his name as I pant and moan through my orgasm.

"That's my girl." The world tilts as Asher lays back and bucks his hips up in the air, suspending me so my knees barely reach the mattress. He proves those muscles aren't purely for show as he holds the position while thrusting up inside me.

My hips rock, grinding my clit into his pelvis and sending me over the edge again. The orgasm hangs, or maybe it's multiple—I can't tell where one ends and another begins as wave after wave of sensation rolls through me.

My name spills from his lips as he swells inside me. I don't want the moment to end; I lean back, gripping the muscles of his thighs as I rock on him, trying to prolong this for both of us.

As Asher's shudders slow, he clutches me and shifts us so we're face-to-face on our sides. We're smiling as our breaths come in tired pants.

A spiral of emotions dances across his face, leaving his expression more serious.

"What are you thinking about?" I say.

"How happy I am Jessie asked me to change the keg that night." His expression softens as he tucks a curl behind my ear.

I lean into his hand as warmth spreads in my chest. "Me too."

CHAPTER 32

Gut Reactions

The bar is buzzing, but it's all background noise to me. As I sling bottles and smile at faceless customers, my mind is on my novel. I'll run a scene through my head a thousand times before I ever put it to paper. Each time getting a little further, or tweaking the action slightly until it's right. What can I say? I think best on my feet.

"Here you go." I drop off two martinis and keep moving.

Gabby slipped out a while ago. It's not that I miss her, not really. I've been too busy filling orders to do more than look at her on and off. There's undeniably something comforting about her presence, though.

And inspiring.

Since she arrived, my word count has skyrocketed. Not that I've had much time to sit in front of the keyboard lately. My lip curls as I think back to last night's lesson. I honestly don't know who's enjoying them more.

"What are you smiling about?" Jessie asks as she loads glasses into the dishwasher. "Or do I not want to know?" I mime locking my lips shut. She looks over at the bar stool that Gabby usually haunts. "Where is your little friend?"

"She decided not to join me today." I try to keep the disappointment out of my voice, but obviously fail as Jessie turns and studies my face. "What?"

"I've never seen you like this. She must be different."

"She is."

"Be careful. With a look like that on your face, you're in danger of getting your heart broken."

I'm touched that she cares. "I'll be fine."

"Someone always gets hurt when you do back-to-backs." Pain flickers in her eyes for a moment before she pushes it back and her normal don't-give-a-damn expression returns. "Anyway, I actually came over to remind you it's time for your break."

My stomach grumbles, telling me it's later than I thought. Another glance at the empty barstool shows Gabby still hasn't returned. I push aside the disappointment; I had hoped to eat lunch together. Oh well.

After a quick run through of the customers at the bar, I head back to the kitchen to grab some food. Anna hands me a plate, and my feet automatically take me to the little table we use for meals.

Tony is already taking up one of the seats, a worn paperback in his hand. He gives me a goofy grin as I sit. "Hey man, how's it hanging?"

"It hangs."

He looks around behind me. "No Gabby today?"

"Nope, she's writing over at the bookshop. She's hoping the smell of books inspires her." I smile, remembering how serious she was this morning when she made that declaration.

"So you and Gabby are a thing, right?" Tony's tone is casual, but what is his motivation? He did ask her out for coffee after all, maybe his interest in Gabby wasn't purely literary.

A rush of jealousy hits me, followed swiftly by a Neanderthal voice internally grunting "mine." Emotions overwhelm me, freezing me in place. I've never gotten possessive like that over a girl before—then again, I've never had more than one night with someone.

Tony looks up from his burger, and he rushes to defend himself, his eyes wide. "Woah, man, I think it's great. I like Gabby," he pales, "for you! You guys make a cute couple."

"Yeah, we're a thing." I force an easy tone, but my gut is still churning despite Anna's delicious food. He still watches me with wide eyes. "Tony, relax. You caught me off guard. We're good, man."

"Great." His voice cracks. "Remind me not to get on your bad side, Ash. No wonder there's never any trouble in the bar—who the fuck would cross you?"

I wolf down the rest of my meal, no longer in the mood to chat. It's not that I'm upset with Tony. An uneasy swirl of thoughts and feelings distracts me from any meaningful conversation—completely unfamiliar emotions, and I'm not a fan of new things.

Younger me may have been a thrill-seeker, always hunting that next big rush, but I've outgrown that. Re-planning your entire future because of one careless moment will do that to a person real quick. I like order and routine in my life.

Well, I did—it's hard to keep to a routine with a walking chaos factory in your apartment.

Is that all this is with Gabby? Am I simply chasing the dopamine high? It feels wrong to reduce our connection down to that.

Still mulling over that train of thought, I wave goodbye to Tony and head back out front, barely halfway through my break. A lone man at the bar catches my attention. I head over and refill his soda.

"Hey, Ronnie, haven't seen you in a while." I hold my fist out for a bump.

"Business has been crazy. I've been driving all over the state lately, it's good to have lunch here in Friendship Springs for once." He takes a bite of the hamburger dripping with barbecue sauce and fried onions and lets out a healthy moan. "Nothing beats Anna's cooking."

"I'd imagine you'd feast on her food all the time, what with being best friends with her husband and all."

"Selfish bastard keeps her goodies all to himself! Says they're still newlyweds like they haven't been married six months." I chuckle at Ronnie's comment. "Sometimes I think he's forgotten who saved his damn life."

Anna's husband David and Ronnie met in the Marines. Neither talks much about their deployment, but I've heard they damn near didn't make it home. When they got back, David convinced him to put down roots here in Friendship Springs so he could win Anna back. Together, they run a security firm and manage the surveillance systems for most of the local businesses and residences.

"Still listening to those damn crime podcasts?" Ronnie and I met while trying to catch the asshole who attacked Anna in our kitchen. David pulled me in as an inside man at the restaurant, and I dragged Johnson in because he's a good planner. Suffice it to say, Ronnie wasn't impressed with our credentials, but we amateur sleuths cracked the case two Marines had been sweating over for weeks. Caught the bastard and made a new friend, though he still busts my balls about my choice of entertainment.

As I open my mouth to answer, Ronnie's cell blares in his pocket. He pulls it out and frowns at the screen. "Dammit, that's a panic button for one of the stores down the street. Can you put this on my tab?"

My stomach drops, and dread fills me. "Which store?"

CHAPTER 33

Clearing the Pipes

I sink deeper into the velvet couch, my hands poised over the keys. My writing playlist plays through my wireless headphones—fantasy movie soundtracks, of course. The smell of books and coffee surrounds me, soothing my senses but doing nothing to inspire the story to flow from my fingers to the blank screen before me.

It's official—I'm well and truly stuck. Blocked. Clogged up. Dried out. How come the only words I can come up with are to insult myself?

Desperate times call for desperate measures. I save and close the doc and open another. Sometimes, when you hit a wall on your current draft, you need to write about anything else. Start a new project, journal, doesn't matter—the goal is to prime the pump, if you will. Like those old-timey faucets. Now, instead of mocking me, the fresh page welcomes me, begging me to fill it with words and ideas, and I, the ever humble servant, oblige.

Once the flow starts, it's impossible to control. I can only hold on and pray that my fingers keep up with the flood of scenes coming from my brain—and that the keyboard survives. All sense of time and space disappears as I'm swept into a new world of my own. I'm completely lost in the story.

A clatter startles me. Cassie gives me a sheepish smile as she hovers by my side. "Sorry, I thought you might need some fuel. I misjudged the distance to the table." There's a steaming mug on a plate with two scones.

Making sure the project saves, I close my laptop and slip off my headset. "It's cool. I could use a break." I grin up at her and nod at the chair nearby. As Cassie runs off to grab her own cup, I take a sip of the decadent roast. Hints of chocolate and raspberry dance across my tongue, followed by the delicious caress of sweet cream. I don't understand why more people don't stop in for the coffee alone.

"Good session?" Cassie asks. I groan as I savor more of my brew and slouch against the cushion. "No? You certainly seemed to get a lot of words down."

"I got a good six thousand down." My tone drips with sarcasm.

"So, what's the problem?"

"In a new book. In a completely different series." I lift my cup in mock salute.

"Oh... What's this one about?"

"A princess who discovers she has magic and runs away to use it when her parents want her to hide it away and marry some stupid prince instead."

"That sounds really good. Not sure that's going to help your deadline, though. Any idea what's blocking you on *War of the Witches*?"

With a frustrated yowl, I shove a scone in my mouth. "I can see the whole story; I know exactly how I want it to end." Crumbs fly from my lips as I speak. I hold the plate out to Cassie.

She delicately picks one up and nibbles at the side. "So, what's the problem?"

"It's these damn sex scenes!"

"Even with live-in inspiration like Asher?" She waggles her eyebrows at me, and my face immediately flames up.

"Inspiration isn't the issue. I could draft some decent smut now—if it was about any other characters. Every time I try to write about Catrina and Lucian specifically, the words jam up. Wicked frustrating."

"Do you have to include the spice? The first book didn't have any spice, just a hella lotta tension, and it was a bestseller. I loved it anyway."

"Thanks. According to my agent, the sex is nonnegotiable."

Cassie opens her mouth to reply, but the bells over the door interrupt her as the shop door flies open. The sun glares in behind a figure, blinding us. "There you are," a masculine voice booms in the silent room.

"Roger?"

Speak of the devil. He stomps across the floor, a scowl clear on his face and his normally neat hair mussed. "What the fuck are you doing here?"

Beside me, Cassie bristles. "Everything okay, Gabby? Do you know this man?"

"This is my agent." I turn back to the angry man in front of me. "Roger, how did you find me?"

"I have Google Alerts on you. When I saw a post about signed copies in this store, I knew you had to have been here because I didn't send any. What the fuck are you doing on vacation when you have work to do?"

Cassie pales as she pulls out her cell from her pocket, keeping it between her leg and the chair. Her eyes stay glued to Roger as her finger hits a button on the screen.

"This isn't... I am on an intensive writing retreat."

He scoffs. "With a ladies' tea time? What the fuck, Gabriella? Do you know how much I have riding on this book?" Roger looms over me.

My stomach drops like I'm on a roller coaster. What happened to the man who bought me a cupcake after my debut? *Red velvet—after you'd already told him you avoid excess food coloring... and cream cheese.* I stand, refusing to cower any longer. "O-of course I do. It's my name on the cover!"

"You ungrateful little... Pack your shit; you are coming back to Boston." Roger lurches forward, his hand stretched towards me, and I jerk away as the door opens again.

CHAPTER 34

Deadly Serious

"Is there a problem here, ladies?" The stranger is wearing a red polo shirt with "S&H Security" on the breast. He's about Asher's height and build. His lips form an easy smile on his dark skin, but his eyes are sharp and calculating as they take in the scene.

A mask settles over Roger's face—the one he uses for PR—as he turns to the newcomer. "No problem here. I was simply collecting my client. She hasn't been answering my calls, and I was worried."

The bell rings again, and Asher rushes in. "I told you to wait for me, Ronnie. Gabs, you okay?" He's by my side in a moment, his arm around me as he puts himself between me and Roger.

"You? I know you." Roger's facade flickers as he stares at Asher. My Viking simply holds me in his arms and glares back. "You're the bartender from the signing. What the fuck are you doing here?"

"I should be asking you that. A long way from Boston. Do all your clients receive such attention? Or is there a reason you're stalking Gabby?"

Roger's eyes drop to Asher's hand at my waist, and my hands fisted in his shirt. "You ran from your responsibilities to shack up with some himbo? I'm disappointed in you, Gabriella. How did he get his hooks into you so quickly?"

I jerk as if his words physically wound me. "You don't even know him, and my personal time is none of your fucking business, Roger. The pages are almost ready. He's been helping me."

Roger's lip curls as if he suddenly found shit on his five-hundred-dollar shoes. "There are millions on the line, do you realize that?"

"Watch the way you talk to her if you want to keep those veneers, bub." Asher's arm turns to steel around me. I clutch him tighter, worried he'll deck Roger. *That would be wicked hot.* My inner voice seriously needs therapy.

In a moment, Roger's face transforms, and he appears remorseful. "I'm sorry, Gabriella. You've been acting so strangely lately, I worry. You're so close to really making it, and I don't want to see you lose it all over a lack of discipline."

"My work ethic has never been a problem. I told you, these scenes the publisher wants are not my usual style and are taking extra time, but you'll have them very soon, and I'm already brimming with ideas for the next book."

He nods, his eyes casting around the store. "Maybe we should hire a ghostwriter for the adult content if you are struggling." I bristle, and Asher rubs my arm soothingly. "Just consider it."

The security guard now stands by Cassie. "I think it's time for you to leave if you won't be buying anything in Miss Cassie's shop."

Roger gives me one last look. "Yeah, Okay. I'll be at the airport hotel tonight if you change your mind. Answer my calls, Gabriella, I worry about you."

The anger dims as guilt twists my stomach. Roger has been looking out for me for years—a sort of surrogate father figure. He's not wrong; my behavior has been a bit erratic lately. "Sorry, I'll be better about sending updates."

Roger leaves without another look back. With a nod to us, Ronnie follows him out and down the street.

Asher pulls me against his chest in a tight hug. I breathe in his smoky, clean smell, and some of the tension melts away.

"Oh, Gabby, I'm so sorry. I had no idea." Cassie's eyes are brimming with tears, and she twists her fingers in her lap.

"Whatever for?" Leaving the comfort of Asher's arms, I grab my friend's hands.

"It's my fault he found you. I posted about the signed copies online—thought maybe it would help with foot traffic or tourists. I didn't realize you were hiding from your agent or that he'd use it to find you." She sniffles, and a tear trickles down her face. "He was so angry."

"This is not your fault, Cass. Of course, you should advertise them! Hell, I'll order you more to post about or take a selfie. Roger has just been... extra lately. This book deal has him super stressed. I swear he's not usually like this. He's been my agent for years."

She still doesn't look sure.

Asher squats down next to me and draws her eyes. "Hey, you did the right thing, Cassie. You didn't like the body language in the room, felt threatened and hit the silent alarm without engaging him. That's exactly what you're supposed to do."

Her phone rings, startling her. "That's my roommate—as my emergency contact, he gets the alert. I should take this."

Asher and I step aside to give her privacy, and he immediately wraps me in his arms again. "Are you okay?"

"Yeah, how did you get here so fast?"

"Ronnie was having lunch at the bar when he got the notification. I knew you were here, so I ran after him when he said it was Books and Brews."

"That's wicked smart." I settle against his chest, refusing to overthink the moment.

"Yeah, well, they were both security specialists in the Marines. For a small town, we've had our share of crime lately, so we make sure all the girls know how to use the app. We'll put it on your phone, too."

Cassie approaches us. "Gabe's on his way. He left work when the alert went off, so he should be here soon." She is still pale, and more subdued than usual. I'm glad she has someone to come sit with her. "I'm so sorry, Gabby."

My arms wrap her in a sisterly hug. "Please don't apologize. I'm sorry he scared you." Her hands tremble as she hugs me back. She stiffens as the doorbell rings again.

"Cass?" A man bursts in. From the way Cassie relaxes at his voice, this must be Gabe. He's fairly unassuming, not quite as tall as Asher, with pitch-black hair, brown eyes, and golden skin. His eyes pinch in concern as he looks her over. "Want me to take you home?"

"I can't afford to close up. I'm barely keeping the lights on as it is. You didn't have to leave work."

"Well, I'm here, and I have too much PTO to roll over, anyway. Why don't you catch up on paperwork in the office and I'll mind the front? I'll bring you some tea in a minute."

"That would actually be helpful. I'm behind on taxes, and the register keeps glitching. Thanks, Gabe." As she smiles up at him, his entire face softens.

"If you're all good," Asher starts, "we're going to head out."

I blow a curl off my forehead. "Yeah, I better get back to writing. I'm going to finish that scene even if it kills me."

Asher stiffens, and his voice is rough when he speaks. "Don't joke about that."

"Ash, sex scenes can't kill people. Unless you're reading them while walking off a cliff or something."

He snorts. "Come on, Imp, let's grab you some fuel on the way home. I'll even buy you a cupcake as a treat for when you ace it. Cookies and cream."

Our favorite, my inner voice preens.

His arm settles around my shoulder as we wave our goodbyes and head out to the car, my unpleasant meeting with Roger almost completely forgotten.

War of the Witches – Book 3 – V2

by Gabriella Boyle

~~~

As Lucian looked at Catrina, he felt a rising surge
of arousal, no doubt the result of the love potion
the enemy had dosed them with. From the blush of
her cheeks and the way she bit her lip, Catrina was
feeling it too. No longer able to resist the pull,
he pushed her back against the tree and lifted her
skirts. "I want you," he growled.

She wrapped her legs around him and opened herself
to him. "Finally," she breathed as her head tilted
back to give him better access to her neck. Tiny bolts
of electricity danced across her skin, radiating
from each point his lips caressed. She gripped his
shoulders, whimpering as the thick leather of his
armor barred her path.

A dark chuckle rumbled, the vibrations stoking the
flames higher. "Easy, kitty cat. Tonight may be my
~~~

only chance to have you, and I have no intention of rushing it."

Easing her fingers down the back of his tunic, Catrina dug her nails into his muscled back for leverage as she rubbed herself more firmly on his arousal. "Even kittens have claws, Lucian."

Tongues and hands clashed in a fevered dance, both desperate for more contact, neither wanting this to stop.

Catrina lowered her hand to the ties of his britches, but in her haste she tightened the knot instead of loosening it. When tugging only made things worse, she twisted her fingers into a spell, burning through the string.

"Careful there."

"Am I or am I not the most powerful witch in Orcain." She took him in hand, running her fingers over the silk-wrapped steel of his manhood, silencing his words. He melted into her, lowering his head to her shoulder with a groan.

The potion made her bold. Catrina guided him to her entrance, a place no man had dared enter before. As he rushed forward, she gave herself over to the sensation of being filled by him. Her senses overloaded by him, his hands on her thighs, his lips on her throat, his muscles under her fingers.

With flashes of light, she exploded as the sensations sent her over the edge. He quickly followed, crying out her name as he filled her with his seed.

~~~
~~~

Anatomy of a Sex Scene

S eed? Seriously, Gabby? My palms dig into my eyes and scrape down my face.

Objectively, it is better, but something is still missing. I just can't put my finger on exactly what it is. When I read AR Storm's novels, the characters jump off the page during sex. There's no shift in tone between the plotty bits and the spicy bits.

I groan as I look around for Asher. He'd come back from the gym some time ago and disappeared into the bedroom but hadn't reappeared. My feet carry me automatically seeking him out—whether for comfort or advice, I'm not sure, and frankly, I'm not going to think about it too much. I collapse on the bed like a dramatic cartoon princess beside the pile of laundry he's sorting.

Asher chuckles as he pulls out an earbud. "Writing going that well?" I grunt, my face still buried in the comforter. He tosses a pair of socks at me. "What's wrong with the scene this time?"

The stack shifts as I sit up, and I pull a mound of socks closer to sort. "I don't know. It's better—less mechanical and more sensual."

"But?" He pauses folding, his entire attention on me.

"But I find myself thinking, 'So what?' as I read it."

"Well, what is the answer you came up with?"

"What do you mean?"

"What is the purpose of the scene? How does it lend to the plot?"

"It doesn't. I'm only writing it because my publisher is making me?" I can't help my voice lifting at the end. What is he getting at?

"There's your problem. Sex scenes aren't filler; they further the story. Your characters reveal things about themselves, their feelings, and the relationship shifts during the scene." I look at him like he's crazy. "You know why they call it spice? Because it enhances the flavor of the plot. It would still be a novel without it, but the spice gives nuance."

"So you're saying the sexy bits do more than make the reader horny?"

He laughs. "Well, hopefully they do that, too. What is shifting for your characters in this scene? What are their secret wants or wounds?"

I mull that over as I absentmindedly match socks. "They want each other, but are too focused on saving the world to give in to the urges until a potion forces them to. Maybe there's a bit of fear? They've been partners of a sort for a long time on this quest, so this would change everything."

"There you go. Forbidden lust, the thrill of finally getting what you never thought you'd have. That would bring some urgency and desperation to the situation." He tosses gym shorts onto a growing pile.

"Have they ever admitted even to themselves they want more from this partnership?"

"No, not really. Obviously, there's been some tension since readers ship them so hard, but no overt statements." The pieces slowly connect in my brain. That is the dimension in AR Storm's romance novels that I'm missing in mine. "You're wicked good at this. Maybe you should write the sex scenes. You certainly have the life experience."

When Asher doesn't respond with the expected quip, I look up; the smile falling off my face as I take in his wide eyes and the pallor under his tan. Maybe calling him a man whore wasn't the best move. *Way to put your foot in your mouth.*

"Listen, Gabby..." His voice is hesitant, with a bit of a waver at the end.

He's totally going to end things. Blinking away tears, I look down at the pink sock in my hand with black cats on it. My sock. "You did my laundry?"

Asher stands at the foot of the bed, a hand cupping his neck as the other holds a purple Salem t-shirt. "Yeah, you were busy, and I was doing it anyway, so I threw it in. Was that wrong?"

"No, I just... I don't want to be a bother." I clutch the sock in my lap.

"Gabriella, you could never be a bother." His eyes are intense as they bore into mine. I give him a slight smile, which seems to satisfy him. "How about you heat up some dinner while I finish this and then we go see a movie? That new dragon one sounded good."

I jerk up, then fall back down as I try to save a precarious stack of laundry. "The one with the lost princess? How do burgers and tots sound?"

"Perfect." His expression softens, and he reaches down to help me off the bed.

As I'm tossing frozen potatoes on a sheet pan and listening to the patties sizzle, a thought occurs to me. I've never been in a fuck-buddy situation before, but dinner and a movie sounds more like a date. Maybe that's the "friends" part of "friends with benefits."

Yeah, that makes sense; friends can go to the movies and hang out. Why does that thought make my stomach hurt?

What about rushing to your rescue? Asher was sure friendly at Books and Brews. He didn't react any differently than Cassie's roommate did, and those two are only friends. *The way Gabe looked at Cassie wasn't entirely friendly.*

I try to ignore the dangerous spark of hope that ignites in my belly.

Lesson 5

Asher sits up, still straddling me on the bed, a black sleep mask between his fingers.

"Woah, I've seen this porn. You put that on and a friend comes out of the closet and starts fucking me instead, and next thing I know I'm in a three-way." I dart my eyes from him to the doors. My lady bits are whispering they might not hate the idea while my brain screams we are so not ready for that. "Is it Johnson?" I whisper.

His eyes darken in a way that's both scary and exhilarating. A muscle spasms across his cheek. I think I've poked the dragon, but I'm kind of excited to see what happens. Asher's voice is a low growl when he speaks.

"There's no one in the fucking closet. I would never spring a threesome on you, Jesus Christ, especially not with my best friend."

He actually looks hurt. My stomach twists with guilt. I'm not sure if it's the idea of sleeping with Johnson or that I basically accused him of rape when he's done nothing but take things at my pace and asked if I was okay every step of the way.

"I'm sorry." His jaw is still marble under my hands. "I freaked out a bit, and my mouth took off without my brain again. You would never push for something I wasn't comfortable with; I know that." His eyes soften, and he turns to kiss my palm, sending my heart into a freaking frenzy. "So what is the blindfold really for?"

"You're too in your head. We need to limit the senses you are using so that you can concentrate on the sensations. That way, you can describe them in your writing." It makes sense. "Do you trust me?" There's a vulnerability in his eyes.

My lips curve. There's no way he knows Aladdin was my sexual awakening, but it is exactly what I need to hear. "Always."

He smiles too, and in that moment I know I'd do anything to be the one who makes him do that.

I lower the blindfold, plunging myself into darkness. My heart pounds. With no way of knowing what is going on around me, I cannot predict what sensation will come next, and I jump at the first touch before settling again.

Asher's fingers sweep over my skin, gentle enough so they don't drag, but firm enough to send tingles along my nerve endings, spreading like ripples across the pond. A stroke along my hip, then thigh. Each pass tantalizingly closer to the aching center but torturously too far.

An uneven whoosh of air reaches my ears, and I realize it's from my breathing and not the vents. The chirp of cicadas and the faint sounds of traffic fill out the soundtrack.

Smoky hints of Asher's body wash grow stronger. The mattress dips, the pull of gravity telling me he's between my legs. Now both of his hands are free to travel up my thighs, doubling each sensation. My knees fall open, inviting him to finally touch that weeping center.

Ever the gentleman, Asher complies.

His fingers hook the sides of my panties, dragging them down. Cool sheets caress my back as he lifts my feet above his shoulders. The straps scrape over my skin, leaving it raw and sensitive. His touch eases the sting as he strokes my body. The muscles of his fingers press into my hips, lifting me higher so he nestles deeper into the valley between.

A soft but firm bump against my clit—a gentle request for entry, a promise of more to come. "Can you feel my cock, Imp? How it yearns to be inside you."

The smoothness of his blunt end nudges my opening, the latex of a condom providing the slightest friction. He rubs again from clit to crack, then eases in.

With my knees over his arms, I'm already exposed to him. It's not enough. I open myself impossibly more, wanting him deeper.

"It's so tight from this angle," he groans as he pulls out and then pushes back in. "Such a greedy little pussy." His lips kiss my throat, the stubble on his chin leaving scratches, the bite of pain bringing an intoxicating contrast to the gentle caress.

"Don't forget your other senses," he whispers. "What do you smell?"

The smokiness of his body wash is even stronger this close, mixed with the sharpness of sweat.

"What do you hear? Do you hear the wetness of your pussy against my cock?" he asks.

Yes, it's a purely sexual sound—panting breaths and his skin slapping against mine with each thrust.

He picks up the pace, locking his hands under my ass to maintain that perfect angle as his piercing caresses my G-spot with every movement. Every stroke pushes me closer to the brink, but I'm not ready for it to end.

The blindfold unlocks a side of me I didn't know existed. Something about the freedom from perception allows me to give in to my body's urges. My nails claw at the skin of his thighs, and moans louder than I've ever made before escape my lips, thanks to a simple scrap of silk.

"That's it, feel how your pussy clenches around me?" Gentle, almost reverent strokes on my ankle belie the harsh tone. "You have my cock in a fucking vice. How does it feel, Imp?"

"S-so g-good."

The building sensations crest within me, overwhelming in the absence of sight. I rip off the blindfold, desperate to see his blue eyes as I cum. As I meet his gaze, pleasure blinding my thoughts, my thighs shake uncontrollably.

Every muscle tenses—knees, fingers, core—as if every part wants to bind him to me. Loud, undecipherable cries wrack my body, and I give myself wholly to the passions.

He grips my hips as his thrusts intensify and lose their rhythm, as lost to this connection as I am. He swells within me, and as he leans forward, my name a whisper on his lips moments before he captures mine. There are so many emotions in the kiss, but I can't read them fast enough. Shudders wrack his body as he gives in to his own orgasm.

The spasms set off another climax for me, and I clutch him, never wanting to let go.

With a groan, Asher collapses beside me. He pulls me against him as he strokes my back. Neither of us speaks, but words almost seem irrelevant.

I struggle for breath, but a foreign satisfaction radiates through me. My eyes drift closed. I need a moment to recover. Silky fabric brushes my face.

When did Asher put on a shirt? It feels like seconds but must be hours, because when I open my eyes the room is dark and instead of a warm chest, I'm cuddling with my body pillow.

Beside me, Asher splays across the bed on his stomach, blond hair pooling. He transferred me to my "nest," as he calls it, after I fell asleep, so my back wouldn't hurt. My heart gives a little lurch—he truly is an incredibly thoughtful man.

The cold tile is shocking as I tiptoe to the bathroom to freshen up. Crazy how hiding in a supply closet got me here. Where would I be right now if he hadn't found me that day?

I slip back under the warm blankets, wiggling back into my pillows. A slight pressure on my hip has my eyes popping back open. Shifting the pile, I find a set of manly fingers has infiltrated my pillow wall. A smile stays on my lips as I fall back asleep.

CHAPTER 38

Cataclysm

Pop is packed tonight—there's a bachelorette party here on Ladies' Night, and I haven't stopped moving. A quick glance to the corner confirms that Gabby is happily eating her bar food while reading her book—yet another one of those fucking romance novels. I swear she must be about out of them by now.

Feeling my eyes on her, she looks up and finds me. She gives me that impish smile, and something in my chest loosens. She lifts a pretzel roll dripping with cheese to her lips. Her tongue darts out to catch a bead of sauce, completely unaware of how fucking hot she is. I'm hard in an instant thinking about her licking me.

I have no clue what idiot convinced her she needed lessons. Can you be both insanely grateful and want to murder someone at the same time? Because that's about where I am.

Taking a deep breath, I turn back as a customer slides onto the stool in front of me. "How can I help... you?"

I look up and find a vaguely familiar blond making aggressive eye contact. From the "Bride Tribe" sash and the slightly glassy look in her eyes, it doesn't take a rocket scientist to figure out she's from the bachelorette party.

"Oh, I think there are a few things you could help me with." There's no slur, so she's not drunk, but still tipsy enough to be brave. Trick of the trade—I can grade a buzz a mile away. She leans forward, squeezing her breasts together and angling them at me.

I keep my eyes squarely on hers as I clench my fists on the bar top and work to maintain a professional smile. "Hopefully, a drink is one of them. What will you have?"

"Is the bartender on the menu?"

Four things happen in quick succession. Time slows as I see it all coming one second too late, completely powerless to stop it as everything goes to fucking hell.

First, a memory tickles the back of my brain, and I realize this is the same blond from the night I met Gabby. The damn thoughts move too slow, and I stare at her a little too long.

Taking my lack of comment for consent—which it abso-fucking-lutely wasn't—the blond leans over the bar, clutching my arm.

As I'm trying to remove her hand as quickly as possible without hurting her or risking a lawsuit, Jessie swoops in thinking this is a perfect time to play avenging girlfriend. It's not her fault; it's what we always do. She pushes her body in front of mine to handle the blond, looking to the room like a woman claiming her territory.

"Hey, babe, grabbing someone else's man isn't a good look. Not very mindful or demure. You feel me?" Thunderclouds gather on the blond's face. Jessie pitches her voice low and continues, "It's also fucking assault, so unless you want me to call the sheriff, I suggest you go back to your friends."

"I'll send a round of drinks to your table. On the house," I say.

"You okay, boss?" Jessie is still standing in my space, her hand resting on my arm and genuine concern in her eyes.

A stool screeches in the corner.

I turn. Pain fills Gabby's eyes as she backs away.

It's too crowded to jump over the bar, so I slide under the server pass and catch her in two strides. I thread my fingers through her curls, holding her still as I lower my lips to hers with a bit too much force. She whimpers, and I gentle my touch.

A series of whoops and cheers breaks the moment.

Glaring at the crowd, I grab Gabby's hand and pull her into the nearby supply closet—the same one we met in.

Tears glitter on her eyelashes, stabbing me in the heart. "Don't cry, little Imp."

"I know I don't have any right—we're not anything." Her words rip at my chest more than her cries did.

I wipe her tears with my thumbs. "We're sleeping together, Gabby. Exclusively. Doesn't matter if it's casual; you have every right to be upset at someone else touching me."

"Just seeing both those girls fighting over you..." Her eyes are full of pain, and it's fucking killing me. "Why did you flex for her?"

"What?"

A flicker of anger spreads through her eyes. "Just before, you flexed. Like you were inviting her to touch you."

"Oh my god, no. I was clenching my fists, but because I was pissed the fuck off, not because I wanted her to feel. The only hands I want on me are yours." I lean down to kiss her, but her hand on my chest stops me.

"What about Jessie? Have you two ever…"

"Fuck no. I would never sleep with someone I work with." Her eyes pin me, clearly not believing me. "As bartenders, we're hit on every night. Sometimes the customers become aggressive, don't take rejection very well, and it can lead to problems for the restaurant."

"Especially when you're the hot bartender from the reviews. What does that have to do with Jessie, though?"

"We look out for each other. I scare off the handsy guys; she cockblocks the eager women. It's only so the customer saves face, but there's nothing there. She's like a little sister—all the girls here are. I swear."

She searches my eyes, a spark of hope in her gaze. "You wouldn't lie to me, right?"

Is omission the same as a lie? A flicker of guilt runs through me, which I quickly squash. "Not about something this important."

Gabby releases her pressure on my chest and melts against me, her shoulders still trembling with emotion.

My arms lock around her, holding her like they can keep her from ever leaving. I lower my lips to the top of her head and shut my eyes as my heart breaks in two, because the truth is I am lying to her.

CHAPTER 39

Plotting World Domination

The next day, I'm still troubled as I walk into Pop—alone. Gabby decided not to come to work with me anymore. She says she trusts me, but seeing it is too hard. Her eyes were red, with dark smudges underneath, as I kissed her goodbye. A day on the couch is probably exactly what she needs.

Meeka waves me over as I head into the kitchen for a sandwich. "Anna and Bree are in an all-day meeting today, so you're in charge front of the house."

I check my phone, brows pinching. "Huh. Did they say where they're going?"

"They're upstairs."

That's weird. My fingers fly over the screen, already sending off a text. "Thanks, Meeka."

Me

Everything good?

Anna

At Pop... yes. For Nic... no.

As I'm puzzling over that response, none other than Nic herself sweeps through the back doors, looking absolutely pissed. She barely spares a wave to the rest of the room before stomping up the back stairs to the offices above.

Me

She looks pissed

Anna

Not half as much as she's going to be. Block the exit.

I chuckle to myself as I prep the bar for the day. Ever since Nic got married to some British lord a few months ago, there's been tension between those three. Her husband is a decent enough guy, but she's been spending a lot more time away—and keeping secrets from Bree and Anna.

After so many years of working together, it hurts me to see them fighting. They'll work it out.

A few hours pass with no sign of the girls—which I'm choosing to see as a positive, though we may have to do a proof of life check later. It's been relatively uneventful at the restaurant. A group of Karens complains about their food, asking to speak to a manager. Between the designer clothes, diamond rings, and frown lines, it's fairly easy to assess them. Most likely wives of big-time Orlando execs, ignored by their husbands who are probably sleeping with their secretaries, dissatisfied with the life they chose and looking for validation in all the wrong ways.

Instead of comping the meal—which they finished—I send over a free dessert—which they wouldn't have ordered without the excuse, anyway. I give them a little bit of attention, some guilty pleasure, and they don't leave a bad review. Win-win.

Overall, the slow day allows my mind to wander back to Gabby. I miss her.

The thought freezes me in place. I know I look to the world like a textbook extrovert. It's true I'm a social creature—you have to be to do this job—but it's not how I restore my energy. Nope, I'm that rare breed: an outgoing introvert. My time away from work is exactly that: me time. I'll hang out with the guys, go to the gym, but I've never wanted someone there when I walk through the door.

Now I do.

There's a lightness, an excitement to go home and tell her about my day that I've never experienced. The rut I was stuck in is gone, and I've never felt more creative than I have in the past few weeks. Speaking of which, thinking of Gabby sparked an idea for my novel.

Resting a hip on the counter, I pull out my phone and type away in the notes app before the thought disappears.

"Plotting world domination?" My head jerks up, and I see Nic behind the bar, scanning the bottles. "Or texting your girlfriend?"

"I don't have one." The words taste like a lie.

"So now you're kissing random patrons and dragging them into supply closets?" She arches one whip-thin black brow at me.

"Just Gabby, but we haven't put a label on it." She merely hums as she eyes me, those hazel eyes calculating like they can see into my soul. I'll never say it out loud, but Nic scares me sometimes. "Aren't you supposed to be in a meeting?"

She scoffs and turns back to the bottles. "More like a damn intervention! Daisy Duke and June Cleaver sent me down for booze." She spots her target and grabs the bottle with a triumphant hoot. "Why is the rum always gone?" Nic is definitely a little tipsy, but it only makes her pirate impression better.

"Fireball is a whiskey." I grin as I point at the yellow and red bottle in her hand.

"Eh, toe-may-toe, tah-ma-toe. I should probably remind you that half the ladies come in here for the hot bartender and not the drinks."

I ruffle. "So I'm not allowed to date?"

"I thought you hadn't put a label on it?" Her lip curls in a Cheshire grin. "I meant hire a new hot bartender. Interesting reaction, though."

"This has nothing to do with Gabby. I was clear when I bought in that I wanted to still tend bar. Now you're pushing me out because I don't want the crazies touching me?"

"Asher, we are plenty busy on the weekends to support another bartender, not to mention the events side. I'm honestly surprised you haven't done it already. Unless there's some other reason."

No argument comes to mind that I can use. I can't tell her about my outside activities. No one knows about my hobby, not even my family. A new bartender would take the attention off me, but what about when Gabby leaves?

My stomach drops.

She's going to leave soon. The scene is almost complete, and then she'll have no excuse to stay. I'll have no reason to avoid handsy blonds at the bar. It'll be another meaningless string of one-night stands like it was before.

Isn't that what I wanted? My work has always been enough, and it will be again.

"Great. So we'll put out feelers for a new bartender, and you can go back to plotting on your phone and kissing the same woman every night."

The pit in my stomach doubles—can't kiss her if she's in Boston. Who the fuck am I kidding? I don't want to go back to before, but what choice do I have?

I slap on my bar smile and deflect. "Don't you have bigger worries than my sex life? Or is being a fancy artist and society wife not enough?"

"We all have hobbies, darling. And secrets... even dark and stormy ones." She leans in closer and whispers, "Such a shame to hide that face, though—from a purely professional standpoint." Nic sashays out of the room, waving a bottle of Fireball.

I stand frozen as I try to work out what she means by that. And what she knows.

CHAPTER 40

Say Hello to My Little Friend

It's a lazy Saturday afternoon. I'm lying on the couch reading the latest AR Storm novel I could get my hands on while he's in the shower getting ready for work. The male main character pins our female lead against the hotel wall, finally about to ravish her, when the doorbell rings.

"Ash," I yell, "you expecting anybody?"

"Could you grab it?" he yells as the water shuts off.

Sighing at the interruption, I place my bookmark and pad to the door in my socks. The peephole doesn't show anyone waiting, so I slowly open the door and check up and down the hallway. I'm about to close it when I see the small package on the ground.

As I lay the box on the counter, Asher emerges from the bedroom looking delectable in his work jeans and polo. It's curious; when I first arrived, I'd get so tongue-tied seeing him like this. The sight of him still makes my ovaries combust, but mostly I see Asher, the funny, supportive guy I've grown fond of. "You've got a delivery." I push the package towards him.

He pushes it back to me. "Actually, that's for you."

I raise an eyebrow at him, but rip open the tape and cardboard. Inside sits another box. The words "hands-free" are about the only thing I can figure out. "What's this?"

He stands behind me, boxing me in at the counter. "This is a remote-controlled vibrator you place in your underwear." I arch my neck to see his face better. "You have no problem using your words when we're in bed now. I figured the key to unlocking your scene was to draft in a stimulated state." His lips find my bare throat.

A weight drops in my chest, nerves and adrenaline mixing. "I don't know..."

"You need to feel sexy to write sexy, Imp. Wear something slinky and try it tonight while I'm at work." I search for arguments, but his mouth on my skin evaporates every word. "Worst case, you write nothing, but you're horny and ready for me when I get home." His teeth nip at my shoulder.

"Well, when you put it like that." My voice sounds husky.

"That's my girl." I don't want to admit how my heart leaps at those words. He deftly sets up the app on both our phones. "I can control it remotely, too, if you give me access." He puts it on the charger, and with another drugging kiss goodbye, leaves for work.

I eye the device like it might explode at any moment, suddenly losing my nerve without Asher's body distracting me.

A bubble bath is probably the right place to start.

An hour later, I wander back out to sit at my keyboard. I reread the scene I've been working on, and yep, it's still shit. Groaning, I bang my head on the desk.

"I need wine for this."

I grab a bottle of white from the fridge and fill a glass. As I sip, I lean back against the counter and stare at that fucking vibrator. The green charger light taunts me. Or maybe it's a siren call. A dare?

"Fuck it."

Tossing back the rest of the wine, I quickly shove the device into my underwear and against my clit. Feeling absolutely stupid, yet strangely determined. My thumb stabs the app icon, then hovers for only a second over the big play symbol.

The first vibration has me squealing and nearly jumping out of my skin as I dive for the stop button. I turn down the intensity and try again.

Okay, this isn't bad. Kind of interesting.

I sit at my computer again with another half-glass of wine.

Now what?

I reread the scene, trying to immerse myself in my world.

Slowly, a warmth spreads in my belly. The soft tee I stole from Asher brushes my nipples, which harden. My mind revisits our nights together. The touch of his fingers as they skim over my skin, leaving a trail of goosebumps in their wake. How alive I feel when I ride him, his hands gripping my waist as I arch my back, lost to the sensations.

A moan escapes my throat. I fall back into my body and realize I'm rocking my hips, grinding my pussy against the seat. Seeking friction, riding the vibrator like it's Asher's face.

Another needy cry echoes in the empty room, but my fingers start typing. They fly across the keyboard as the scene takes shape. It's raw. As Catrina begs for release at Lucian's hands, I'm nearly as desperate.

The lovers lay entwined under the moon, satisfied and renewed in their determination to save the world so they can be together, but I need more.

My phone lights up with an incoming text.

Asher

How's it going?

I bite my lip. High on actually completing the scene that's evaded me for months, and with hormones running rampant, I only debate for a second, then switch to camera mode and send him a pic. His shirt is falling off my shoulder, exposing pale skin, and has ridden up to the swell of my thighs. The light on the vibrator is clearly visible through my underwear, but it's my face that somehow looks the most sensual. Flushed cheeks, blown pupils, and biting my lip.

Three dots dance at the bottom of the screen, then disappear. I stare, my confidence waning with each minute. He left me on read?

A loud crash behind me nearly sends me out of the chair with a shriek. Asher rushes in, eyes wild as he searches the room. He kicks the door closed and stalks towards me, looking every inch the conquering Viking.

My legs shake as I stand. "What happened? Your shift isn't over yet." I manage two halting steps before he meets me in the center of the room.

He grips the backs of my thighs and lifts me so I straddle him, the vibrator still pulsing between us. Asher buries his face in my neck with a groan. "I left when I got your text. It was that or jack off in the supply closet."

I glance at the clock. "That was not enough time to drive home."

"I drove fast." Open-mouth kisses trail across my shoulder. "Did you finish your scene?" He tugs the shirt down with his teeth, exposing one nipple before latching on with his lips.

"Uh-huh," I manage in a barely intelligible moan.

"So I was right." A scorching trail up my throat, then his teeth graze my ear. "The vibrator helped."

My heart pounds and the room spins. "Shut up and fuck me already."

He strides into the bedroom and drops me on the bed with a bounce. His smile is practically devilish. "Yes, ma'am. After we both cum once, you're reading me the scene while I eat you, though."

I groan my enthusiastic agreement as I lift my hips for him to remove my underwear.

A tease along my slit, then he groans as he lifts his fingers to his lips. "You're absolutely soaked. We're going to have to change the sheets."

"I'm sorry."

"I'm not."

War of the Witches - Book 3 - V3

by Gabriella Boyle

~~~

As Lucian looked at Catrina, his cock stirred to life.
He could blame the love potion, but deep down, he
knew he'd always felt this way. No longer able to
resist his longing, he pinned her against the tree,
running his palm up her thigh. "Catrina," he groaned,
as his nose caressed the shell of her ear. "Tell me
this is alright. If you don't want this... even if you
have to tie me to this tree, I'll find a way to stop."

She was familiar with this brew; it would last until
the drinker climaxed. There was no way but forward,
and they had been denying this hunger for too long.
Catrina wrapped her legs around him and opened
herself to him. "Don't you dare," she breathed as
her head tilted back to give him better access to
her neck. Tiny bolts of electricity danced across
her skin, radiating from each point of contact. She
gripped his shoulders, barred by the thick leather
of his armor, with a frustrated whimper.
~~~

His fingers found their destination, and it was unclear who moaned more. Unhurried, light strokes that left her panting and aching. More friction, more contact, more of him.

A dark chuckle rumbled against her shoulder. "Easy, kitty cat. Tonight may be my only chance to have you, and I have no intention of rushing it."

Easing her hands down the neck of his tunic, Catrina dug her nails into his muscled back for leverage as she rubbed her core more firmly against his hand. "Even kittens have claws, Lucian."

His lips caressed her jaw, leaving sweet promises of the hours ahead of them before finally capturing her mouth. She could now admit to herself she'd wondered what a kiss from Lucian would be like—every time they posed as a married couple at an inn, or she witnessed ardent couples in the shadowy corners of the street—but the reality was far different than what she ever imagined. His wide mouth, usually so firm in a severe expression, felt surprisingly soft against her own.

They remained entwined, both desperate for more contact. The world could have burned to the ground around them, and neither would have stopped or cared. That was precisely why they had never dared acknowledge this connection between them, and exactly why the dark coven had spelled them.

Catrina lowered her hand to the ties of his britches, but in her haste she tightened the knot instead of loosening it. When tugging only made things worse, she twisted her fingers into a spell, burning through the strings.

"Careful there." His voice held no real concern as he nipped her earlobe.

"Am I or am I not the most powerful witch in Orcain?" She took him in hand, running her fingers over the silk-wrapped steel of his manhood, silencing his words. He melted into her, lowering his head to her shoulder with a groan, his mighty arms still holding her against the tree.

The potion made her bold. For the first time, Catrina focused on what she wanted. Lucian. She guided him to her entrance, a place no man had dared enter before. As he rushed forward, she gave herself over to the experience of being filled by him. Her senses overwhelmed by him, his hands on her thighs, his lips on her throat, his muscles under her fingers.

With each stroke, lightning bolts of awareness rippled across their skin, and pressure built deep within her belly. Desperation transformed to ecstasy and with flashes of light, Catrina exploded around him. Lucian quickly followed, crying out her name as he gave her all of himself.

~~~
~~~

CHAPTER 42

Post Coital Cuddle

As my hands glide over Asher's torso, my fingers trace the ridges of each muscle. "Do you wax?" We've already gone two rounds—exactly how he promised.

"Random." He chuckles as his lips brush my head. "Got it lasered."

"Seriously?"

"Yeah. I used to wax, but I'd forget appointments or get ingrown hairs—which are a nightmare—so I got laser hair treatments."

"Huh."

"What? Do you prefer hairy chests or something?"

"No, at least I don't think so—never really thought about it." My fingers dance across his skin with a new appreciation. "I like your chest. It's so smooth, except right here." A rough patch along his ribs by the swell of his pec catches on my finger. "What happened?"

Asher shifts, propping his head up on the pillow more. "I was a bit of a wild child, always getting into scrapes. Jumping off the furniture, trying to do crazy stunts. One of my friends dared me to jump my bike off a ramp we set up—it didn't go well."

"You built a ramp?"

"Well, built is a strong word—we leaned some leftover plywood on a trash can. As the bike reached the end, the wood slipped, and I fell on the corner. Broke two ribs and needed twenty stitches."

"Holy fuck."

"Yeah, it was the last straw for my parents. After I healed, they threw me into every sport they could find. They figured if they tired me out enough, I wouldn't be climbing the walls at home."

"Did it work?"

He laughs. "A little too well. I became obsessed—football in the fall, basketball in the winter, lacrosse in the spring, ultimate Frisbee in the summer. Honestly, anything where I could run and play rough."

"I bet you were good."

"I was great—some said the best running back of my year. Got a full ride on a football scholarship, and scouts were circling for the draft."

"So what happened?" He stiffens, and guilt floods my cheeks. "I'm sorry, you don't have to tell me. I shouldn't have pried."

"No, I like talking to you." He pushes an escaped curl behind my ear and pulls me down to cuddle against his shoulder. "It was stupid. A week before the big game, I played ultimate Frisbee with some fraternity brothers. Someone had the brilliant idea of playing at night with a light-up disc and glow sticks in the goals. I jumped for the catch and didn't see a hole in the dark, landed wrong and tore my ACL. One impulsive decision and I lost my scholarship and ended a pro career before it began."

"Oh, Asher, I'm so sorry."

His hand glides across my hair and down my back. "Shit happens. Physical therapy introduced me to weight training, which I still do. The guys felt responsible, so they started floating me odd jobs to help pay for college."

"The bartending."

"Yup, and fitness training. Plus, I had more time for my studies and realized I actually like psychology—which also helped me cope."

"You're wicked impressive, Asher Ramstead." He scoffs, so I push up and look him in the eye. "Seriously. The way you kept going and made lemons into lemonade. Not everyone could do that. I've seen plenty of people give up at the first hiccup."

"Maybe that's why we get along."

"What do you mean?"

"Look at everything you've overcome. Your parents, your health—so many people would have given up. Not you, Imp. You face whatever life throws at you with a smile on your face and a never-ending sense of wonder. You inspire me."

My face flames, and I'm unsure how to respond. Asher smiles at me, his fingers gently clasping the back of my head, pulling me in for a sweet and lingering kiss before settling me back against him.

I trace invisible shapes on his chest as I relax in his hold. "So you never have to shave again? That sounds amazing." His laugh vibrates under my ear. "So, did you mean it?"

His fingers pause as they play with my curls. "That I don't have to shave?"

I smack his chest. "No, that you liked the scene."

"Oh! Of course, I meant every word." His lips caress my forehead. "We should go out and celebrate tomorrow night."

"Really?" My stomach flips—at once happy with his praise and terrified about what finishing the spice means for my time with Asher. I'm not ready for this to end.

"Damn right, Imp. You deserve to be celebrated." As I listen to his steady heartbeat under my ear, I believe him, and wonder if just maybe he wants this, too.

CHAPTER 43

Down We Go

The music swells and the bodies press in. My heart beats a little off-tune in pace with the thumping bass. This is so not my usual scene, but I want to celebrate, and the idea of pressing up close to Asher all night, of being the one in his gorgeous arms, excites me more than the crowd terrifies me.

His fingers wrap firmly around mine as he leads me deeper into the throng of dancers. Asher looks back over his shoulder at me, flashing a white smile that practically glows under the strobing lights.

I can't help but beam back.

He tugs me against him, and I go willingly, molding my body to his. A firm hand trails down my back before landing on the curve of my butt and grips the folds of the ruched bodycon dress Cassie lent me. I skipped the matching heels she tried to push on me in favor of balance and foot comfort, so Asher towers over me, making me feel very much like a princess with her dashing knight.

One song blends into another. I breathe him in, narrowing my focus to the two of us and documenting all the places our bodies touch—like he taught me.

He drops his lips to the shell of my ear to be heard. "Want something to drink?" I nod, and he leads me back to a roped-off area with our friends. The booth is small, but the club is so packed we were lucky to snag one to begin with. Asher sits, pulling me onto his lap, one arm anchored around my waist, keeping me secure.

A waitress in nothing much more than lingerie comes by with a tray of shots. I take two and shoot them both back, needing the liquid courage to combat my rising nerves. The liquor singes straight down to my belly, where it lights a fire.

Asher leans into my neck, his nose leaving a scorching trail along my jaw. "Who do I have to thank for this dress, Imp? You look delectable." I wiggle slightly in his lap, eliciting a groan. His fingers flex, digging into my skin as he centers me more fully on him, pressing the proof of his comment against me. A fire of a different sort burns lower. "Maybe I should call you 'Siren' instead."

"Get a room, you two." Cassie tosses a cocktail napkin at us from her seat deeper in the booth.

Next to her sits her roommate, Gabe, smirking over a glass of water. I don't think I've heard him say more than a dozen words since we all piled into his van. Johnson rounds out our little party. Turns out, although I met him as Asher's best friend, Johnson and Gabe work together with Brianna.

It really is a small town.

"I come bearing shots!" Johnson appears at the table's edge with a tray full of slightly glowing liquid. We each grab one. "To Gabby, for overcoming her writer's block. May Catrina and Lucian have many more adventures."

With a round of cheers, we all throw back the drinks.

"I want to dance more." I stand a little too fast, setting off an immediate buzzing in my ears as my vision dims. Blinking through some slow breaths. Coolness coats my tongue as I chug a nearby water, waiting for the world to stabilize.

The booze kicks in first, though, and that stability never quite returns. I may lean on Asher a bit more than before on the dance floor, but he doesn't complain, and the press of his body is stronger than all the liquor in the bar.

All night, Barbie-looking women have openly stared at my Viking. I can't even blame them. He looks particularly appetizing in a blue button-down shirt and jeans, his hair slicked back from his face, those electric eyes on full display. Those eyes haven't looked once, though. He's all mine.

For tonight, at least.

I don't know if it's the success with my writing, the dress, or the man, but I'm filled with a foreign confidence. I've never felt more comfortable in my own body.

"What are you thinking, Imp?" Asher's breath tickles my ear.

"I'm glad you suggested this. I'm having fun."

"It's not too people-y?" The smile is clear in his tone.

I laugh as he reminds me of our first meeting. "Not with you here."

His eyes find mine, and the intensity steals my breath. He leans down and I meet him halfway, pouring into the kiss every confused emotion in my own heart. My fingers thread through his long hair as he palms my back.

I have no idea what this is, but I'm holding on tight with both hands until it ends.

I wake up with a start, an unknown sense of dread filling my body. My heart hammers as if it's trying to escape my chest.

Did I have a nightmare?

I reach out to the nightstand for my water but find it empty. My mouth is so dry, my tongue might as well be sand. The covers weigh a million pounds as I push them off, my limbs leaden.

With my glasses off, I can't make out more than vague shapes, but I can barely keep my eyes open right now, anyway. I just need some water, and then I can go back to sleep.

My feet touch the icy floor. The room spins like it always does when I sit up too fast. I sway a little, head bowed as I wait it out.

Maybe I'm still drunk? Ugh, I haven't felt like this since college.

I stumble, catching myself on the wall, my breaths coming in short pants.

Come on Gabby, it's only a few steps to the bathroom. Get some water from the sink, and you can crawl back in bed.

My hair tingles as I reach the threshold. The sparks of electricity spread to my face and then my fingers go numb.

Already beating faster than I thought possible, my heart gives a painful lurch. The little light fades from my vision. Slowly, I try to lower myself to the floor, but it's hard to control my movements.

"Asher," I call to him.

The cold tile against my burning cheek is strangely soothing. Little shots of lightning still dance over my skin.

"Ash..." My voice is weak; I doubt he can hear me. Oh, god, Asher. I never told him how I feel about him.

My heart isn't pounding anymore. It's slowed, but is still so heavy in my chest. Short, shallow breaths are all I can manage as my eyes drift closed. I'm sorry, my sweet Viking.

CHAPTER 44

Darkest Fears

I wake with a start, unsure of what disturbed me. Rolling towards Gabby's side of the bed, my fingers search for her. Strange how I already think of it as hers. My lips twist into a smile, thinking of my little Imp. Her nest of pillows is empty but still warm.

"Gabs?"

There's no answer. Maybe she's in the bathroom. She drank quite a bit, better go make sure she's not praying to the porcelain gods.

"Gabs, babe, you okay?"

Rubbing the sleep from my eyes, I pad across the floor. I freeze in the doorway, the sight of Gabby collapsed on the floor sending my heart into my throat.

I sprint to her side, calling her name. She's breathing, but won't wake up. I can't think, refuse to let my mind go to all the places it wants to. Running back to the bedroom, I nearly trip over the comforter as I scramble for my phone.

I couldn't tell you what the dispatcher said, but I could describe exactly how cold her face felt against my fingers. It killed me to leave her alone there as I answered the door for the cops.

Why the hell did they send cops?

"Asher, go put some clothes on. The EMTs will be here soon." Deputy Ramirez's words cut through the haze.

I glance down at my boxers and bare legs. Woodenly, I grab the first pair of shorts and t-shirt I find, then hustle back to her side.

It feels like hours before the ambulance arrives; I hold her hand the entire ride.

They rush her straight back. I jog to keep up, but a nurse blocks me at the door. "Immediate family only."

Family?

Intense pain twists my chest. My heart is breaking because it knows its other half is lying on a hospital bed in there.

Alone.

I'm in love with Gabriella Boyle, and I never got to tell her.

CHAPTER 45

Answers

My head pounds. I want to stay asleep, but the beeping of my alarm is incessant. Why the fuck did I set an alarm after a night of drinking?

I crack my eyes open, and bright light immediately invades my peace. My eyes dart around, taking in the sterile white room. A deep breath fills my nose with an astringent scent I somehow missed before. I struggle to sit up, but I'm much too heavy to move. The beeping grows increasingly frantic.

"Shhh, it's okay." A woman in scrubs appears by my side, silencing the noise.

Still weighted by drowsiness, my mind struggles to process. Woman plus scrubs equals nurse. Beeping heart monitor, not alarm clock. Hospital room, not Asher's apartment.

How did I get here though?

"If I had a fiancé like that, my heart would be going crazy, too. Lucky girl. I think that's the first sleep he's gotten all night." The nurse has a kind smile.

I follow her eyes and find Asher collapsed in a chair by me, his hand tightly holding my own. He looks terrible. His blond hair falling limp and dull, clothes mismatched and rumpled.

Wait, a tick... did she say fiancé?

I open my mouth to ask if I'm hallucinating, but she shoves a thermometer under my tongue. The cuff tightens around my arm painfully.

"Hmm, blood pressure's a little high."

"I 'on' 'eally 'ike 'opitals." My words are comically jumbled around the instrument.

She rips off the cuff, and Asher stirs at the sound. Those icy blue eyes snap to me. He pushes out of his seat, sending the chair screeching across the floor.

"Gabby." His fingers tenderly cup my jaw, and he lowers his forehead to mine.

"I told you she'd be fine. Just had to sleep off all those drugs." Drugs? What drugs? Did someone slip something into my drink? "I'll go let the doctor know you're awake."

"What happened?" My voice croaks, and I clear my throat.

Asher reaches for the jug of water and brings the straw to my mouth. "You were on the bathroom floor, passed out. They don't think you hit your head, though. How are you doing?"

I wince slightly as I shift in the bed. My entire body aches. "Like somebody stuffed cotton in my head."

He brushes my curls away from my face, gently rubbing his thumb over my temple. "They said the meds would make you tired. You've been sleeping most of the day."

A woman in a white coat, a little older than me, walks into the room. "Good afternoon, Miss Boyle, I'm Dr. Carmack. How are you feeling?"

"Okay, a little sore and groggy."

"We'll get you some Tylenol and up and moving soon. Can you tell me what happened?"

My brow pinches as I try to remember. "I woke up and needed a drink of water. When I sat up, I got a little dizzy. On the way to the bathroom, I started getting really tingly and faint, so I got down on the floor and called for Asher."

He squeezes my hand, more panicky than comforting, and the color drains from his face.

"How often would you say this happens? The lightheadedness and fainting?" She looks up from her tablet with patient brown eyes.

"Never. I mean, the normal amount, like when I stand up too fast."

She smiles kindly. "What about when you reach over your head? Like styling your hair or changing a lightbulb."

"Yeah, I guess." What a weird question. Doesn't that happen to everyone?

Dr. Carmack taps on her screen a couple of times. "Do you have trouble standing for long periods of time?"

My brows pinch, making my headache worse, so I force them to lower. "I try not to stand perfectly still—I usually sway or lean, and that helps."

She nods. "What did you eat or drink before going to bed? Anything new?"

I shake my head. "No. We went out dancing. I had a few drinks, but I don't think there was anything unusual in those shots." I look to Asher, who shakes his head. "That was hours before it happened, anyway."

"Miss Boyle, you experienced anaphylaxis, which then caused a hypotensive crisis."

I blink at Asher, hoping he'll translate, but he only blinks back at me. We turn to the doctor.

Her lip quivers as if she's trying not to smile. "You had a severe allergic response, which impacted multiple organ systems and triggered low blood pressure, and you passed out."

None of this makes sense. "But I'm not allergic to anything. I've done that stupid skin prick test twice, and it's always negative."

The doctor taps some more on her tablet and then turns it to show me some graphs. "We ran some bloodwork, and your tryptase was extremely high, telling us you were having a histamine reaction."

Asher squeezes my hand as he squints at the screen. "She has food sensitivities. Could those actually be allergies?"

My head shakes as I rush to recite the normal reply. "It's not that serious; certain foods give me a stomach ache. My parents always said I was just sensitive."

She faces me. "If you eat those foods, do you experience diarrhea?"

My cheeks burn. "Yeah."

"Always the same foods? Like only with apples or tomatoes?" Her eyes are sharp as she waits for an answer.

"Not really. Generally, if it's rich, greasy, or creamy, I know it's not going to sit well. Or if I'm stressed—they said it was IBS." My face tingles as my ears join the burning.

"I see. And have you been more stressed than usual recently?"

"No," I say as Asher says, "Yes."

"And this flushing," she points to my face, "does it happen often?" Again, we give opposite answers in near unison. Her lips quirk again. "Have you ever been assessed for a mast cell disorder? Or POTS?"

I stare at her blankly, trying to figure out what cookware has to do with anything.

She stops trying to hide her amusement. "I'll take that as a no. Mast cells are part of the immune system and help the body with allergic reactions, inflammation, and tissue repair. We don't fully know why, but sometimes these cells go a little haywire, overreacting to things the body isn't actually allergic to—including exercise and emotions—causing hives, flushing, and even anaphylaxis."

My stomach drops. "Well, that explains... a lot. What about the pan thing?"

Her smile expands. "POTS, or postural orthostatic tachycardia syndrome. You are correct; a slight dip in blood pressure upon standing is normal, as gravity pulls blood from the head. Our autonomic nervous system kicks in, speeding up your heart to regulate your pressure. For most people it's seamless; for people with POTS, the response happens too late, the heart overcompensates, and their heart rate goes too high."

"How do we fix it?" Asher asks, his hand still in mine.

"There is no cure, but with lifestyle changes and medication, we can manage all of your symptoms. I'd like to observe you for a couple more hours, run a few more tests, but then we can send you home with a pamphlet and a referral to some specialists. Any questions?"

Tons, but I can't find any words, so I simply shake my head. With another nod to us, she leaves the room.

CHAPTER 46

New Normal

I reach for the jug of water and find it empty.

Asher takes it from my hands. "I'll go refill it. Do you want anything besides water?" I shake my head, still reeling too much to form words. "I'll be right back." With another forehead kiss, he exits the room.

I can't say I ever understood the purpose of forehead kisses. They always sounded so... paternal? There's nothing fatherly when Asher does it though. It's caring and affectionate without any expectations. All in all, I'm becoming a fan.

My phone rings on the nearby table.

"Hello?"

"Where the fuck are you? Why haven't you answered any of my emails? Your publisher wants to talk about the new chapter—you only sent one sex scene—and Netflix needs your approval of the script."

A simmering rage boils in my belly. Heat prickles across my skin and, right on cue, the machines start beeping faster.

"What is that fucking noise?"

"I'm in the hospital. I collapsed last night." My voice is impressively even. Well done, Gabby.

"Did the press see you? The last thing we need is a rumor you're having a nervous breakdown."

The phone shakes in my hand as I double-check caller ID, almost hoping I've hallucinated. Is this the same man who took a chance on me years ago? Who supported me and encouraged me when my own parents didn't?

"Are you fucking kidding me? I tell you I had a medical emergency, and that's your first question? You know what, I'm done." The words fall from my lips with no thought, shocking us both.

"Excuse me?"

I hadn't planned this, but my inner voice cheers the idea on. For years I created excuses for Roger. The pathetic truth is I thought he had my best interests in mind because he was the first person to believe in me besides Dee. My time here in Friendship Springs has taught me what supportive relationships are, and this right here is not it. "This isn't working for me anymore. I will be seeking alternative representation."

"Who the fuck do you think you are? I made you!"

"And I made you rich. You're fired. Don't call me again; my lawyer will be in touch."

As I pull the phone away from my ear to disconnect, Roger shouts, "You'll regret this, bitch!"

I take a deep breath through my nose, waiting for remorse to sink in. In less than a minute, I blew up my entire career—with barely any thought! Dee is going to love this.

"You okay?" Asher's voice is gruff and filled with concern.

Instead of anxiety, a calmness settles over me. There's been an incessant twist in my belly for months over the direction of this book and compromising my vision. I didn't even notice it until it was gone.

A second deep breath. My shoulders relax into the pillow, and the machine's beeping slows. "Yeah, I really think I am."

"I never liked your agent."

I laugh. "Oh, I know. You made that perfectly clear when you met him."

He hands me the water, and I happily take a sip.

"What are you going to do now?"

I tilt my head as I consider my options—I'm not even sure I know what all of them are. Maybe that's the right place to start. "I have no idea. Focus on my health? Write Catrina's story the way I want to and see where it takes me?"

He sits on the edge of the bed and lifts my hand, not meeting my eyes. "I know without the publisher pushing for the sex scenes, our arrangement no longer applies."

My stomach drops. I hadn't even thought of that. I always knew we had an expiration date, and now we're here.

His thumb strokes the back of my hand as he continues, "You have your health to worry about, and figuring out the next steps of your career, but do you think you could do all that here in Florida?" His eyes shine with a new vulnerability as he speaks. "This time together has been the happiest of my life and, selfishly, I don't want you to leave. Stay with me; give this a real shot. I can't say I have much experience with relationships, but I've never felt this way about anyone before, and I want to see where this goes."

My heart races, but this time with excitement. "I'd be a shitty fiancée if I went back to Boston now."

His ears redden as he gives me a boyish grin. "Uh, they wouldn't let me back here, so I improvised. You might also want to call your sister. I had to ask her for some of your medical history, and she's pretty scary." His Adam's apple bobs as he gulps. "She threatened to hop on a plane and beat my ass, and I think she might do it."

"Naw, Dee wouldn't hit you." Asher relaxes until I add, "She'd sue you so badly even your grandchildren will be in debt and ensure you never worked again."

Asher lowers himself into the empty chair, looking a bit lost.

I grab his hand. "But she loves her baby sister and won't do anything if I tell her not to. I should call her about Roger anyway; she'll have to look at my contracts and help me figure out the next steps."

We share a gentle kiss, then he squeezes my hand. "I'm so proud of you for speaking up for yourself."

"Me too."

We're still grinning at each other when the nurse comes back in. "Okay, I got your Tylenol. Let's take that catheter out. The sooner we have you up and moving, the sooner your young man can bring you home."

CHAPTER 47

Juicing

I roll over, reaching for Asher in the bed, frowning when I find his side cold.

Despite my assurances that I was fine, Dee and Corinne flew down for the weekend. I expected Dee to demand I return to Boston immediately as soon as she landed, but she was surprisingly supportive of the idea of this indefinite vacation—she even brought a suitcase filled with my stuff. We showed them around Friendship Springs, and while I loved seeing my sisters, it wasn't exactly how I planned on spending the first days of a new relationship.

So much for my hope of starting the day with some lazy cuddling in bed. Pushing up onto an elbow, I blow my curls out of my face as I squint around the room. A thump from the kitchen gives me a clue, so I swipe my glasses and pad out of the bedroom in only Asher's t-shirt.

He's standing in the center with at least fifteen bags of groceries and a giant box. The basketball shorts hug his muscular ass and thighs as he bends over for a bunch of bananas and a bag of apples.

My mouth waters, and it's not for the fruit. *Well, maybe for a peach.* Can you even call a man's ass a peach? *Whatever, it looks yummy.*

"What's all this?" I step over the sacks as I approach him.

Asher turns, his face breaking into a grin, then quickly shadowing with guilt. "I didn't mean to wake you."

"Then you shouldn't have left the bed." I push up on my tiptoes to kiss him, resting my hands on his ribs, enjoying the way the muscles dance under my fingertips. The fact that I'm allowed to touch this man whenever I want is still shocking. And I do—I want to touch him all the time.

Asher deepens the embrace and grips the back of my thighs to lift me to the counter before stepping fully between my legs. "Good morning."

"I can think of how it could be better." He chuckles and goes back to unpacking the bags. I frown at the loss of his warmth. "What's all this?"

"Went to the next town to pick up supplies." He unloads fruits and vegetables of every color onto the counter. "The doctor said you should eat more whole foods."

"Okay... what is this thing?" I look closer at the box. "A juicer?"

"Well, neither of us is too big on cooking, figured this was a way to get all the veggies in." He shrugs and goes back to unpacking even more produce.

I eye the purple leafy ball in his hand. "Is that cabbage? You expect me to drink cabbage?"

"Would you give it a try before you make that face? Go get dressed."

Grumbling the entire way, I go through my morning routine with zero rush to experience cabbage juice. When I finally walk back out to the kitchen, Asher has the new contraption washed and assembled with a rainbow of produce across the counter.

"Okay, now what?"

He hands me a carrot and a peeler. "Now we prep the veggies."

My lip curls as I eye the mountain of vegetables. "I thought you said this would be easier than cooking?"

"It is. You only have to peel the hard skin off and cut everything into pieces that fit in the juicer. No oven, measuring, or hot skillets necessary."

As I work, my mind finds some comfort in the brainless, repetitive task. Asher and I work side by side, chatting about various topics—the gossip at Pop, possible plot angles for my series, the news. It's all surprisingly easy—and maybe a little fun.

Half an hour later, we finally have a glass of juice each. It is literally a rainbow—beets, oranges, carrots, celery, apples, kale, red cabbage, ginger.

We both take a sip at the same time. "So," Asher asks, "what do you think?"

I take another taste as I consider. "Not bad. Who knew cabbage juice was spicy? We need to adjust our ratio. The celery's a bit strong."

"Successful first try, though!" He leans down and gives me a kiss.

I smile at him as we rinse the machine parts and load the prep tools in the dishwasher. This all seems like a lot of effort—the juice isn't worth the squeeze—but he sounds so proud of himself I can't bring myself to disappoint him.

It's not that bad, but it's one more change too damn fast. Yes, I've always avoided certain meals unless I could handle the consequences, and that list of "safe foods" has dwindled over the years. That was my choice, though. Now that I have "doctor's orders" to avoid ingredients, I want to rebel. I believe the shrinks call it oppositional defiance disorder—or maybe I'm grieving my loss of autonomy.

I know that diagnosing a chronic condition doesn't make a difference—a disease by any other name and all that—but the validation does. After thirty years of "it's all in your head" or "stop being so difficult," you learn to tune out your body. Then one day, a doctor tells you all those little symptoms you've explained away are part of this bigger thing. You can't ignore it anymore because Schrödinger's disorder is out of the box meowing in your face.

Okay, I may have picked up one—fine, three—of Asher's psych textbooks while I was bored. Philosophers shouldn't have pets...or children. Not exactly a nurturing bunch.

None of this is Asher's fault. The juicer was a thoughtful gesture, and he's not wrong that drinking it is easier than cooking and eating all those greens.

CHAPTER 48

Change of Plans

I sprint up the stairs to my apartment, anxious to see Gabby. Poor little imp has been down lately. Ever since her sister's visit, there's been a cloud over her head. She's still the filter-free chaos machine bumping about my place, but it's like someone turned her volume down.

She's still not joining me at the restaurant anymore. She's either in bed or on the couch when I leave, and usually in the same spot when I get home. There're bananas and grapes missing, so I know she's eating something, but I'm starting to worry she's depressed. All she does is lie around reading those damn romance novels. They're scattered across the apartment, taunting me at every turn.

Okay, I wasn't complaining a week ago when she wanted to reenact a couple of the scenes to check if the position was possible—spoiler alert, it was, and fucking amazing—but sex doesn't solve everything. Never thought I'd say that, but this girl has me saying and thinking things I never thought possible. I guess that's the power of love.

And yet, I'm still keeping secrets from her. It may have started as a white lie, but I've hidden a huge part of my life from her. There were chances to confess, but I let them all pass by, and now this little omission has grown so big. I can't keep this up forever, but coming clean now could destroy everything.

Gabby looks up at me from her spot on the couch with a rare smile. She's wearing one of my shirts, a pair of fuzzy socks, and nothing else. Her curls a frizzy halo around her head and glasses slipping off her nose.

I've never come home to a more welcoming sight.

My gut twists all over again. I can't lose her.

"Hey, Imp, I switched shifts with Jessie so I can take you out tonight."

Her eyes drop to her lap, where she frets with the hem of my shirt. "Oh, where are we going?"

I push back the stab of disappointment her words create. It was damn hard convincing Jessie to come in—I had to trade for a future favor that I know will bite me in the ass. "Dinner and a movie. You'd better change." I run my hand up her thigh, finding only panties underneath. "I'm loving the easy access, but pretty sure the restaurant would prefer pants."

My lips latch onto her neck as I nibble and tickle her, getting a squeal and a tiny giggle. Gabby's nails dig into my arms as she tries to pull me closer, making my cock twitch in my jeans. Our sex-life has been practically nonexistent since the hospital. I could blame it on her book or her general low mood, but the truth is I'm the one holding us back. There isn't a moment I don't want this woman, but now I'm the one stuck in my head, so damn worried about her I can't act on it.

I'm hyperaware of the slightest shift in her posture or mood. She's chewing her lip with an unsure expression. "What's wrong?" I ask.

"Which restaurant?"

I caress the indentation between her brows until it relaxes. "There's a burger place by the movie theater I thought you might like."

She nods, but still worries her lip. "Do they have gluten-free buns?"

Fuck. "Oh, good point. Chinese is probably out, too. Indian?"

"The spices don't usually sit well. Hot pot?" Her eyes widen hopefully.

Now my brow is furrowing. "I don't know of any around here."

Her lip quivers. "I'm sorry." Her voice cracks, and tears pour down her face.

Something breaks inside me. I've never liked it when women cry, and having two sisters, I've seen my fair share of tears, but none has hurt me as much as Gabby's. In a smooth motion, I scoop her up against my chest, turning us so that I cradle her in my arms as I sit on the couch in her place. "Hey now, whatever for?"

"I make everything so difficult."

"What?" This is not where I saw this conversation going.

"We can't even go out and eat dinner like a n-normal couple because I have to w-worry about all these dietary restrictions. I can't even have popcorn at the movie theater! What do you even get out of this relationship? I'm just a burden."

Pinching her chin, I turn her face up to mine, making her meet my eyes. "Don't ever say that."

"It's true! My parents always highlighted how difficult it was when I was sick."

"Your parents are assholes, Imp."

"Well, yeah, but two things can be true. Whenever they had to come pick me up from school, or take me to a specialist, it was abundantly clear what a hardship I was."

"Bullshit. You have a medical condition, but even if you straight up refused to eat a certain type of food I loved, it wouldn't matter." She looks unconvinced. "If I were allergic to peanuts, would you call me a burden?"

"No..."

"If I were diabetic and couldn't go out for ice cream cones anymore? Or I was afraid of clowns, and we could never go to a circus?"

She sniffles as her lips curl slightly. "No."

"You are not a burden. You are funny, and brave, and beautiful. My life was numbingly boring before I found you in that supply closet, and I never want it to go back to that. Do you hear me?"

She buries her face in my shoulder, her tears leaving scalding trails down my shirt. I hold her close, rubbing my hand soothingly down her back as I whisper encouraging words to the top of her head. When her sobs subside, her shoulders relax and her breaths even out.

"Why don't we order in? There's that Mexican food truck you like—no cheese or sour cream—and then we can pop some fresh popcorn and watch something on the couch."

She hesitates. I can see the gears churning in that beautiful brain of hers, making excuses and turning this around on herself. It's clear her parents did a number on her self-esteem—I don't need my psych degree to tell me that. If I ever meet them, we're going to have words.

I squeeze her hip where my shirt has ridden up to her waist, leaving her bare. "I've decided I can't stand the idea of you in pants, after all."

She laughs, and it's good to see a flash of my Gabby again. I smack her butt lightly. "Okay then, you order; I'm going to go change into something more comfortable." She's nibbling her lip again. "What now?"

"But your ass looks so good in those jeans." Her eyes darken with hunger, and not for nachos from a food truck.

Standing with her still in my arms, I drop her onto the cushions with a squeal. She bounces back up to stare over the back of the couch.

Do I swagger a bit more as I walk away? Fuck yeah, I'm a red-blooded male. I turn back, and she blushes as I catch her. "Am I forgiven if I put on gray sweatpants?"

She bites her lip harder and nods at me, wide-eyed.

I can't help but smirk as I change. This isn't shaping up to be the night I planned, but I'm meeting my main objectives of cheering up Gabby and spending a fun night together. If she's half-naked for it, all the better.

Kaboom

I slam the car door a bit harder than strictly necessary.

"You good?" Asher raises an eyebrow at me.

"Peachy." I cross my arms and stare out the window.

This morning, Asher told me to dress in something I could move in because he had something fun in mind. I was expecting more mini-golf or maybe a day at one of the local theme parks. Did we do either of those things? No! The damn Viking dragged me to work out with him, like getting "swole" is everyone's idea of a good time.

So not my thing, but I convinced myself that he's trying to include me in his interests like a couple does. Plus, if I'm going to enjoy the rewards of his gym time, I might as well show some interest. I quickly realized this was not, in fact, a casual trip.

For over an hour, he ran me through various machines—leg presses, leg curls, and a dozen other torture devices I can't remember the names of. Gone was happy-go-lucky Asher. Instead, I was stuck with a serious personal trainer, completely focused on my form and barely completing any exercises himself.

He wouldn't even listen when I suggested something different. I pointed to a girl doing burpees and wanted to try it, but he said absolutely not with the jumping. That's when he let slip he's been researching exercises for managing POTS symptoms. I told myself he cares.

It wasn't until the end that I got good and pissed off, though. Another couple was using the machine next to us. Where her boyfriend was driving her to do one more rep or push a little harder, mine kept asking if it was too heavy or if I wanted to stop. The difference was so stark; it hit me how much he'd coddled me the entire time. I thought maybe it was because I was new to this, but a sinking realization took root. After the last one, I stood up too quickly and stumbled over the machine leg. Asher was hovering over me in a second, clutching my elbow, and asking if I'd remembered to take my medicine.

There was nothing normal about this excursion, and sure as fuck nothing fun.

I'm still pissy as we enter his apartment, so as Asher heads into the shower, I head to the fridge to grab ingredients for a smoothie instead of joining him. Frozen banana, spinach, coconut water, and a jar of vegetable juice. While I'll admit I like the juicing a hell of a lot more than the exercise regime Asher has gotten into his head, making everything fresh is a real pain in the ass. So, I've come up with a little workaround.

When he's at Pop, I put on my favorite music and prep a whole bunch of veggies at once to juice! Celery, carrots, cabbage, beets. Do you have any idea what a bitch it is to wash beet juice off your hands? That shit stains everything. I like the way it tastes, but I do not want to be dealing with the mess every day.

I hum to myself as I peel an avocado for my smoothie. My mind wanders as I go through the now routine task. I haven't written anything in weeks, and I'm feeling a bit restless. I always have something going, even if it's a side project, or a short story I want to explore, but there's something blocking me. This has never happened before. Usually, that means something isn't working in the plot, but maybe this time it's because my life is so chaotic that my brain can't focus on churning out the narrative.

I miss it. The escape of getting lost in my own world. Letting the words take shape—honestly surprising the fuck out of me. Sure, I have a vague idea of where the story is going, but if I'm in a good flow, I'm finding out the plot as it appears on the screen. We give birth to these characters, but they take on a life of their own on the page.

The motor stops, pulling me back to reality. I remove the blender and walk over to the ready cup. Oh boy, this one is a pretty magenta color; must be extra beets and red cabbage. Excitedly, I go to twist the blade cap off and... nothing. It's on there good and tight today.

I grunt and glare at the bottle. The sound of the shower still filters in behind me, so asking Asher for help is out of the question. *Plus, that would ruin our silent treatment.* I try again, my fingers whitening as I grip and turn until my vision goes black.

Fuck.

Panting, I look around the kitchen, considering my options. A silicon heat pad catches my eye. Gripping power! I try again. The lid budges a millimeter, but it's still progress and gives me hope. Victory swells within me with another burst of strength. The cap twists another centimeter as a hissing sound escapes. Before I can think better of it, I give the cover one more little jerk, and... BANG.

I scream as the lid flies off and I'm showered in cold liquid. My heart pounds and I pant for breath, trying to figure out if I'm injured. I can't see anything; pink slush completely coats my glasses.

Then the smell hits me.

Cabbage. The whole kitchen smells of cabbage. Holy fuck, that is disgusting. I try to wipe off my face, but it makes little difference when I'm this soaked. *I'll never watch Ghostbusters the same way again...*

"Gabs, are you okay? What happened?" Asher comes tearing into the room in only a pair of boxers. His eyes widen as he steps towards me, his foot sliding on a puddle of smoothie. He skates across the tile floor, loses his balance, and lands flat on his back in a lake of pink liquid.

I rush to help him, slipping in the same damn puddle and landing on top of him with a grunt.

We lay there stunned for a moment, then burst into laughter.

"What the hell happened? Are you hurt?" he asks, his eyes darting over my face.

I try to shift my weight off him, holding myself up with my arms. "Just my pride. I was making a smoothie, and it exploded."

His eyes widen. "What the hell did you put in it? Gunpowder?"

"No. The usual: celery, carrots, beets, red cabbage." A glob of pink drops from my hair and onto his chest.

A deep V forms on his forehead. "But I haven't bought cabbage in like a week."

"Yeah, I juiced it all a few days ago and kept it for smoothies. It's more efficient than cleaning that damn machine every day."

His expression slackens. "When fruits and vegetables age, they give off gas. You basically made a cabbage pipe bomb."

I freeze as his words sink in. "Oops."

We both laugh again, and he pulls me against him. "Fuck, Imp, it's on the ceiling."

I groan as I stand up, careful to avoid the puddles. Sure enough, he's right. There are pink polka dots across the white plaster, blinds, counters, and all the clean dishes. "It looks like someone murdered a Barbie doll in here. I'll clean this up."

"I'll help. I'm already covered in it anyway." We work together to scoop the clumps into the sink and wipe down surfaces. My anger from earlier settles as I scrub; the combination of physical activity and visible progress soothes my nerves.

Asher shoots me weighted looks as he mops until he finally breaks the silence. "You ready to tell me why you were so upset in the car?"

I sigh. "Sometimes I feel like all you see is my disease. Like you're trying to fix me, instead of letting me be me."

He freezes and turns to me wide-eyed. "What?"

"It's too much. The diet, the juicer, asking if I've taken my medicine, and now the exercise? All our interactions are now about my health, and I'm sick of being a burden."

He steps towards me, sliding only slightly in the puddle, pinches my chin, and forces me to meet his gaze. "You are not a burden. I can see I've gone a tad overboard with the health stuff." I glare at him. "Okay, more than a tad, but it's only because I care. I have never felt more helpless than when I found you on that floor. Watching you suffer and being unable to do a damn thing was the worst experience of my life. Working out, researching diets—those are things I can do. This was never about you being less than... it was about me."

I gulp back the lump in my throat. I hadn't thought of it from his perspective. Yes, I've called myself a burden but hadn't thought about what that meant to him. It doesn't excuse his actions or invalidate my feelings, but maybe it explains them a bit.

"I appreciate you want to help, but could you try not to obsess quite so much? This is a big change in my life, but I'm craving some sense of normalcy, too. We haven't gone on a date since I left the hospital. We always had fun together, but it's been so serious lately."

His lip curls. "Fun I can do, Imp." He pulls me into a bear hug. I'm painfully aware that he is mostly naked. My fingers trace his abs, enjoying the feel of the muscles dancing beneath my touch.

"Your hair smells like cabbage." Well, that certainly kills the mood. "Come on, let's go jump in the shower. I'll show you why there's a bench in there, then we can go out and find some fun."

Who knew that shower benches are useful for more than shaving your legs? *The Viking did, obviously.* Or that makeup sex could be so good? *Um... everybody.*

CHAPTER 50

Batter Up

The two plates on the counter taunt me—ground turkey, zucchini, and rice. It all looks about as appetizing as wet dog food, but it's all ingredients on Gabby's allowed list—and things I can manage to cook. Pretty fucking pathetic to be a thirty-two-year-old man with zero skills in the kitchen, but in my defense, I have access to a five-star chef at work every day. Who wouldn't take advantage?

"Dinner," I call towards the bedroom where Gabby is finishing up her hair for date night.

Eating out has still been difficult. The last time we tried, Gabby ended up running to the bathroom halfway through the meal, then spent the rest of the night doubled over in pain. I held her on the couch while we binge-watched some mind-fuck sci-fi show on Netflix. She was mortified, but I'll never complain about a night with her in my arms. Since then, I haven't suggested going out.

Gabby emerges looking hot as fuck, luscious curves on full display in a pair of denim shorts and my baseball jersey open over a tight white tank. "Thanks." She smiles at me, but it quickly fades as she sits. She pushes the meal around with her fork, then looks at my plate, frowning. "You really don't have to share this with me. I can handle watching you eat real food, you know."

"What are you talking about? This is great." I scoop up a heaving forkful and shove it in my mouth to prove my point. As the mushy vegetables, crusty rice, and bland meat mix on my tongue, it takes every ounce of self-control not to grimace. "Plus, it's efficient." From Gabby's raised eyebrow, I assume I failed.

With a sigh, she pushes away from the counter and rummages through the fridge, returning with a bottle of ketchup. "At least put some sauce on yours." I squeeze a generous helping onto my plate, then hold it out for her, but she only shakes her head. "Added sugar and fillers."

"We could try that organic brand—the one that's unsweetened."

She shrugs, moving the mush around. "Maybe when I can start adding food back in. I'm still supposed to avoid high-histamine foods like tomatoes and vinegar." She squints at a zucchini, then pops it in her mouth, chewing slowly. "What seasoning is this? Pepper?"

My fingers dig into the back of my neck as I wince. "Um... that might be char from the meat and rice... they stuck to the pans and burned a little." I'm not a great chef on my best days, but the solution to a massive plot hole hit me out of nowhere, and I lost all track of time. The pieces suddenly fell together for how the female lead recognized the pattern of the book pages left at the scene.

I caught a fictional serial killer, but dinner was a very real casualty.

"It's fine, or it will be when I adjust. I'm sorry, thank you for cooking. I think I'm just cranky because I'm in sugar detox. Fuck, I miss those little sweet treats of pure dopamine." The rice crunches in her mouth, and she winces. "So what's this baseball-themed date?"

There's got to be something I can do for her. I can research more diets and recipes—there's got to be some popular diet that matches her list! Or I can ask Anna. Why didn't I think of that before? That woman could definitely make this dog food delectable. She once fed her husband a grilled cheese with ghost pepper jelly in it, and he told me it tasted good—after he regained feeling in his tastebuds.

"You'll see. I promise it's actually fun this time." The rest of the meal goes down in four giant, hard to swallow bites, and then we're in the car and off.

Gabby's eyes are round as we pull into the sports complex in the next town. Florida weather is unpredictable, often too hot or too wet for outdoor sports. This place offers four floors and fifteen thousand square feet of temperature-controlled indoor spaces for everything from swimming to rugby. I guide her to the second floor, where the batting cages are.

A batter hits the ball with a loud crack as we pass the first cage, sending Gabby jumping three feet in the air. I pull her closer to me and rub her arm. "Have you ever played baseball or softball?"

"Not since elementary school gym class. I wasn't very good."

"That's okay. It's about moving your body, not home runs. Plus, sometimes smacking the shit out of something is cathartic. Remember the golf ball?" She blushes, and I laugh as I kiss her temple.

Gabby still looks unsure as I secure the helmet over her head. She's adorable with her round glasses and oversized shirt. "What do I do?"

Cupping her hips, I guide her to the box on the floor and square her up with the machine. "Grip the bat like this and keep your eye on the chute. I'll help you." I wrap my body around hers, marveling at the way she fits perfectly between my arms.

"What if I miss and it hits me? Or what if I actually hit it and it bounces off the walls and comes back to me?"

I squeeze her hand on the bat reassuringly. "It's on the lowest setting, so it might hurt, but it won't do any real damage, and the netting is designed to slow down the ball instead of bouncing it back like the windmill. You'll be fine. I'll block any balls coming at you."

She giggles, wriggling her hips against my crotch slightly. "Hopefully not all balls."

"Settle down, Imp. Tell you what, if you hit one, I'll make it worth your while." That perks her up.

The first pitch startles her, and she tries to back away from the box. The second, she swings too early, and the third, too late. Determination shines in the pinch of her lips as she stares down the chute. She gets a chunk of the fourth, but it goes wide. Fifth and sixth are better, but still not quite a direct hit.

The seventh pitch meets her bat at the perfect angle, bouncing back to the net with a satisfying crack and thud. With a cheer, she drops the bat and jumps up and down, turning to me with excitement clear on her face. "They say seven is a magic number!"

I hug her close, so damn proud of my girl. Her breathing changes to shallow pants that flutter against my chest. Concerned, I pull back and find that telltale faraway look in her eyes. "Gabby?"

She blinks a few times, then gives her head a little shake before meeting my gaze. "I'm good." A flirty smile curves her lips. "Now that I've won my prize, I'm ending on a high note. Show me how it's done, all-star."

I don't press her further, she'll only tell me she's fine anyway—even if she's not. Frowning, I dig in my wallet for a five. "Okay, go grab some waters while I reset the machine. Sit on the bench outside—you don't want to get hit by one of these fast pitches."

My fingers change the settings on autopilot; in my mind, I'm back to the morning I found her on the floor. How many times had she paused and blinked at me like that before that day? Aren't the meds supposed to prevent this? Is the dosage correct? Should I have reminded her to take another pill?

The first swing connects too high, and the ball drives into the astroturf with a dull thud.

I heard her earlier, and I know she gets frustrated when I focus on this stuff, but it's a big part of her life right now, and she's a big part of mine.

The second swing hits too close to my hands as I overreach. With a clunk, the ball strikes the ground to my left. I curse as I shake the vibrations from my fingers and adjust my grip.

It's not that I think she's incapable of taking care of herself, more that I see her load is so heavy and I want to carry it for her—like when I grab all the groceries or beach chairs. Being unprepared and impulsive cost me the entire future I had planned.

That's not going to happen to Gabby if I can help it.

My third swing hits dead-on, the crack of the aluminum bat reverberating through the room. The ball soars straight down the middle of the pitch, hitting the netting in a perfect arc.

Gabby cheers behind me, bringing a smile to my face. "Come on, slugger, I think we both earned that prize."

If I'm gentler with Gabby in bed that night, if I hold her tighter, it's because of my ever-strengthening feelings for her. My lips can't form the words yet to tell her what she means to me, but I sure as hell can show her. No matter what it takes.

CHAPTER 51

Cooking Lessons

I'm strangely nervous as we stand in front of the cute little house nestled in downtown Friendship Springs. It's fucking adorable, like something from a southern postcard. A young magnolia tree grows proudly in the yard, and instead of a planted garden, large planters line the walkway and windows, overflowing with herbs and colorful vegetables. It's clear a chef lives here.

The door opens, and the biggest man I've ever seen appears. I thought Asher was tall, but this man stands another couple of inches over him and has at least fifty pounds of muscle on him. My eyes are probably bugging out, but I can't help it.

Hazel eyes crinkle in humor, his smile half hidden by a dark beard. "Hey Ash, and you must be Gabby. Come on in, Bella is in the kitchen." He has a slight twang of a Southern accent in his deep voice. The giant steps back to let us in and walks deeper into the house.

I lean towards Asher as I take my shoes off. "I thought her name was Anna. Have you let me call her by the wrong name this whole time?"

He chuckles. "Her full name is Annabel. She started going by Anna as an adult, but her family calls her Bella. She and David have known each other since they were kids."

Sure enough, the blond from the restaurant I know as Anna is at the kitchen counter. David has one hand on her hip as he stands behind her, murmuring in her ear. She laughs and holds up a slice of vegetable from her cutting board for him. Instead of grabbing it, he bends down and takes it from her fingers with his lips. Anna smiles at him with such happiness that I almost feel guilty witnessing the exchange. Like I stumbled in on a private moment.

Asher catches up to me and pulls me against his chest, resting his chin on my head.

Noticing us, Anna turns to me. "Hey there, suga', how ya feeling today?"

I try not to sigh. It's nice that people care—truly. I should be touched that they ask, and I am... But I wish every conversation didn't come back to my health these days. "Pretty good, thanks. The medicine is working great, the diet has been a bitch, though—especially since I have no idea what the difference is between a saute and frying pan. Thanks again for offering to do this."

She waves away my words, but it's David who answers. "Bella will take any excuse to cook. The woman is happiest when she's feeding people."

"Well, it's a good thing I married a man who eats so much." He kisses her temple as she smiles. "Don't you have football practice, Asher? Why don't you take David with you and leave us to our girl time?"

"Are you sure?" Asher looks down at me, clearly conflicted. He's still been hovering a bit since our talk. He doesn't say anything, but the worry is still written across his face.

"I'll be fine. You shouldn't miss another practice, Mr. Assistant Coach. What will the boys think?"

"Okay, call me if you need me to come back." He kisses me, then heads off with David in tow. Asher only glances over his shoulder twice more—a marked improvement from when he headed to work yesterday.

"He can be so overbearing when he's worried." Anna pours two glasses of a light brown liquid and hands me one with a knowing smile.

I take the glass, playing with the straw. "And the endless research! Every day there's some new diet or exercise he's read about. I know it's because he cares and I should appreciate it, but sometimes he makes me want to scream." My stomach drops. Maybe I shouldn't be venting about Asher to one of his closest friends.

"When that man fixates on something, he's like a dog with a bone." She rolls her eyes, then gives me a soft smile. "Just because it comes from a caring place doesn't make it any less annoying."

"I don't mean to complain. He's such an awesome guy, but it's been... a lot."

She waves away my words. "Oh, I know it. I've known the man for twenty years, and David still struggles with letting me fight my own battles. If they were perfect, we wouldn't love them as much." My cheeks burn, and her knowing eyes sharpen. "Let's get cookin'. Asher gave me the basics of your diet. He mentioned it's fairly restrictive."

I tick off the items on my fingers as I rattle them off. "Yup. Gluten free, dairy free, sugar free... preservative, color, and alcohol free—so basically fun free. Whole-food centric and organic where possible. So my go-to of spaghetti and jar sauce is out."

She lets out a puff of air. "I can see how that could be challenging if you don't cook, but what are you specifically struggling with?"

"The variety, but mostly the time, I guess? When I'm writing, I don't want to stop working to go make an entire meal, but processed foods are like half the no-no list. I also miss sweets. Stress eating is my only vice—especially if I can't even have a glass of wine."

She nods once. "All that I can help with. Alright, so we're going to make a whole big batch of chicken. I read that leftovers could be an issue, but if we portion and freeze them immediately, that should slow histamine formation. Same thing with these sweet potatoes. I'm going to show you how to make this broccoli fresh, but honestly, the frozen bags are fine and will work with your lifestyle and take five minutes."

"Okay." I can only look at her with wide eyes.

"I know it sounds like a lot of work, but you only need to do it once a week. After you build up a bit of a store in your freezer, you can cycle through meals to spice up the variety. Oh, and I found some rice noodles when we did an Asian-fusion thing at Pop that are tasty. That should help with your boil it and go routine if we find a sauce you tolerate."

"What's that for?" I ask, pointing to some bananas and a bowl of brown wrinkly blobs on the edge of the counter.

Anna's eyes light up. "Dessert. Asher already mentioned your sweet tooth. Refined sugars are out, but we can use natural sweeteners like dates, and the starchiness of the plantain means we don't need flour. Go on and drink your sweet tea, darlin', I cooked down some peaches and dates to sweeten it naturally."

Tentatively, I take a sip. A hint of sweetness floods my tongue, melding perfectly with the tanginess of the tea. "Wow." She smiles proudly, then points to a nearby apron with the tip of her knife before going back to cutting broccoli trees into bushes. "Thank you for doing this. I'm sure you had other things to do on your day off."

Anna's knife clacks against the board as she whirls on me, one hand perched on a cocked hip. Her brown eyes are sharp as they stare into mine. "Don't do that. Asher is family, and you're special to him, so that makes you family too. Nothing is more important than family. Own your space, sweet cheeks."

My sweet cheeks burn as I give her a rueful smile.

Seemingly satisfied, Anna turns back to the prep. "So, first you're going to butterfly the chicken." When I simply gawk at her, Anna chuckles and continues, "Cut the chicken breast in half like a hamburger bun. You can leave a sliver connected and open it like a book, or cut it all the way through for this recipe."

I follow her instructions, careful not to slice my hand—or think too hard about how cold and slimy the raw meat feels. The first breast is in two pieces as I apply too much pressure. The next one is a bit better, but still wonky. Finally, on the third breast, I get the hang of it and stop just short of cutting through. With the strip still connected and flopped open, it does kind of look like a butterfly. Smiling, I turn to Anna, and she nods proudly.

"Who taught you to cook?" I grab the next breast and keep working.

"My Momma. I spent hours with her in that kitchen. It was the only place my brothers left us alone, and I got her all to myself."

"Brothers, plural?"

"Four." I lower the knife and look at her with wide eyes. She laughs. "So you can imagine why one-on-one time with Momma was so special. That kitchen was always so full of love. After she died, I kept cooking her recipes to feel near her, and to comfort my brothers, too."

"I'm so sorry." What's it like to be close to your parent and then lose them?

There's a faraway look in her eyes for a moment and a sad little smile about her lips. Then she shakes her head and grabs her sweet tea for a sip. "I take it your momma wasn't much of a cook?"

I snort as I attack the last chicken breast a bit too violently, slicing it clean in half. "My parents weren't around often. High-powered lawyers and surgeons tend to work long hours and have business dinners. The housekeeper made meals for my sister, Dee, and me to reheat, but I was never home when she cooked them. First-world problems, I guess."

Anna switches out my cutting board and knife for fresh ones, and shows me how to dice the sweet potatoes. The consistent chop of the knives and repetitive task is surprisingly soothing, and per usual my tongue loosens without my consent.

"There was a short time I had their attention. After Dee came out in her twenties, well, it didn't go well. For a little bit, they focused on the defective child, but it was clear I'd never be a good lawyer or doctor, so they quickly lost interest again. I moved out at seventeen and never looked back. Dee and I were just two kids in a cheap apartment trying to finish school on part-time jobs and sheer will." I chuckle at a memory. "We lived off ramen and crap cafeteria food, but anything more complicated than boiling water or frying an egg was beyond us."

The look in Anna's eyes is uncomfortably like pity, so I rush to deflect. "It got easier when Dee got an internship at the law firm. She'd sneak us leftovers from catering, and we'd eat like queens. Then she met her wife, Corinne, and we got home-cooked meals again. My sister-in-law still drops off casseroles for me when they visit."

She smiles at me. "You sound close."

I shrug. "My sister is my best friend. She's going to shit a brick when I cook dinner for her."

Anna laughs. "Here, I'll show you how to make a quick marinade for the chicken, and we'll get this broccoli steaming."

She's a patient teacher and, under her careful guidance, I manage to cook the entire dinner without injuring myself once. Okay, so I got a face-full of steam when I leaned a little too close to check the broccoli, but I'm calling that a facial. Everything is portioned out into glass Tupperware and popped into the freezer for later. Anna even printed out some recipes, and a suggested shopping list for getting started with meal prep.

Chatting with Anna is so easy; I can see why Asher is friends with her. Several times this afternoon I've forgotten why I even needed these lessons in the first place—it's felt like a fun outing learning a new skill.

For the first time, this diagnosis doesn't feel like the end I feared. Maybe this could be a new beginning.

CHAPTER 52

Hidden Words

We find both women doubled over in laughter on the counter when David and I return. "What's all this?" I ask as I close in behind Gabby. My eyes dart between them, trying to catch the joke.

Gabby wipes tears from her eyes as her shrieks quiet. "Anna was telling me about the time a cougar proposed to you at the bar."

The truth is, many a lonely octogenarian has propositioned me at the bar. One was a bit more persistent than the others, though. "Gladys is a lovely woman, and a generous tipper. I could do worse. What's this?" I reach for the nearby plate, deciding to deflect the conversation. The rest of this tale is one I'd rather not relive.

"Real generous, alright." Anna quips, eyes bright with laughter. "Half her fortune, generous. Drafted up a prenup and everything."

If I started dancing on the counter, would they stop telling this story?

Gabby gasps. "No! Then what happened?"

Probably not.

"Her son found it and stormed into the bar, waving the paper in Asher's face," Anna says.

"Did you get into a fight?" Gabby asks as she gazes at me wide-eyed. Her cheeks are flushed, but it's clear it's from amusement and not illness.

Fuck, I guess there's no escaping this, not if it makes my girl smile. "No. Turns out he was gay and tried to convince me to give him a shot instead of being his stepdaddy." I grab a bite of the pancake-looking thing on the plate. Nutty sweetness floods my mouth.

"Didn't the granddaughter come in and hit on you, too? Like some weird family tradition?" David asks from behind Anna's chair.

Anna and Gabby double over again.

"Hey!" I yell. "I thought you were my friend." The traitor only shrugs.

My notoriety as the hot bartender of Pop has been a running gag within my circle. I've never found it funny, but that doesn't stop them from printing out particularly thirsty online reviews. It was fun for a time—in my twenties—but these days I usually feel the overwhelming need for a shower.

I bury my discomfort with another bite of sweet, sweet dopamine disguised as a pancake, closing my eyes on a happy moan. "You're forgiven if you convince your wife to make this for me again."

The girls share a smile. "Actually," Anna says, "Gabby made those."

She beams up at me as I wrap my arms around her. "Maybe I'm a kitchen witch."

I kiss the top of her head, so damn proud of my girl. "These are amazing, Imp. I think I'm officially fired from cooking duty."

"You could be her sous chef. Getting bossed around in the kitchen has its perks." David gives Anna a look that's practically pornographic.

A fork laden with pancake pauses halfway to my lips. "Ew. Please tell me you bleached the countertops before preparing the food I just put in my mouth."

We visit for a bit longer, leaving with the frozen spoils of Gabby's efforts, a handful of recipes to try, and an invite to couple's game night tomorrow.

When we return to the apartment, Gabby rushes off to video chat with her sister. Partway to the bedroom, she spins and tackles me, squeezing her arms around my waist and planting a big kiss on my lips. "Thank you, Asher. Cooking with Anna was so helpful. You always seem to know exactly what I need. I'm sorry if I haven't said that enough."

My arms squeeze her. I'm reluctant to let go but so damn happy to see her back to herself. I have no idea what they talked about, but I owe Anna so much. When I tried to thank her, she only waved me off and simply said, "That's what family does."

I stand in the living room at a loss for what to do. Every moment since Gabby's collapse has been spent with her, or thinking about her, or researching her disease. She doesn't need me right now, so I'm free to spend time with my first love.

Sitting at my computer, I pull up my manuscript and quickly lose myself in the story. Besides that quick burst yesterday, I haven't typed anything of significance in over a week. The plot has been constantly churning away in the back of my mind—forming connections, filling holes. A clever trap, discovered too late. Our heroes caught in the serial killer's clutches, their lives hanging in the balance. A blossoming romance between our detective and the bookstore owner threatened at knifepoint.

So when I start, the words pour forth in a rush as my fingers struggle to keep up with my racing thoughts.

Beauty and the Butcher

by Asher Ramstead

~~~

A splitting headache blossomed in James's head. He tried to rub his temple, where the pain radiated from, but a metal cuff dug into his wrists. James was trapped, but he'd been through tougher scrapes before.

Rolling onto his back to hide his arm behind him, he hit the power button five times to alert 911. Overhead, a single, uncovered bulb provided little light. From the musty smell, he guessed he was in a basement, and from the chittering, he wasn't alone. Hopefully, mice were his only company, though he highly doubted it.

"Finally awake, I see." She stepped out of the shadow, the navy sweats and BPD tee at odds with the surroundings. He had to keep the killer talking to allow the dispatcher to track the signal. Even if he
~~~

became Wilde's next victim, the recording would send her away, and that was satisfaction enough for him.

"Why'd you do it, Trudy?" In hindsight, he should have brought backup instead of confronting her directly. He knew Cathy would never let this case go and wanted to beat her here.

"Because you stuck your nose where it didn't belong! Why couldn't you leave the case closed?"

"You know me, Trudy. I couldn't watch an innocent man die in jail."

"Innocent?" She spat at his feet. "That man is as corrupt as they come."

This was the angle he needed. Now, to keep her talking, get her confession on tape, and maybe buy some time. "If Greyson is guilty, then he'll pay, but for the crimes he actually committed. You're a cop, Trudy, you need to let justice serve out."

"Where was justice for my sister? She reported him—filed all the appropriate forms, got a restraining order. What good did due process do when he attacked her? Left her so broken she felt she had no way out but a needle?" She paced the length of the room as she spoke, her mind far away as she relived the horrors of her past.

"I'm so sorry, the system failed her, Trudy, but this isn't the way."

"Tell that to the others. To the victims who never see their attackers brought to your precious justice." She stopped by a table and picked up an object. A sharpened letter opener glinted in the dim light as she walked towards James.

"Why the books, Trudy?"

"For her." Pain mars her beautiful face. "My sister loved to read. She wanted to be a librarian and help the kids in our old neighborhood."

"Greyson was her professor, wasn't he?"

"Her advisor. She was so elegant, so good, and he wouldn't take no for an answer." Trudy looked down at the dagger in her hand. "Sophia was going to be the first in our family to finish college. I had this made as a gift, but she OD'd before she could graduate."

Her face hardens. "He took everything from her. From me. Now I take the lives of predators exactly like him. I'm their justice, and you won't stop me." She lunged at James, and all he could pray was that the cops arrived before Cathy..............................

CHAPTER 54

It's All Fun & Games

"**W**hat-cha doing?"

I'm in the basement with a serial killer giving a villain monologue when Gabby's voice startles me.

Heart racing, I tab to an open browser window. "Nothing much. How's your sister?"

I should probably tell Gabby about my side project, but I know it's going to lead to a fight—she's made her feelings very well-known about unsolicited manuscripts. Today's the first genuinely good day she's had in a while. Who am I to take that from her?

"Awesome. She's threatening to keep my cat, though. Want to watch that documentary about the cult in Missouri?"

I kiss her forehead as we walk to the couch. "You know I can never turn down a real crime show. Sounds like a perfect night."

I'll tell her about the novel later.

Gabby fidgets beside me. She keeps twisting the ringlet behind her ear; her tell that she's nervous. I shift the cases of beer and sparkling water in my arms so I can wrap one around her. "This is my first time, too."

She turns to me with an incredulous look. "I don't believe that."

I chuckle. "I've been over to Bree and Colin's loads, but couples' night has always been sacred to them. Johnson and I tried to convince them to let us pair up a few times, but they shot us down."

"Really?" Those big eyes look at me, but she's relaxed enough to release her hair.

"Yeah. Take lots of notes. I'm under strict orders to report back on all the details."

I ring the doorbell and a minute later, Bree's husband, Colin, answers. He gives me a smile and then turns to Gabby. "The infamous Gabby. Pleasure t'a meet ya, love." That damn dimple appears as his grin widens.

Gabby's face slackens as she stares at him, and I swear if he weren't so happily married, I'd deck him. I manage to restrain myself to a grunt, and the damn Irish bastard only grins wider.

Something about her makes my inner caveman shine through.

Colin quickly takes the drinks from me and points us to the living room. Bree sits on a navy couch with a glass of wine in her hand and a white fur-ball of a dog in her lap. Nearby, Anna lounges in an overstuffed chair,

David on the floor at her feet. Everyone's attention focuses on the rug in front of them.

Baby Nora sits up, a green ball in her chubby fist as Bree's first love, her Yorkie mix, Riley, bounces back and forth. His eyes never leave the ball as he squats down, ready to leap, tail wagging in the air, with little yips. With a wet giggle, Nora rolls the ball—well at least she tries to—it only moves a foot or so, but the dog jumps on it like it flew a mile before dropping it in the baby's lap with a lick against her dimpled cheek.

"Riley, not the face," Bree calls absently as everyone laughs.

Nora arches her arm back to chuck the ball and loses her balance. David steadies her immediately, his giant hand covering her entire back. She turns to him with wide blue-green eyes and then smiles as drool drips down the side of her face.

I look at Gabby and see her eyes shining with absolute baby fever. The thought should terrify me—we've only barely started dating—but it doesn't. An image forms in my mind of Gabby round with our child, her face glowing with happiness, and I want it. I want everything with this woman.

Bree smiles up at us and pats the seat beside her, beckoning Gabby over.

"She's beautiful," Gabby says. "How old is she?"

"Eight months." Bree beams with pride, the love for her daughter clear in her eyes. Colin walks behind the sofa, laying his hand on his wife's shoulder, with a similar expression on his face.

Nora gives a yawn and almost tumbles over again as she rubs her eyes.

"That's my cue to put the little miss to bed. Why don't ye all get settled in the dining room and set up the game?"

Everyone demands a last baby cuddle, which is definitely a first for me on a Saturday night, but I don't hate it.

"If you're all here, who's at Pop?" Gabby asks as we sit around the big table.

"Between Meeka and Jessie, they can handle most things," Anna answers as she lays out trays of snacks on a sideboard.

"Plus, Johnson is there tonight. With the banquet space getting so popular, I can't keep up with all the work anymore. He's offered to take on more event planning," Bree adds.

David devours a potato skin in one bite. "What about his job at CAE? Don't a lot of people want to meet during the day?"

Bree shakes her head as she chews a popover. "Honestly, he's such a strong PM he accomplishes in four hours what takes anyone else eight. It's not fair to give him twice the work for the same pay." She smiles. "Sometimes it's good to be the boss."

"What are we playing?" Anna asks as she sits next to her husband.

"I got this new one called Knowledge Knockout. Teams complete challenges in different categories, and the first to reach the center of the board wins. We'll do couples as teams."

I lean back in my chair and sling my arm over the back of Gabby's. "You ready, Imp?"

She turns to me with a challenging glint in her eyes. "Born ready."

My lips are inches from hers as they twist into a confident smile. "Good, because I hate losing."

Gabby tosses her curls at me. "Oh, I don't lose trivia games. My 'very particular set of skills' was made for this."

"Hey! That sounded exactly like Colin!" David says, and the entire group breaks into laughter.

Colin walks into the room with a baby monitor on his hip. "Wha'd I miss?" Which only sends the room into hysterics again. He grins at everyone as he sits by his wife.

Bree wipes tears from her eyes as she settles down. "Just Gabby's stellar Irish accent."

Gabby turns beet red next to me, but she's still smiling. "It's honestly only that one line! I swear, I'm a one-trick pony."

I pull her close and kiss her temple. Taking pity on her, I steer the conversation away. "Come on, we're going to whoop your asses. We're blue."

Colin takes the green token, and David takes the red.

"Directions say oldest goes first, so that's Colin," Bree explains. "Pick a category—sports, math, lifestyle, history, geography, literature, science, or art. Each team has thirty seconds to answer. We'll choose math."

Gabby draws a card and reads it aloud. "What's the derivative of x?"

"One," they both shout together, then kiss.

Gabby chooses science. "What is the powerhouse of the cell?" Anna reads.

"Mitochondria!" Gabby grins and claps her hands. She looks so happy.

During the next round, Anna answers a lifestyle question about the difference between baking powder and baking soda, and Bree correctly names all the sisters in *Little Women*.

I choose history.

"What was the cause of the Chicago Fire of 1871?" David reads, then flips the timer.

"No one knows," I answer.

"Are you sure?" Gabby asks. "I definitely remember my teacher talking about a cow kicking a lantern."

"That's one of the theories, but so are arson and lightning. There's not enough evidence."

"Time's up," Bree calls. She scans the instructions. "If no consensus is reached or a clear answer given, the team receives no points. Sorry, guys."

"Asher was right," David says, "though the card mentions the cow thing as a possibility." A heavy silence falls around the table.

Great. I sigh, sitting back. Whoever designed this game is a sadist.

Gabby stands up. "I'm going to grab a soda." She stumbles slightly, gripping the back of the chair for support as she blinks a few times.

"Are you okay? Did you take your meds? Do you need another dose?" I'm on my feet, hovering, in a moment.

Gabby glances around the room, finding all eyes on her. She glares at me, pulling away from my hands. "I'm fine; I just stood up too fast."

I sink back down, watching her walk into the kitchen, fighting every urge to go after her.

Anna pats my hand. "I'll go make sure she's okay and grab some more snacks." With a kiss for David on the way by, she follows Gabby.

The room is quiet. The baby monitor crackles, and whimpers turn into cries. Bree stands and says, "Sounds like everybody needs a snack break." She slips out of the room, taking the baby monitor with her.

David's deep voice rumbles in the quiet. "You want to talk about it?"

I fist my hands on the table. "Every time I close my eyes, I see her on that floor. I wake up from a dead sleep and check to make sure she's breathing next to me."

David nods. "I get it. After that asshole attacked Bella, I checked on her all the time. Why do you think I went so crazy installing the security cameras?"

"Yeah, but you can kick an attacker's ass. How do you fight an illness?" My fingers spear through my hair.

Colin's beer clanks on the tabletop. "You can't. When Bree was on bed rest with Nora, all I wanted to do was fix it. I ended up annoying her so much, she threw a book at my head."

"What did you do?" I ask.

"I stopped asking her how she felt and started finding little ways to make her laugh or smile. Her favorite takeout. Things to take her mind off the worry and the boredom of being stuck at home. That's when we started watching some of her shows together, because it made her smile."

"Gabby is a big girl—they all are. It's in our DNA to want to fix it, but that's the fastest way to piss them off. Believe me." David salutes me with his bottle, then takes a swig.

That's exactly what Gabby said after the smoothie incident. I've been doing my best not to hover, to plan fun date nights or dinners in, but one stumble from her and my fears come back with a vengeance.

"You worry because you care," David continues. "That's not wrong. You need to channel it the right way, though."

How the hell do I do that?

Until Somebody Loses

Storming off before I made a scene seemed like a good idea at the time. Now I'm standing in a strange kitchen with a can of seltzer and no clue where the glasses are. Do I just drink it out of the can? God, my mother would have a shit fit over that.

Perfect.

With a rebellious giggle, I pop the can and take a giant swig, letting the bubbles soothe my annoyance.

I was only dizzy for a moment—anyone who stood up that fast would have felt the same.

The metal hits my teeth with an unpleasant buzz. Dammit, I can't even enjoy this, because Mom was right; soda belongs in a glass.

Anna sweeps into the kitchen behind me, making a beeline for the fridge, completely at ease in Bree's home. A pang of unexpected envy floods me at their closeness. I know they've all been together since college, but I've never had friends like that. I've always been too weird and prone to zoning out, visiting my fantasy worlds in my head, to form actual friendships.

Without a word, Anna hands me a glass with ice in it.

"Thanks," I say, wasting no time pouring my drink into it. She leans against the counter next to me, holding out a plate of deviled eggs. With a grateful smile, I pop one into my mouth. Fuck, these are good. I need her to teach me how to make these.

"It's got to be difficult, all this change."

"People deal with food allergies all the time, Anna. Plus, technically, I've had this my whole life, only thing new is the fancy name for it. I've had no major flares or POTS attacks in a week."

Her chocolate eyes pin me to the spot. "Just 'cause you carry it well, don't mean it ain't heavy." She pushes the plate towards me, and I take another egg. "How are you honestly doing? And I'm not talking physically; you've been taking care of yourself for a long time, how you doing in here?" She taps her blond head.

"I'm fine. Yes, the diet stuff is a complication I could do without. It is significantly better than the alternative, though."

"But...?"

I take a deep breath and let the floodgates open. "Everyone looks at me like I'm broken, and I hate it. Do you think I want to be like this? Having to plan out every fucking moment, everything I eat? Research every restaurant to see if it can accommodate my diet? Make sure wherever we go has seating, so I'm not on my feet for too long?"

Her only response is to hold the plate up again. I shove another in my mouth and keep going, no longer able to keep back the words in my heart.

"I'm dating one of the sportiest guys I've ever met, and I can't even do any of the active shit he likes. He tried to take me to the batting cages, and I broke out in a cold sweat from standing. Fuck, I was doing dishes the other day and started getting woozy. I know this is hard for him too, I do, but if he looks at me like I'm about to shatter one more time, I honestly might knee him in the balls."

With a last exhale, the energy drains from me. "Then I remember I'm mad at life, not Asher, and promptly dive into a shame spiral over yelling at him. It's an endless cycle. I'm angry I can't do things like other people, then guilty for messing up Asher's plans, then I'm just sad. So fucking sad."

"That's grief, sugar. You're grieving for the life you knew, adjusting to the new state of normal."

"Does it get better?"

She gives me a wistful smile. "It does, but it never fully goes away. Oh, you'll feel it less often as you adjust, but the pain itself stays just as sharp. That's why you need to surround yourself with good people who care about you." She wraps an arm around me, squeezing me into her side.

"Thanks, Anna."

"Don't mention it, suga'. You're family." We look down at the empty plate. "Oops."

"Why is it that the idea of eating six hard-boiled eggs is disgusting, but a dozen deviled eggs go down like water?"

She gives me a conspiratorial wink. "It's the mayonnaise. Fat makes everything better."

We're both still laughing as we reenter the dining room—snackless.

My eyes meet Asher's. There's still too much worry for my liking, but there is also a flicker of contrition. He doesn't ask if I'm okay again at least, so I guess that's progress.

I sit back down in my chair and lay my hand on Asher's muscular thigh to silently convey we're fine.

His arm snakes around my shoulders, tugging me into his side so he can kiss my temple, then lower his lips to my ear. "I'm sorry, Imp, I know I hover too much. I thought I'd lost you, and it broke something in me. This is about me lacking, not you."

When I turn to meet his eyes, there is nothing but sincerity shining in their icy blue depths. My heart lurches painfully, but it has nothing to do with my condition. "You can apologize by helping me kick their asses. I don't like losing."

"Hell's Bells, where are those deviled eggs you made?" David asks.

Anna and I share a look across the table while trying not to laugh. "I think we forgot them."

"No, I distinctly remember carrying in a whole plate of them."

Anna turns to her husband and shoves a jalapeño popper into his mouth before he can argue any more. "Here, eat this. If you're still hungry later, I'll make you a grilled cheese." David's eyes soften as he looks at his wife, evidently forgetting all about the missing snack.

CHAPTER 56

Winner Takes It All

"Ha!" I cry as I move our piece onto the finish space, where it joins the red and green tokens. It wasn't easy, but Gabby and I managed to catch up. "This is it, the last question."

Brianna consults the rules. "In the event multiple teams reach the final spot on the same round, there will be a sudden death round. A question will be asked, and one member of each team will attempt to answer. The other teammate must say whose answer they think is correct. This will continue until a question is answered incorrectly."

"Huh?" Gabby asks.

"I ask a question. All the guys give an answer. The girls take turns saying which guy they think is right. The girl needs to choose the correct response; first to choose wrong loses."

"Well, why didn't they just say that?" I deadpan.

"I don't know. Okay, Anna, you're first. What psychologist's cat was both alive and dead in the box?"

"I have no fucking clue," David says.

"Schrödinger," I answer.

Colin points to me. "That's the one! Schrödinger's cat."

"Guess I'll go with Schrödinger," Anna says.

"Correct. Okay read for me." Bree hands Anna a card.

"Well, fudge. Why didn't I get this one? In baseball, what does it mean when an umpire holds one finger in the air?"

"Fly ball," David says. Close, but not quite accurate.

Colin's brows pinch. "Strike one?" His voice sounds unsure.

This is our chance—baseball is America's pastime after all. "Strike," I say. Anna raises an eyebrow at me, but luckily Bree doesn't notice. If I can eliminate Bree and Colin here, then Gabs and I can win the whole thing.

It's not cheating—I'm being strategic and using their psychology against them!

"Strike," Bree says.

"The correct choice was an infield fly. Y'all are eliminated."

Bree's eyes whip to me as she takes the card box back. "Didn't you play in college?"

"All's fair in love and board games, sweetheart. Nowhere in the rules did it say I have to respond correctly if my girl isn't the one guessing." I lounge back in my seat, laying my arm across Gabby's shoulders.

David shakes his head. "You're savage, man. Maybe a little too competitive for game night."

I shrug and wait for Bree to read the next question.

"What country is known by its inhabitants as Misr?"

David purses his lips for a moment as he scratches his beard. "Morocco."

I know this one! When I was a kid, I loved *The Mummy* and spent a year learning about Cairo and the culture. "Egypt."

We both turn to Gabby, waiting for her. I'm already smiling, knowing we have this in the bag. There's no way my girl can lose.

"Morocco."

My neck cracks as I whip towards her. "What?"

Bree's eyes are even larger than they normally are as they dart between us. Colin leans over her shoulder to read the card, and a hiss leaves his lips. "The answer was Egypt. Anna and David win."

Gabby blanches and then flushes bright red. When her eyes meet mine, the flicker of guilt in them stabs me in the gut. She didn't think I knew it.

I thought she was different, but she sees me as a slab of meat like everyone else—only good for a laugh or a fuck or two.

The chair scrapes slightly as I stand, the noise breaking me from my spiral long enough to realize everyone is staring at me. My skin feels too tight. I have to get out of here.

I grab the stack of plates and flee to the kitchen with a mumbled excuse. On autopilot, I walk to the sink and start washing dishes. The sound of the running water and the familiar action are soothing.

No sooner does the first dish sparkle than a large hand grabs it. "I'll dry." David already has a towel in his hand.

With a nod, we fall into the chore silently. As I hand him the last cup and shut off the faucet, I feel slightly better, but there's still a dull ache where my heart should be.

David holds out the dishtowel for me to dry my hands, and I numbly take it. "It's only a game, man. Try not to take it so personally."

I rest a hip against the sink, clutching the cloth. "I know it's a game—I do. It's just..." Sighing, I squeeze the back of my neck, lost for words.

He bumps my shoulder with his as he mirrors my stance. "It's just...?"

"I'm sick of being the hot comic relief. It's getting old. Hell, I'm getting old, and I thought Gabby saw me as more than that, but..."

"She's still here, isn't she? Yeah, y'all started as fuck buddies, but it's progressed, right?" I smirk at his slip of Southern drawl. "Yeah? Then tell her how you're feeling and listen to her response. That's the difference between hitting and quitting and relationships. It's not all fun and fucking, there's going to be rocky bits where you fight. That's when you're tested, when all y'all have to decide to stay and work through it or not. Couples challenge each other to be the best versions of themselves and grow together."

"Grow together. Is that why you're suddenly throwing out y'alls?" I toss the towel at him with a laugh.

"Hey now, I grew up in Georgia, too, thank you very much."

Gabby appears in the doorway, fidgeting with the edge of her sweater. "Ready to go?"

My heart twists. She's doubting herself again, and it's because of me. I tug her against me and kiss her forehead, desperate to hold her in my arms and reassure her. "Yeah, Imp, let's go home."

The drive is somber. Gabby keeps glancing over at me, and her mouth opens and snaps shut a dozen times. It's not like her to be this restrained. Guilt rises again, mingling with the hurt that's still there.

It's not all her fault. This is an old scab she's accidentally picked, but it's still bleeding all the same. No one's ever expected me to be smart. Even as a kid, my mother and sisters babied me, never allowing me to figure out things for myself—and I ate it up like a damn king. Then I coasted through school. Popular, a top athlete, and I did the bare minimum to earn As and

Bs without taking away from my social life. It wasn't until my knee blew that I bothered focusing on my studies.

Oh, there were always topics that I would obsess over for a time, dive into until I knew every factoid about a subject. A lot of them were sports-based, but there was plenty of history and geography too. Then I discovered podcasts. Suddenly, endless information was at my fingertips—er, eardrums?

I've accepted that at the bar everyone sees my face first. The staff respects me, and that's always been enough. With Gabby, though, I want her to see the real me.

David's got a point. I need to talk to her—I'm a goddamn trained professional, I can do this. Right? A lump forms in my throat as I glance over at her staring out the car window.

I'll think of a way to make it up to her, and show her how much she means to me.

CHAPTER 57

Secrets Discovered

I shake my hips to the music blasting as I gather ingredients and prep vegetables. I'm still not a whiz in the kitchen, but thanks to Anna I'm a bit more comfortable around a stove.

Asher went into Pop to work an event because someone called out, and I want to surprise him with dinner when he gets home. Things have been a little off since game night this weekend. I know dealing with my health can be a lot, and I want to show him I appreciate everything he's done for me. Even if I'm shit at saying it.

I may have gone down a little TikTok rabbit hole looking for recipes, but I finally came up with a menu I'm happy with. There's steak marinating for fajitas, which will go in the oven on a cookie sheet with sliced veggies.

I even made flour-free protein cookies out of chickpeas! Now I only need to make the flourless tortillas out of plantains.

The music cuts off, throwing off my groove.

Hitting the screen key does nothing. Dammit, I doomscrolled too much, and my battery is dead. I plug my phone in, and it starts loading an update with a warning that it will take up to fifteen minutes and reboot multiple times.

No worries, before we had cells there were laptops! It's buried under my growing pile of paperbacks from Cassie's store. Last time I was in there, she made a joke that I'm single-handedly keeping her in business. Eh, what are book-obsessed friends for?

Opening the lid reveals the dreaded blue screen with a spinning wheel of death. My heart drops. Nightmares of lost manuscripts dance in my head. Did I back it up? Just because I've been avoiding writing lately doesn't mean I never want to again. As I pray to every deity I can think of, the display changes to "Working on updates... 2%. Don't turn off your PC. This will take a while."

Dammit! *We really should stop postponing those updates.*

The clock on the stove reads six-thirty p.m. Shit, Asher will be home soon, and I want to get these ready and cool. My eyes scan the apartment as I try to think of a solution. Then I see it—Asher's desktop computer in the corner of the living room. *Winner, winner, chicken dinner!*

Er, steak dinner? *Whatever.*

The screen springs to life as I jiggle the mouse. Thank god there isn't a password. I waste no time and search for the recipe. Technology won't defeat me this time! I grab a pen and scrap of paper and write down the ingredients. Victorious, I close out the browser, revealing a word processor document.

I push away from the desk to get back to cooking, but the words jump out at me and keep me locked in my seat.

Cathy tried to escape the event. These blueberry tarts may be delicious, but the crowd was proving to be too much for her. As she rushed from the room, she ran straight into a wall. Bouncing back with a grunt, her eyes slowly traveled up a man's chest, and she realized it was no wall.

"Shit, I'm sorry. Are you okay?" Her eyes widened in horror as she saw a purple stain blossoming on his white dress shirt. They dropped to the tart in her hand, now reduced to a smashed ball of crumbs and gooey jam. "Oh my god, I'll pay for the dry cleaning, or a new one. Blueberry is such a bitch to get out. I'm so sorry. I was trying to escape the mob, not murder your shirt."

Her words flowed like an overflowing cup of water. Matched with the chaotic halo of red curls around her head, she struck him as not of this world.

My cheeks sparkle with pinpricks of energy as my heart pounds. What is this? Why does the character sound so much like me?

I scroll up further until I reach the first page of the document.

Beauty and the Butcher

by Asher Ramstead

A Psychological Thriller

What the fuck is this?

CHAPTER 58

Truths Revealed

My feet take the stairs two at a time as I rush towards my apartment door. It's bad enough I got called in to Pop while Gabby and I are still in a bit of a fight, but to then be an hour late? I'm so in the doghouse.

"Gabs, I'm so sorry, babe. You will not believe what happened at the event." It's quiet, with no sign of my little imp anywhere. "They had to call the cops, and I had to wait to give a statement."

The place is eerily still. The kitchen has the fixings for dinner spread across the counter. Dammit, she's probably mad. Please be that and not that she's on the floor again. My heart speeds up as I look for her.

"I should have called or texted. Do you want me to heat up something or take you..." My words stall as I reach the bedroom door. Gabby is sitting on the edge of the bed, her purple suitcase by her feet and tears staining her cheeks.

"What's the matter?" I kneel in front of her, reaching for her, trying to meet her eyes, but she turns away. My stomach twists. Something is very wrong, but I have no idea what. "Gabs, you're scaring me. What happened?"

"Why didn't you tell me you were writing a book?"

I jerk back as if shot. "What? How did you…"

"I found the manuscript. Were you ever going to tell me about it?"

"Eventually." The need to move is overwhelming, so I don't fight it. I stand up and pace. So many emotions bombard me at once—betrayal, embarrassment, anger, fear—I don't know which one to explore first.

Anger seems like a good place to start. "Why were you on my computer?"

"My phone died while I was trying to surprise you with dinner. I needed the recipe quickly, and my laptop was frozen. I wasn't snooping, if that's what you think. It was open on the screen when I closed the browser. Did you base Cathy on me?"

"In a way. I started writing it months ago when we first met, when I thought I'd never see you again."

She nods, her eyes far away and sad. "All this time you could have told me about it, and you didn't. When things were only casual, I could excuse it. But after? Were you hoping I'd help you?" She freezes as the color drains from her face. "That's all this was to you, wasn't it? A way to get published."

I turn to her slowly, ice penetrating my voice. Every insecurity and doubt dialed up to ten. "I'm not sure who you just insulted more, me or you. It's not even the same genre, Gabriella. How would your fantasy contacts help with a psychological thriller?"

She shoots to her feet; her face a mottled mask of rage. "Why is it everyone thinks they can write a book? How do I attract the same type every time?"

Anger was definitely the right choice. "This is bullshit. The fucked-up part is, I've published more books than you have! I don't need you or your contacts."

Gabby stops halfway to the door. "What?"

"Those romance novels you've been devouring? I wrote them and self-published every single one." Somewhere in the back of my head, I realize I've blurted out the secret I've never told anyone, and in the worst way possible, but the adrenaline is too high to pull back now.

"You're AR Storm?"

"Damn right, sweetheart."

"I thought AR Storm was a woman."

"Everyone assumes that, but that's me on all the covers you've been drooling over. So, no, I don't need your contacts and I don't need your help with my book."

She pulls a paperback out of her bag, her eyes studying every inch of the model before catching that damn scar along the ribs. Almost desperately, she flips to the back cover, then thumbs through the back matter. She won't find anything there because I've never included any details. All the color drains from her face, and it takes every ounce of my willpower not to step to her and make sure she doesn't fall.

"Why didn't you tell me? We spent hours talking about plot and character development for my books." The book falls to the floor as her fingers grip her hair. "I read how many of these in front of you? You never said a damn thing—just let me believe you were somebody else."

"My job is not who I am. You know me."

She stares off into the distance. When she turns back to me, an eerie calm takes over her features, like a mask descending. "I never understood what you got out of this arrangement. We're so different. You were laughing at me the whole time, like some big joke. Why else would you be with someone like me?"

"Maybe because I fucking love you. You honestly believe I would use you? That I'd be with you just to get ahead or for a laugh? Maybe you're not who I thought you were."

She turns away. Watching her roll that purple suitcase to the door breaks my heart, but I won't beg.

My feet move without conscious thought. I catch up to her as she reaches the door, my hand palming the surface over her head as I lean over her.

"If you walk out that door, I won't stop you. But I want to be absolutely clear about something. The only person who sees you as broken here is you. If you truly can't believe someone would love you for everything that makes you incredible, there's nothing I can do to convince you."

Her body shakes with emotion. My arms ache to hold her, pull her against my chest and soothe the hurt away, but I restrain myself. All the words in the world can't fix this.

I love her, but this will never work if she doesn't love herself.

Releasing the door, I step back, praying she turns around, knowing she won't. The handle twists, the door opens, seconds drag like hours. She steps over the threshold and doesn't look back. I stand there staring until the door clicks, the finality echoing through my heart.

"FUCK," I yell to the empty room.

Angry feet carry me to the kitchen. The remnants of Gabby's surprise are still spread everywhere. I grab the trash can and throw it all out. Wasteful, I know, but I don't want anything that reminds me of her.

This place was once my haven. It will be again.

Next, I ransack the bathroom, tossing the shampoo and conditioner in a shopping bag under the sink. Her scent still clings to the air.

I need to get the fuck out of here.

He answers on the second ring—I know better than to text him if I want a reply this year. "What's up?" The sounds of guns and sirens trickle through the line.

"I need to burn off some energy. Meet me at the gym?"

He must hear something in my voice, because the video game sounds abruptly end. "Yeah, man. Give me fifteen to change."

I can always count on Johnson. This is what I need. Some weights, some time with the guys, maybe a couple of beers, then back to my quiet refuge. As I grab my keys, I only hope I'm not lying to myself.

Harsh Reality

My muscles blaze, but I push through. The metal bar digs into my palms; the sweat stings my eyes. It's all a welcome distraction from the pain in my chest. It's been days, but it still burns fresh, and I can't help ranting yet again.

"And then she had the nerve to accuse me of only sleeping with her for her publishing contacts. What does that make me? A prostitute?"

"I thought guys were gigolos." Johnson helps me guide the barbell to the brackets with a clang.

I glare at him. "Dude. Not the point." He tosses a towel at me, and I sit up, scraping the terry cloth over my face. "I let her into my home, the innermost part of my life. Have you ever seen my place?"

"Well, no."

I toss the cloth onto my gym bag. "Exactly! She saw parts of me no one has. I took a chance and let her in, and this is where it gets me."

Johnson clears plates from the bar and says nothing.

"She turned out to be just like everyone else; only sees me for the pretty package and not what's inside."

He still stays quiet.

"What?"

Johnson turns to me with a sigh. "Did you honestly let her in?"

"Of course I did. More than anyone before."

He gives a harsh laugh. "You never even told her you were a writer. The biggest thing you had in common. Constantly being judged on appearances sucks—I know that—but for better or worse, the outside is the only part people can see. Unless you tell them what's going on inside, they have no clue."

"You're one to talk. You dress like a model and act like a geek. Isn't that false advertising?"

The plate clanks on the stand. "Okay, one, I prefer nerd, thank you very much. Two, I never hide the fact that I'm into gaming and comic books. The topic is worked into every conversation I have. On purpose. We don't walk around with subtext and introspection like in one of your novels."

I freeze, the hair on the back of my neck standing on end. "You've read my stuff?"

"Oh, yeah. My sister is a big fan, and I borrowed a couple—I expect you to sign them for her." I groan, and he chuckles as he takes my place on the bench. "Why all the secrecy, man?"

"I don't know. It started as an assignment in college—write a short story from a very different perspective using our psychology skills. With two older sisters, I felt like that made sense for an angle. Everyone loved it, and so did I. When I blew my knee and lost my scholarship, bartending wasn't enough. Romance is the top-grossing genre in publishing, so I figured, why not?"

"Why hide it, though? Were you ashamed?"

I debate my answer as I spot his reps. "Romance written by men rarely does well. It's escapism for women—they want men written by women."

"Like that cartoon hero that was created by a female focus group!"

"Exactly. I have a lot of respect for romance as a genre. It gets a bad rep for being all about smut, but there is so much emotional depth and nuance in character-led stories. For a while now, I've been wanting to try something different, though. Something darker, but I couldn't quite grasp the plot. Then I met Gabby, and the words exploded on the page."

"So, what are you going to do?"

"Publish it—scheduled to release next Friday. No pseudonyms this time, either."

"That's awesome. We can have a little launch party at Pop." The bar clinks into place and he sits up. "I was talking about Gabby, though."

I take a deep breath. My heart flips at the sound of her name. Despite everything, I miss her. Maybe Johnson has a point; maybe I didn't give her the chance I thought I did. Was she truly as shallow as I painted her? Or did she simply have a lot going on? In reality, we were only together for weeks, and in that time she had major challenges with her health and her career.

Maybe I sabotaged my own love story.

Nothing I can do about it now.

"Nothing. It was a temporary relationship. This isn't a novel where the guy sweeps in with a grand gesture after some insta-love." I slap him on the shoulder. "At least I still have the true love of my life. You'll never leave me, right, buddy?"

He laughs as he wipes his face with a towel. "Hate to kick a man when he's down, but there's someone else, and I don't share."

"No shit? Does she know you're a massive nerd?"

"Considering we met gaming, yeah, my cover is blown."

"When do I get to meet her? Bring her for drinks on Friday."

His cheeks color. "Um, about that..."

"Oh, is it a dude? That's cool."

A deep V forms between his brows as his flush deepens. "No, it's a woman. Why does everyone assume I'm gay? You've seen me pick up women!"

"You're always so well dressed, and you spend all your free time with me. I don't know, you could be bisexual!"

"Way to lean into stereotypes, asshole. My sister is a stylist, dude. I let her buy me clothes so I don't have to bother with it."

"Oh, is she single?" I duck with a chuckle as he tries to smack the back of my head. "So what's the big deal with meeting your mystery woman, then?"

"I haven't exactly met her in person yet. We've been playing that new online co-op game together for a couple of months."

"So, was it her body count that attracted you? Still say she could be a dude catfishing you."

He laughs. "No, man. We chat over headsets while we play. We've stayed up all night talking before. She's incredible."

"And you have absolutely no idea what she looks like?"

He smiles in the same way Colin and David do when they're thinking about their wives. "None—and I don't care. If she's half as amazing in person, I'd be crazy not to marry her."

"What if she's not your physical type? Sexual chemistry is important."

"Not to me. The body is a shell. You can dress it up, decorate it however you want; it doesn't change who you are. It's someone's mind and soul that makes them attractive to me. I want a partner whose personality turns me on. Someone who doesn't see only this." He gestures to himself. "I'm more than my face, and so are you, man." He tosses me a water bottle.

Wasn't that my entire issue with my relationship with Gabby? That she only saw my muscles and not me? I was looking for more, and she was looking for a hot fuck.

My stomach sours, the thought sounding off even in my own head. All the times we laughed together, or debated plot structure, or simply walked holding hands—none of that was sexual. When she was reading my books, yes, she'd comment on the cover, but it was the stories she'd gush over for hours. My words. My mind.

Was it I who made it about the physical? Maybe I'm cynical, or maybe I'm insecure.

I guess we both have to learn to love ourselves.

CHAPTER 60

Ante Up

The bitter bubbles dance across my tongue as I take a swig of my beer.

"Your bid, Ash." Ronnie is looking at me with a calculating expression.

The cards scrape against my fingers as I space out my hand. Ace, king, jack, ten, eight, all hearts. "Raise two." I toss the chips into the middle.

My next card is another eight, not what I want, but at least I have a pair.

"I'm out." Johnson tosses his cards on the table and leans back. "It's great having you out again. Between Pop, the gym, and poker night, I think I've seen you every day."

The truth is, I'd rather be anywhere than in my apartment these days. What was once my haven is now my hell.

Johnson's words have rattled in my head nonstop. I torture myself, replaying our time together in my mind, analyzing where I could have done better. Seeing all the opportunities I ignored to be honest with her. Our split wasn't wholly on me, but I need to own my shit.

Once I admitted my share of the blame, a Gabby-shaped hole appeared in my apartment. At first I could pretend she was in the other room, but one morning I woke up and felt she was truly gone. Her smell is gone, that ever so slight scent of rose. It's not in her pillows—all fucking five of them I left on my bed—or my shower.

"Okay, final card." Gabe deals to the remaining players.

I even spent an hour at the store in the next town sniffing all the products, trying to find a match. Yeah, I know I have a problem, and her name is Gabriella Boyle.

I hold my breath as I flip it over. I'm so close to a royal flush I can taste it. A jack smiles up at me mockingly. Two pair isn't a bad hand though; I could still win this thing.

"Raise two." I'm bluffing a bit, but hey my degree has to be good for something.

"Fuck. Too rich for me." Gabe folds.

Now to psych out Ronnie. He looks at me, his careless grin at odds with the intensity of his eyes. "I'll call." He tosses two more chips into the center.

I splay my hand on the surface and wait.

Ronnie taps his cards on the table twice, then lays them flat. Four queens smile up at me. "Tough break, not catching your queen of hearts."

"That seems to be a trend in my life," I mutter before draining my bottle. "I'm going to grab another beer. Who needs one?" A round of grunts or waves answers me as I stand.

I walk over to Johnson's kitchen and stare into his fridge. Grabbing four beers, I rise and find Gabe standing on the other side of the door.

He nods as I hand him one. "How are you doing?"

"Great. Why wouldn't I be? My book is number one in the Kindle store."

"Cut the shit."

With a grunt, I pop the cap off and throw back my beer.

Fuck, I miss her.

"I'll be fine. Eventually."

"Cassie says you should call her about doing a signing." He squeezes the back of his neck as he winces. "And, uh, if you sign her stock of AR Storm novels, she'll think about forgiving you."

My head falls back against the cabinet with a clunk. "She talked to Gabby. Are they still talking often then?"

"Yeah, man. Mostly a lot of memes back and forth that I don't understand, but they video chat sometimes too. Mostly to meal prep together and talk about books."

"How's she doing?" I try for casual, but based on his look, I miss the mark.

"Why don't you ask her yourself?"

"She's got a lot going on right now—between her book and her whole life blowing up, the last thing she needs is me bugging her. I knew how she felt about people using her for her contacts, and I still chose not to tell her about my writing."

"If you knew it was going to be a problem, why didn't you tell her?"

I scrub a hand down my face. It's something I've asked myself a dozen times—after the righteous anger died down, anyway. "At first I didn't think it was a big deal. It's not like I was actually trying to use her connections and we were just casual."

"And after things got more serious?"

That's the question that keeps me up at night. "I was scared. It now felt like this giant thing instead of a small one. I argued with myself about telling her countless times, but I couldn't find the right words."

He salutes me with his bottle. "Ironic for a best-selling author."

With a mirthless laugh, I finish my beer. "The ultimate irony is a man with a psychology degree, who also writes romance, fucking up his own relationship so completely."

"Naw, man, that's just life. We're too close to our own shit to see it clearly. I could spend five hours trying to debug my own code and never see the problem but spot the issue in someone else's in five minutes. Our minds are constantly playing games on us, showing us what we expect to see and not what's actually there. Don't be so hard on yourself for that."

"What can I be hard on myself for, then?"

"Letting her walk out without a fight. If I had the woman I love in my arms, I'd never let her go. I already know life without her sucks, and I'll do anything to keep her close. Make any sacrifice." His eyes flash with conviction. Pretty sure he's not talking about me anymore.

"How would I even begin?"

The asshole shrugs. "Beats me. You're the romance writer. Figure it out. Or butter Cassie up with a bunch of signed books and pick her brain." He slaps me on the arm. "Now let's go play some poker. I want to win more of your book money."

War of the Witches – Final

by Gabriella Boyle

~~~

Catrina and Lucian, having vanquished the evil
threatening Orcain, hung up their capes and swords.
There would be other threats to their world, other
evils—for the fight against darkness is never truly
won—but those would be battles for someone else.
They had done enough and had now earned a quiet life
in a cottage on a hill overlooking a small village,
where they lived out their days. Together.

The End
~~~

CHAPTER 62

What's After The End?

I expected to feel something as I typed "The End." A sense of accomplishment, joy—hell, I'd even take grief that the biggest thing in my life was now over.

Pushing away from the computer, I stretch as I pad to the kitchen. I grab a few bags of frozen fruit, a handful of spinach, dates, and coconut water, and throw them into the blender with a few scoops of protein powder. As the motor whirls, I contemplate my next move. Like the liquid, my mind equally swirls in circles.

The machine stops, but I stare at it, unseeing.

"Yo, Gabby, where are you?"

"Kitchen."

Deidre appears in the doorway with a plastic bag. "I brought lunch. Figured I'd have to drag you away from the computer, but here you are."

"Here I am." I grab a cup from the cabinet and meet her at the island.

Dee unpacks two bowls and chopsticks, setting them out in front of us. "I got that poke you've been raving about. So, is this break from the keyboard a good or bad thing? Breakthrough or block?"

I pick up a piece of salmon, enjoying the buttery texture before replying. "I finished."

"With book three? That's awesome, Gabby!"

"Book five." I look up in time to see Dee staring at me slack-jawed. "I finished the whole series."

"Wow."

"Yeah, once I let go of what everyone else wanted from the story, it just flowed. I've never drafted anything this fast before."

"What are you going to do with it?"

I blow out a breath, sending the curls around my face fluttering. "No clue. A new agent is probably a good start. I was going to ask you to reread my contracts—I don't even know if I have the rights to my characters to re-query or self-publish the series."

She lays her hand over mine. "If you don't, we'll buy the rights back. I'll get the contracts team onto it. Lawyers are only assholes when they're not on your side."

I squeeze her hand with a grateful smile.

"So why are you so down? Would it have something to do with a certain Neanderthal?" She looks smug as she plops a chunk of pineapple in her mouth.

"Deidre..."

"Come on. You've been avoiding this conversation since you got back. At some point, we need to talk about it. What happened down there? I can see you're hurting, Gabby. I thought it was supposed to be a friends with benefits situation."

With a groan, I sit back on the stool. "Yeah, it started that way—guess I'm not capable of separating sex and feelings. He was great at first, but after my little episode, things changed. I didn't want to spend every minute talking about vegetables and heart rate. I'm not broken, dammit."

The chopsticks slip on a piece of edamame, adding to my frustration.

"Sometimes people aren't who we want them to be, Gabby, and often they're not who we deserve them to be. Look at our parents—I did everything they wanted, I'm a partner at a major law firm, but because of who I love they couldn't accept me. It's up to us to decide what we're worth and what we're willing to tolerate from people. When someone shows you who they are, believe them."

"He showed me." My chopsticks squeeze a second bean too hard, and it shoots across the room. "The whole time he was saying he cared about me, he was only using me to write a book."

"You mean this book?" She pulls a paperback out of her bag and lays it on the counter. A bookshelf in muted blues, blood dripping from a knife impaling a novel, and the title in bold yellow font stare back at me. "You read it, right? Isn't the main character inspired by you?"

I nod, stabbing a piece of fish with my chopsticks, imagining it is Asher's stupid face.

"Did you help him?"

"No." My eyes stay firmly on my bowl. Maybe if I ignore her, she'll drop it.

"How was it distributed then? You said he was using you."

I mix my food but make no move to eat more. "Turned out he was a self-published author and never told me. Watched me read his books for weeks while he wrote a character based on me."

"This one, right?" I nod. Dee flips to a dog-eared page and narrates. "Cathy stared down the police captain, completely unmoved by a glare that made grown men cry. 'I'm telling you, you have the wrong man, and I can prove it.' The pile of notebooks in her arms hit the desk with a thud, sending three nearby detectives to their feet. Point made, Cathy turned her back on the still-scowling captain, and with her head held high, she marched out of the precinct. The heroes had given up, but she would save the day."

The room falls silent. My chopsticks still hover over the bowl.

"Does that sound like a weak woman in need of fixing?" She barely waits for a response. "Did you actually read this? If you know the main character is based on you, it reads like a damn love letter. So, is it him who sees you as broken? Or you?"

Her words hit the sore spot in my chest, a little too close to Asher's own. "I may have been a bit emotional when I skimmed it the first time." With a gasp, I look up at her. "Did you just lawyer me?"

With a cocky smile, Dee lifts her Diet Coke in a cheer. "Yup. You're not the only brain in the family, kid." She pushes a card across the counter. "There's a therapist at our couples counseling who specializes in medical trauma. You should give her a call."

I lift the card and jerk my head at my sister. "You go to couples therapy? But you two are perfect together."

"Yes, because we go to couples therapy." She laughs. "You think relationships are easy? It takes communication and compromise—even when you don't have a stupid man in the mix. Our therapist helps us develop tools to handle the little things before they become big things. Think about it."

"Okay. Since you're feeling so helpful, do you want to beta-read my book?"

"Thought you'd never ask! Can Corinne read it too? She's been dying for an update."

I laugh. As always, talking with my sister lightens the load. She's not the softest and squishiest person, but she's always in my corner to tell me what I need. Even if it's not what I want to hear.

My phone rings. I don't recognize the number, but a small voice tells me to answer it. "Hello?"

"Hi, is this Miss Boyle?"

"May I ask who's calling?" Dee raises an eyebrow questioningly. I can only shrug in response.

A relieved sigh comes through the speaker. "This is Patricia from Orchid Publishing. I'm so sorry to bother you directly, but we've been trying to reach Roger Altman, and he's not responding."

"That's because I fired him."

"Oh. Damn. Well, that explains a lot."

"Look, I'm sorry to have wasted your time, but I'm not comfortable with the direction you want the series to go. Catrina's story is about overcoming adversity and finding your way in a world not made for you. Yes, she and Lucian fall in love along the way, but that's only a subplot. Including graphic sex scenes doesn't add to the plot."

"We agree."

"You do?" I slump, all this built-up adrenaline for an argument suddenly gone. "But Roger said..."

"Well, I'm glad you fired him, then, because we weren't the ones pushing for the romance angle. We would be thrilled to publish this as a young adult novel. If you are happy to continue this relationship."

"As long as you are open to me telling the story I want, I am. The series is finished, all five books."

"That's amazing. We'll draft a new contract for the remaining manuscripts and be in touch with your counsel."

I give her the number for my sister's firm, and we end the call.

Dee and I stare at each other in a moment of silence, then we both jump out of our seats yelling and dancing around the kitchen before collapsing in a fit of giggles against the counter. We finish our lunches, and as I walk Dee to the door, she promises to set up an appointment with her media division for tomorrow.

When I grab my half-finished smoothie, Asher's novel sits conspicuously beside it.

I should read it again. Remind myself of all the reasons why we would never work. Rip apart the prose and delight in how terrible it is. *Not that we did that with the fifteen other books of his we devoured.* On second thought, maybe later.

My computer pings loudly, startling me. A message from Netflix stares back at me, so I dive to open it.

Ms. Boyle,

We spoke with your publisher and understand you are under new representation. Orchid Publishing also shared that the series is taking a more YA angle. This would fit better with the teenager and family demographic we've been looking to serve. If you are interested in continuing our

agreement, please provide contact information
for your media agent so we can set up a meeting.

Regards,

Perry Smith

They still want to make my books into a movie? Even without all the sex? How much was Roger hiding? How long was I blind to what was going on?

After I've caught up on housework, done some yoga, and taken a shower, I sweep through the kitchen for my nightly cup of tea. The paperback taunts me from the counter.

One chapter can't hurt, right?

Tea and book in hand, I settle into my reading nook with my weighted blanket, ready for my nighttime routine. As Cathy uncovers the first clue and starts her journey to unmask the serial killer, I'm hooked. By the end, I'm sobbing.

Beauty and the Butcher

Cathy rushed down the stairs. James struggled on
the floor, hands cuffed and blood dripping from his
temple as Officer Wilde knelt over him, the murder
weapon held aloft for the killing blow. Pausing for
only a moment, she threw herself onto the killer's
back.

She'd damn well make sure the Butcher had claimed
her last victim.

CHAPTER 64

Boiling Point

Another ladies' night at Pop, another night of distraction. After poker night, I stayed up until three a.m. stalking Gabby on social media. I started and deleted a couple of texts and emails after I saw the deal announcement on Publishers Marketplace. A three book YA contract, no less—I'm so proud of her for standing up for herself and the story she wanted.

A woman in jeans and a crop top approaches the bar with a wide smile, holding up a credit card. "Six lemon drops, please. Keep the tab open."

I give her a curt nod and grab the bottles and tools automatically as my brain continues to mull over my problems.

Would fighting for her have made a difference? Was she ready to listen? All the talking in the world is useless if she doesn't believe she's worthy of love, which requires therapy and self-reflection. I can't muscle through it for her.

The crowd splits as she carries the tray of drinks, and a young guy takes her place. "Two IPAs." Easy. Crack off the caps onto the floor, grab his twenty, and send him off.

The orders blur together, and I find comfort in the routine of it all. Blender drinks, mixed drinks, shots, beers. I'm a machine behind the bar, completely in my element. I'm lighter than I have been since Gabby left, and if when the keg runs out I suggest Johnson change it instead of facing the supply closet, well, that's because it's a training exercise.

"This is insane, man. No wonder you work out so much. I can barely keep up. I'm glad the event side won't be like this." Johnson can't tackle more than pouring a beer or soda, but he can run tabs and manage the drink tickets for the front of the house which is a big help on a night this packed.

"Yeah, these muscles aren't purely for show." I flex for him with a wink. My cheeks sting, and I realize I'm grinning for the first time in what feels like forever. Having Johnson here is exactly what I needed. "What can I get you?" The smile is still in place as I turn to the new customer, but it quickly freezes as I recognize the handsy blond. My stomach clenches at the memory of her last visit.

Her eyes are a little glassy, and the flush on her face tells me she's already had a few drinks—probably pre-gamed some liquid courage, if the determined glint in her eye means anything.

"I'll have the bartender." She lays her hand on mine on the bar top, then bites her lip.

"I'm not on the menu. Is there a drink you'd like to order?"

The pink deepens. I'm reminded of Gabby, but where her blushing always made me smile, this woman purely looks blotchy. "Do you always play this hard to get?"

"I'm not playing, ma'am. I'm simply not interested."

The flirty eyelashes stop fluttering as her entire face pinches with fury. "What the fuck is your problem?"

I'm vaguely aware of the din of the bar quieting around the thrumming of my pulse in my temple. She's attracting a lot of eyes. "My problem is that you won't take no for an answer. This isn't a strip club, but even if it were, there would still be a no touching rule."

"Why, I never... How dare you talk to a customer that way? I demand to speak to the manager!"

A snarl escapes my lips before I can stop it. "I am the manager and part owner."

"Okay, now that's enough of that." Anna pushes in behind the bar in her chef's coat. "Miss, I've called the sheriff's office. A deputy will be here for your statement shortly. Johnson, suga', can you see this young lady over to a booth to wait? With maybe a cola?"

The anger in the blond's eyes dims slightly as she takes in Johnson. He smiles at her, but shoots concerned looks back at me as he leads her away.

"Show's over, folks, please go back to your meals." Anna turns on me with the hellfire her husband nicknamed her for shining in her eyes. "You march your ass into that office right now, mister."

I slam through the kitchen doors and into the small room, but all the vindicated rage quickly flickers out. Anna never cusses—like, ever. She always says she can still taste her momma's soap if she even thinks of cursing, so I know she's mad. I collapse in the chair, hanging my head like a schoolboy waiting for the principal.

She comes in a few minutes later and shuts the door behind her.

"Look, I'm sorry, Anna. She wouldn't take no for an answer, but I should have stayed professional or tapped Jessie in."

"It was Jessie who ran for me. She mentioned this happens often and recognized this woman as having done this before?"

I nod. "She's the same one who caused that issue while Gabby was here. Also, the night of the book signing." I ignore the pang in my chest at saying her name.

"I was just thinking about you, Hell's Bells. Are you coming home yet? I'm craving dessert." David's voice rumbles in the small office. I jerk my head up and see Anna holding her phone out on speaker.

"Sorry, darling, this is business. Can you pull the camera footage of the bar from tonight?"

"What happened? Are you all right?" It's amazing how quickly his tone shifts when he thinks his wife is in danger.

"I'm fine. A customer got fresh with Asher and caused a fuss. There will also be footage from February 10th and sometime in April." She looks at me.

"It was the night before your little meeting with Nic."

"Ah yes, April 25th. Can you transfer all that to a drive and bring it to Pop?"

"Of course." The sound of a keyboard clacking already thunders through the speaker.

"Thanks, doll, Billy is on his way to take her statement, so if you could give it to him that would be fantastic."

"Billy?" His deep voice almost whines. "Hell's Bells, you know I can't stand that man."

"Yes, but you'll still do this for me." Her lips twist in a devilish smile. "And later I'll bake you cookies—in your favorite apron."

David literally growls through the phone. "You better." I don't want to know what that was about, but I can certainly guess.

Anna hangs up and sits down on top of the desk with a sigh. "What are we going to do with you, Asher?"

My shoulders round. "You're going to take me off bartending, aren't you?"

"I definitely think hiring another bartender is in order—which I thought you were already doing. We've been packed, especially with the event side."

Pushing out of the chair, I pace the small room. "I couldn't take it anymore. The constant innuendo, the pickup lines that are always the same. I don't judge a woman for shooting her shot or knowing what she wants, but I'm a fucking person, too. I'm more than the hot bartender of Pop from the reviews. Some of these women act like I'm a fucking tourist attraction or something. So, I'm sorry I yelled at the woman, but I'm not sorry I stood up for myself."

My chest is heaving as I finish and turn back to Anna.

Her brown eyes glitter, and her mouth falls open. "You think I'm mad because you yelled at her?" At my nod, she stands and grabs my hands. "I'm mad because you didn't tell me what was going on. You are one of my closest friends, Asher—or at least I thought so."

I squeeze her hands, a lump forming in my throat. "I am."

"We should have seen it. I had no idea it was this bad. I'm so sorry we encouraged you to keep up the hot bartender thing when you hated it. No business is worth that."

"I didn't hate it at the beginning—I'm still a guy—but at some point I realized I wanted more from my life."

She searches my eyes, moving her hand to cup my face. "You listen to me, Asher Ramstead. You are a kind and caring man with more emotional intelligence than anyone I know. You are a freaking best-selling author, and you make a mean drink. Yeah, you happen to be easy on the eyes, too, but anyone who doesn't see past that is a fool."

My eyes burn as I pull Anna to me in a hug I didn't realize I needed.

"We're going to get through this, Ash. Together. It's not the end, just a new chapter."

That sounds nice. Maybe it is time to step back from the front of the house, let someone else take up the mantle.

CHAPTER 65

Turning the Page

The bitter drizzle matches my mood. Only in Boston can it be cold in the morning and sweltering by the afternoon. The mix of historic brick and modern glass normally puts a smile on my face, but as I trudge down the street, I long for pastel stucco and palm trees.

There's so much culture here—stories written into every cobbled road or ancient graveyard, waiting to be told. Usually they whisper to me as I walk past, but today all is silent. Maybe even the ghosts are judging me. *Hell, I judge us, too.*

They say karma is a bitch, but I think hindsight is the real cunt. With distance, I see that I fucked up, but I don't even know where to start fixing it. Hallmark doesn't exactly sell a "Sorry I accused you of being a leech and making your accomplishment about me" card, and Edible Arrangements doesn't have a "Sorry I'm insecure and walked out" basket. I checked.

My hair tingles as my meds kick in from the extended standing, disrupting my train of thought. Probably for the best. Can't dwell on it now, anyway, because I have shit to do. *Better to obsess about it in bed instead of sleeping like normal people.*

With a sigh, I push through the rotating door of Reilly, Morgan, and Tate and give my name to the receptionist. I've barely sat on the leather sofa when a young man exits the elevator.

His eyes sweep the lobby until they hone in on me, and he strides my way. He's handsome, with dark hair and striking pale green eyes with a deep brown outer ring, made all the more so by his navy suit.

"Miss Boyle, Jack Parker, pleasure to meet you. Let's take a look at these contracts, shall we?"

His smile is dazzling, but does nothing for me—my tastes seem to have switched to the Viking variety permanently. I muster a half-assed smile of my own and let him lead me to the elevator and the twentieth floor. An elegant woman brings me a sparkling water before I can ask and then shuts the door behind her.

Well, fuck me. This is some fancy shit.

"What did my sister do to convince you to take me on?" I was expecting some associate in a conference room, but this man must be fairly high on the food chain to have the corner office and a dedicated assistant.

He grins. "I stole your folder for myself. I'm a big fan of your first book and wanted to guarantee we handled this contract correctly. Plus, I'm pretty sure Diedre would have terrified any of my associates, and I actually like most of them." He gestures for me to take the seat across from his desk.

He's not wrong. With a genuine smile, I sit. "So, where do we start?"

"I've read the summary from you and got some extra details from your sister. I understand your previous agent was misrepresenting you, and now both your publisher and Netflix would like to renegotiate the terms of your deal?"

"That's the gist of it."

"Did you have an entertainment lawyer look over your first contract?"

I shake my head. "Dee read them when I got my first offer, but it was years ago. I trusted Roger, but obviously put my faith in the wrong person."

"Happens to the best of us. It's not my area of expertise, but I think you might have a case against your former agent if you wanted to sue him. If you're interested, my colleague can discuss the particulars with you today and start drawing up documents."

It's on the tip of my tongue to say no. Old Gabby doesn't want to be a bother or make a fuss. Better to avoid conflict and keep moving forward.

Fuck that. I want Jolly Roger to pay. He almost cost me my entire career, my love for writing, and landed me in the hospital. "Let's do it."

His smile is all teeth; looks like I got myself a shark. "Excellent. If you haven't secured new representation, we've brought on a literary agent here at Reilly, Morgan, and Tate. You can meet her today to see if she's a good fit, unless you'd rather shop around. We could handle your foreign translations and publication rights in-house, too."

"That all sounds great. One-stop shopping."

"Terrific. Now, this Netflix deal, I think it's a good start, but we can do better."

My head tilts. "How so?"

"Well, first off, you should be listed as an executive producer. Also, I'd like you to have final approval on the script, and a percentage of the profits."

I sit back in my chair, shocked. "I can get all that?"

"Oh, Miss Boyle, I'm only getting started. Shall we order lunch and introduce you to your new team?"

In a blur, Jack's efficient assistant has the rest of them in the room, seated at a conversation area in his office with a spread of fruit and nuts. I like my new agent, Victoria, immediately. She has ideas for conventions and panels but seems genuinely interested in hearing my intentions for the series rather than pushing hers on me.

Michael, my litigation attorney, thinks he has a solid case for breach of fiduciary duty, fraud, negligence, emotional distress, and breach of contract. At a minimum, my hospital bills from Florida will be covered, but if we're awarded the full million dollars he's asking for, I could take some time to plan my next project.

It's the most productive four hours of my life, and my head spins a bit as we adjourn the meeting. After another round of handshakes, Victoria leads me to the elevator banks. The doors open, but I pause.

"Is there something else, Miss Boyle?"

Pausing for only a moment, I reach into my bag and pull out the paperback. This hadn't been my intention when I threw it in my purse, but it feels right. "I've never done this before, so I'm sorry if this is inappropriate. Have you read this? It would make a great TV series." She gives me a calculating look. "Absolutely no pressure—don't even bring my name into it—but this book is special."

With a slow nod, Victoria takes the novel from me. "I'll give it a look."

I hate it when Dee is right. Cathy is strong and capable, and if she's actually based on me, it's quite the compliment. It's James that twists my heart, though, the handsome and supportive detective who doesn't see what he offers the partnership. The way he trusts her completely when no one else does. And she saves him. By the time I'd finished, it was well past two a.m. and tears were pouring down my face.

Maybe he was who I needed him to be, but I was too scared to see it.

* * *

My feet drag by the time I walk through my apartment door. Draco meows mournfully as he winds between my legs. Chuckling, I head to the cabinet for his food. "How about the good stuff tonight? Mommy's celebrating."

My cell rings as I struggle with the can tab. I swipe and put the call on speaker as I go back to wrestling with the can. "Hello?"

"I can't wait anymore. How did the meeting go?" Cassie sounds breathless.

"Awesome. They even set me up with a whole team—and they're going after Roger in court."

"Woo-hoo! Love it." There's a bang and a crash. "Ow."

"What are you doing?"

"Unloading a shit ton of new stock. Listen, I know you don't want to talk about it, but Asher is having a signing here in a few weeks." I freeze as her words sink in. "I'm still team Gabby one-hundred-percent, but his book is doing really well and I need this for the store. It's just business."

"No, it's fine, Cassie. It's a small town, and you have a business to run. Of course you should do a signing." After dumping the food into a bowl, I lower it to a waiting Draco.

There's a loud exhale into the speaker. "Thank god, if it helps, I'm torturing him and blackmailing him into autographing all my AR Storm stock too. So I'm earning a fortune online on these since no one else has signed copies." She giggles, and it ends a bit maniacally, making me smile.

"H-how is he?"

She hesitates. "Gabe says he's okay; they've been having a lot of poker nights."

I grab a banana from the bowl on the counter, but pause. "Doesn't he usually work nights at Pop?" The other end falls silent. "Cass? What's going on?"

She sighs, and the phone rustles. When she speaks, her voice is clearer, like she's switched it off speaker. "Look, he got into a little trouble and has taken a step back from bartending. He hired a new guy—also super hot—I'm telling you there's something in the water down here."

I'm frozen, stuck on the first bit. "What sort of trouble?"

"A girl hit on him, and he kind of snarled at her. Johnson had to jump in. She was apparently overly pushy, and the sheriff trespassed her, but there was a whole thing because someone got it on camera."

"He must be devastated. Staying behind the bar was so important to him." Cassie makes a noncommittal sound. "What? What else aren't you telling me?"

"Look, I don't think it's the job making him miserable. He's been pretty low since you left. Not that he shouldn't be, he definitely fucked up. All I'm saying is, for what it's worth, I think he genuinely misses you."

With distance, I can see I used the health stuff to push him away. It's not like Dee and Corinne don't hover too—not nearly as much as Asher did, but they also didn't live through the wait for the ambulance alone.

Hiding his writing was wrong, and I had every reason to be pissed off. He had so many opportunities to come forward as AR Storm. Did he try to, and I missed it? He said on the first day in his apartment that sex lessons weren't what he had in mind. Was that what he meant in the first place when he offered to help?

We were reading his book when he offered—in that closet...while we were staring at his ass.

That's right, he blushed at the cover and stared at it just before. Then Roger interrupted. Could this have all been a simple mistake that snowballed out of control?

The truth is, my weeks with Asher were the happiest of my life. For the first time, I felt truly seen and appreciated for who I am as a person—verbal diarrhea, awkward finger guns, and all. I met this caring, thoughtful man and accused him of terrible things that deep down I know he'd never do, then stormed off without letting him explain.

In the end, I wasn't any better than that blond at the bar. I was so busy seeing Asher the fantasy; I rejected him as soon as he showed his humanity. He deserved more.

What he did was wrong, but that doesn't change the facts. "I miss him, too."

CHAPTER 66

The Haunting of Asher

One Month Later

I look around the office of Books and Brews, waiting for this to feel like reality. The last month hasn't felt real. Everyone assumes my overnight success—if you can call it that after ten years and fifteen novels—has been a dream come true, but it's been more akin to a nightmare.

The person I want to share this with the most is gone, because of my damn pride. She's a ghost haunting my every moment. I see her in every redhead at the bar. I fucking miss her.

For the hundredth time, I pull out my cell to text her, not even sure what to say. I almost broke down and called her when her scumbag agent,

Roger, reached out to represent me. In the end, I didn't want to bring her more pain, so I reported the son of a bitch to the Association of American Literary Agents.

"You ready?" Cassie sweeps into the room.

With a sigh, I return my phone to my pocket. "As I'll ever be. Thanks for doing this, after..."

She waves me off. "Don't mention it. This is just good business. Seriously, I think this one event will keep the lights on for another six months."

I nod. "Have you heard from her?" She pales, her eyes widening. Mentally, I curse myself out. "Sorry, you don't have to..."

Cassie gives me a look filled with pity and something else I can't quite place. "She's doing well."

I smile, somehow both relieved and crushed simultaneously. Of course, I want her to be thriving—I'll always love her—but the selfish part of me wants her to need me a bit more. Oh, that would keep a therapist occupied for months. "Good... good."

With one more deep breath, I head out to the main room. Cassie has adjusted the couches to allow for the mob of reporters. A stack of my paperbacks sits by a single table. I move to the wingback behind it and face the crowd.

Johnson gives me a little thumbs-up from the side. That awkward show of support goes a long way to ease my nerves, even as it slashes my heart at the reminder of Gabby. It's scarier than I thought, doing this under my real name.

I feel naked up here.

Cassie addresses the room. "We have time for a few questions, then we'll take a break to set up for the signing."

A journalist stands up. "Mr. Ramstead, I bet there are publishers kicking themselves for passing on this book. What do you have to say to them?"

Annoyance rises, which I push down—the last thing I need is a sound bite going viral for the wrong reasons. "I never queried *Beauty and the Butcher*. From day one, I wanted full creative control, from plot to cover to release date and everything in between. Self-publishing isn't always a second choice. Next question."

"Rumor has it that there is a bidding war for the media rights. Is that true?"

I blink, trying to remember what the lawyers had coached me on. Some fancy practice with a media division reached out to represent me with an offer from Netflix already on the table for a mini-series.

"There are talks of an adaptation, but it's too early to say anything concrete. Next question."

A young woman stands; her press badge says Elysium in bold letters. She must be from the magazine Nic's husband owns. "A debut that topped the retailer charts for weeks and now a potential streaming deal—your overnight success is inspiring. What advice would you give to other authors looking to publish?"

"Although this is my first book under my own name, I've published fifteen other books using a pseudonym." The crowd buzzes, and I lift my hand to quiet them. "No, I won't say which—I used a pen name for a reason. I'm not ashamed of those novels, and probably will continue to write in that series. This book is completely different, and I wanted to keep it separate. I went on a bit of a tangent there, but my point is I don't want anyone to think this was an overnight success story. It's unfair to the years I've spent on my craft, learning the industry, and sets unrealistic expectations for new writers."

The journalist smiles. "Thank you."

"I also want to add that authors shouldn't look at each other as competition. It's easy to compare your journey to someone else's, but we're all running different races. Look at other authors as your peers, learn from them, cheer them on. Building the book community helps us all. Thank you for the question."

Cassie stands up. "We have time for one more, you in the back."

"Reversing the traditional roles, having the damsel save the day instead of the detective, was an interesting twist. What was the strategy there?"

I can't see the speaker, but her voice sends my heart racing. Now I'm hearing Gabby everywhere, too. "No strategy. A very special woman inspired me to write this book. I met her at a point in my life where I felt stuck. Lost. She taught me to stop being afraid and start living. In a lot of ways, she rescued me, so the only option was for Cathy to save the day."

"Sounds like a special lady."

My eyes search the faces again. The similarity is uncanny. It can't be... "She's one of a kind."

The crowd parts in a sea of whispers. At the center remains Gabby in a baby blue sundress, her hair left wild in red ringlets as mischief dances in her eyes.

Every muscle in my body tenses. She's here. It's really her. I can hear my heartbeat in my ears as my legs spring into action. In three steps, I've crossed the distance so I loom over her. The journalists take a step back, but she stands strong, looking up at me with hope. I grab her hand and haul her with me to the back room for some privacy.

The door clicks shut, and I pin her against the surface.

"You're here." Some bestselling author, if that's the best I can come up with.

Back in the Closet

My heart pounds, but it's not an attack—I made doubly sure I took my medicine today. He looks so handsome in his button-down shirt and slacks. He's grown a beard in the weeks we've been apart, but it suits him. My fingers itch to remove his hair elastic and let the blond strands fall free.

"Hi." It's all I can manage.

His eyes caress my face. God, I've missed him.

"I'm sorry," we both say at the same time. He smiles as I laugh. Again, talking simultaneously.

"Let me start," he says, resting his palms on my arms. "I should have told you about the book. All the books. It's something I've always kept to myself, too afraid of people judging me, but I'm realizing I can't be mad at people for not seeing the inner me if I don't share it. I'm so sorry I push—."

I lay my finger on his lips, giving in to the need to touch him. "You were right, too, though. I used finding the manuscript as an excuse to run away because deep down, I didn't believe you possibly wanted me. We both fucked up, but I didn't even give you a chance to explain, and I'm sorry."

We simply stare for a minute, still wrapped in each other's arms.

"The book is wicked good." He goes to interrupt, but my fingers are still on his mouth. "No, really, I read it again and couldn't put it down. The raw emotion, the twists—it's a masterpiece."

His lips curl against my hand in a boyish grin. "You think so? You're not only saying that?"

"I never lie about books. I wouldn't have told my agent to read it if I hadn't believed in it."

The lights dim a little in his eyes as he steps back. "You told them? So I didn't earn it on my own?" He freezes, his eyes widening. "You told them... but you hate it when people ask for your connections. That's why we ended things in the first place."

"You're right." My words are low; if we weren't so close, I doubt he'd hear me.

"Why?" Hope trembles in his voice as he searches my face.

"You know why."

"I never asked..."

I step up to him again, praying he reads the honesty in my eyes. "That's why. The book is so good, Asher. You deserve this. You earned this. I showed them where to look, but you made them pay attention all on your own."

His hands cradle my back, so gentle but desperate at the same time. "I don't see you as broken. You are smart and funny. When you are in a room,

I light up inside and don't want to look away. I love you exactly the way you are. If I hover and try to take care of you, it's only because I'd do anything to make you happy."

"You need to let me figure it out on my own sometimes. Don't treat me like I'm made of glass. I don't want everything in our relationship to be about my health; I want to be a normal couple..." His words catch up with my brain. "Wait, did you just say you love me?"

He chuckles as he leans down to capture my lips. "Took you long enough to hear that."

Pushing up on my tiptoes, I clutch his collar, hauling him close as I kiss him like I've longed to since the moment I walked out of his apartment. He clasps my waist, twisting me and pressing me against a stack of boxes, which tips precariously. Without lifting his mouth, he slams his hands onto the pile, steadying them. I arch my back, clinging to him for support as I tear my mouth from his.

"For the record, I love you too."

"Oh, I wasn't letting you go again, Imp. Even if I had to chain you to my side, you were stuck with me until you changed your mind."

"I thought we just talked about your bad habit of being overbearing and bossy as hell, you damn Viking."

With a devilish smile, he hauls me up so we're eye to eye with my legs locked around his waist. "If I weren't still a little bossy, you'd love me less." His brows pinch into a more serious expression. "In the interest of full honesty, I reported your agent for misconduct."

"Roger?" He nods. "My new team of lawyers is suing his ass into oblivion—I doubt he'll ever work in publishing again."

"That's my bloodthirsty girl. How should I reward you?" He growls as his lips descend on my throat.

A bang on the door sends my heartbeat racing even faster. Cassie's voice comes through the door. "You two better not be fucking in my supply room. That is so unsanitary for the books."

I giggle as Asher groans in frustration. "Why do we always find ourselves in closets?" I ask.

"Why am I not using Cassie's idea in closets?"

"I can hear you talking. Come on, Asher, it's time for the signing. Save the makeup sex for when you get home."

Home.

I finally found my home.

As I watch Asher with his fans, I'm so incredibly proud and humbled that this man picked me. Not because I don't think I'm worthy of love, but because we both came into this relationship a little broken, patched with bubblegum and duct tape.

Our experiences taught us that our cracked exteriors defined our worth. Now, our cracks are filled with gold, like that Japanese pottery, made more beautiful for our imperfections and for what we hold than the sum of our parts.

Will we have more fights? Of course. After all, our entire relationship started with a misunderstanding. Relationships aren't strengthened by a lack of conflict, but rather how you handle it together. Like a sword must first be put through fire, a relationship must be tested to be strong. I've found a love worth fighting for, and I've only just begun.

CHAPTER 68

Epilogue

Three Months Later

Asher walks into my new office and drops a moving box with a thud. "That's the last of it."

"Careful!" I leap from my chair by another half-empty crate towards him.

He stretches his back with an audible pop. "Aw, your concern is touching, Imp."

I dive past him to the box, carefully lifting a book and hugging it to my chest. "Not you, my books! These are all special editions. Look at the sprayed edges!"

Handing my publisher three manuscripts at once has freed me up, and I'm fully taking advantage of the time. After the signing, I traveled with Asher on his book tour. When he wasn't busy doing press, we made up for lost time, filling in the gaps of our courtship on the world's longest third date.

To no one's surprise, I moved to Friendship Springs permanently. I'll miss being close to Dee and Corinne, but small-town life will be much better for my health. We found a house for sale down the street from David and Anna. It's a cute little four-bedroom bungalow with a cozy porch to watch the sunset on, and big enough for two writing spaces.

He shakes his head at me with a laugh. "You about ready for dinner?"

"Do we have to? Can we get takeout instead? We haven't unpacked the kitchen yet, and I still need to find the sheets if we're going to sleep in a bed tonight."

We learned a lot about eating out on the road—a bit of trial by fire, but Asher was a major support. He had a metal card etched with my dietary restrictions on it, so now I simply hand it to the server and know my food will be edible.

Gripping me by my armpits, Asher lifts me up so I'm standing against him, keeping his hands locked behind my back. He drops his head and captures my lips in a too-brief kiss. "Bed's all done." I open my mouth, but he stops me with a finger. "And your fifty pillows. I made sure a set of sheets was in my suitcase when we packed."

He still teases me about my pillows, but I've caught him using one under his knee when his old injury acts up. "What would I do without you?" I tilt my head back for another peck.

Sometimes it still shocks me that it's only been a few months since we got back together. We fully share our writing processes and help each other get unstuck. I'm deep into finishing the first draft of my YA reluctant princess novel, and he's working on a follow up to *Beauty and the Butcher.*

He's learned to give me space and not rush in, but he still shows his support in a thousand quiet ways. Not to say we haven't had fights—we're both flawed humans, after all. Who was going to pay for this house was a doozy of an argument, but we're learning to talk it out with our couple's counselor and individual therapists.

"You'd be fine, but you'll never get the opportunity to find out." What starts as a peck quickly deepens into more. My fingers grip his long hair, and I wrap my legs around his waist as he lifts me. With a pained groan, Asher tears his mouth away. "As much as I'd love to christen that new reading chair, everyone is expecting us at Pop. Can't wait to meet this wedding planner Johnson's been bitching about."

I give him my best pathetic kitten eyes. "But it's going to be people-y. I don't want to share you."

The extended absence helped Asher transition from bartender to author. He still plans to work the bar a few days a week or when they need coverage, but not on ladies' night. The hot bartender from the reviews is well and truly retired.

A deep V forms between his brows as he pouts. "But, Imp, it's trivia night!"

"Is that a good idea? Don't you remember last time?"

"It'll be fine. All the couples are a single team, and we've got every category covered. We'll be unstoppable." He grins, and I don't want to burst his bubble, but he must notice my hesitation. "If it gets to be too much, just slip away. I'll know where to look."

My heart skips a beat thinking about our first meeting. "Oh, yeah? And what will you do when you find me?"

His lips trace a line up my throat, the beard tickling. "What I should have done the first time, lock the door and take you against the shelving." His hands squeeze my ass. "So wear something with easy access." The growl of his voice sends shivers across my skin.

Do we need to go all the way to Pop for that? I mean, we have perfectly good bookshelves right here.

His dark chuckle lets me know I said that out loud. "Save that for when you read my next AR Storm novel, Imp. I'm suddenly taken with the idea of a naughty librarian." I moan as his lips find that perfect spot on my neck. In an abrupt shift, he kisses my forehead and steps back. "Seriously though, if it's overwhelming, give me the sign and we'll come home."

This man is so much more than the sex-god-Viking who strutted into my life all those months ago. He is a story so much richer and more complicated than the pretty cover he displays to the world. I'm so incredibly honored to be the person he lets see his inner pages, and there will never be a day I won't want one more chapter.

Loved Gabby & Asher's story?

The best way you can support indie authors like me is by leaving a review. Even just a few words ("funny," "spicy," "loved it") make a huge difference and help more readers discover my books.

If you enjoyed *One More Chapter*, please consider:

- Leaving a quick review on Amazon, Goodreads, or BookBub.

- Snapping a pic or posting your favorite quotes on Instagram or TikTok — and tagging me so I can squeal over it with you!

Curious about Johnson and his Gamer Girlfriend?

Book 5 in the *Friendship Springs Romance* series is coming **Spring 2026**! A *Gilmore Girls* meets *You've Got Mail* romance full of banter, horrible first impressions, and small-town charm. Follow me online to be the first to know when it's out!

Also by

Want more Friendship Springs?

Friendship Springs Romance:

Stick to the Plan (Brianna & Colin)

Stick to the Recipe (Annabel & David)

Stick to the Deal (Nicolette & Reginald)

Acknowledgements

Thank you for making it this far into *One More Chapter*! I didn't give Gabby chronic illnesses as a gimmick or plot device. For as long as I can remember, books have been my escape from the world, and now writing is healing magic for me as well. It's a safe space where I can work out my feelings and life experiences—like the therapy box in the TV show *Legends*. I pour bits of myself into my characters, and yes, I feel less burdened, but my hope is others feel seen in my characters. I can't properly put into words how it feels when a reader messages me about how one of my characters helped them through a difficult time. My health journey has been long and, frankly, traumatic, but in no way dissimilar from thousands of other women's stories. My goal in this novel was for these women to feel seen.

This book would not have happened without my husband, because I literally might not be here without him. The bathroom scene was not wholly fictitious; this man has lifted me off the tile floor and held my hand wondering if it was goodbye more times than anyone should. In a society where so many leave sick partners, he has stood by my side for sixteen years. Through Mayo Clinic trips, five major surgeries (two I almost bled out during), two hospitalizations, and countless ER and doctor visits where he's advocated for me when no one would listen. Yes, sometimes he gets a bit overprotective, just like Asher, but just like Gabby, if he wasn't so bossy I'd probably love him less. It is a special kind of torture having your body fail you, but I can only imagine how powerless it feels to watch it happen to your person.

And finally, a huge shout-out to my author support network! My author pals who cheered me on and talked me down when I spiraled in the group chat. My amazing cover artist, Lindsey, and her endless patience with me. My editing team—Victoria and Erica—for making sure my ramblings make sense. My beta and ARC readers, who motivated me over the last hurdle. All y'all made this happen.

About the Author

R.S. Barry, a resident of Central Florida, shares her life with her loving husband and their two kids. A dedicated and passionate reader for many years, R.S. Barry now makes the voices in her head work for her.

Drawing inspiration from life's experiences, R.S. Barry weaves contemporary tales of love, connection, and self-discovery. As a long-time reader and working professional, she brings a unique perspective to her writing, infusing her work with a genuine understanding of the complexities of human emotions.

When she's not writing, R.S. Barry is probably curled up with a novel by the pool, over-analyzing a fictional couple's chemistry, or debating whether to buy just one more book.

Find out more and see her complete book list at www.RSBarry.com
And find her on Facebook, Instagram, and TikTok

facebook.com/profile.php?id=61555639000320

instagram.com/authorrsbarry

tiktok.com/@authorrsbarry